Wish List

Books by Fern Michaels

On the Line
Fear Thy Neighbor
No Way Out
Fearless
Deep Harbor
Fate & Fortune
Sweet Vengeance
Fancy Dancer
No Safe Secret
About Face
Perfect Match
A Family Affair
Forget Me Not
The Blossom Sisters
Balancing Act
Tuesday's Child
Betrayal
Southern Comfort
To Taste the Wine
Sins of the Flesh
Sins of Omission
Return to Sender
Mr. and Miss Anonymous
Up Close and Personal
Fool Me Once
Picture Perfect
The Future Scrolls
Kentucky Sunrise
Kentucky Heat
Kentucky Rich
Plain Jane
Charming Lily
What You Wish For
The Guest List
Listen to Your Heart

Celebration
Yesterday
Finders Keepers
Annie's Rainbow
Sara's Song
Vegas Sunrise
Vegas Heat
Vegas Rich
Whitefire
Wish List
Dear Emily

The Lost and Found Novels:
Secrets
Hidden
Liar!

Holiday Novels:
The Brightest Star
Spirit of the Season
Holly and Ivy
Wishes for Christmas
Christmas at Timberwoods
Santa Cruise
Falling Stars

The Godmothers Series:
Far and Away
Classified
Breaking News
Deadline
Late Edition
Exclusive
The Scoop

Books by Fern Michaels (cont.)

E-Book Exclusives:

Desperate Measures
Seasons of Her Life
To Have and To Hold
Serendipity
Captive Innocence
Captive Embraces
Captive Passions
Captive Secrets
Captive Splendors
Cinders to Satin
For All Their Lives
Texas Heat
Texas Rich
Texas Fury
Texas Sunrise

Anthologies:

In Bloom
Home Sweet Home
A Snowy Little Christmas

Coming Home for Christmas
A Season to Celebrate
Mistletoe Magic
Winter Wishes
The Most Wonderful Time
When the Snow Falls
Secret Santa
A Winter Wonderland
I'll Be Home for Christmas
Making Spirits Bright
Holiday Magic
Snow Angels
Silver Bells
Comfort and Joy
Sugar and Spice
Let it Snow
A Gift of Joy
Five Golden Rings
Deck the Halls
Jingle All the Way

Published by Kensington Publishing Corp.

WISH LIST

FERN MICHAELS

KENSINGTON
PUBLISHING CORP.
www.kensingtonbooks.com

KENSINGTON BOOKS are published by

Kensington Publishing Corp.
900 Third Avenue
New York, NY 10022

All Kensington titles, imprints, and distributed lines are available at special quantity discounts for bulk purchases for sales promotion, premiums, fund-raising, educational, or institutional use.

Special book excerpts or customized printings can also be created to fit specific needs. For details, write or phone the office of the Kensington Sales Manager: Attn.: Sales Department. Kensington Publishing Corp., 119 West 40th Street, New York, NY 10018. Phone: 1-800-221-2647.

KENSINGTON and the K with book logo Reg US Pat. & TM Off.

First trade paperback printing: March 2024
ISBN: 978-1-4967-4310-7

ISBN: 978-1-4201-2304-3 (ebook)

10 9 8 7 6 5 4 3 2 1

Printed in the United States of America

I'd like to dedicate this book
to the memory of Ken's grandfather, Jerry Loyd
1937-1995

Chapter One

It was a frosty day, the kind of day to hurry inside, build a fire, snuggle into warm sweats, and curl up with a hot toddy. A cigarette and a hot, new script would complete the make-believe picture. Like it was really going to happen.

Agnes Bixby, better known as Ariel Hart to fans and movie buffs, entered her house and called out to her longtime friend and housekeeper. "I'm home."

She dropped her briefcase by the front door, sending her high-heeled shoes in two different directions. Her lightweight coat landed on a settee. She reached down to a small foyer table, opened the drawer, withdrew a rubber band, and pulled her thick, blond hair into a ponytail. She closed the drawer with her knee as she struggled with her mane. Long hair was for young people, not women approaching the big Five-0. But, in this perfect place called Hollywood, all the perfect people—and she included herself in that category—tried to appear forever young. Long, flyaway hair was a must along with heavy makeup and outrageous false eyelashes. Don't even think about the skinny bodies that hungered for mashed potatoes and gravy, she cautioned herself as she fired up her second cigarette of the day.

Ariel felt out of sorts as she stared around at the pleasant room she basically lived in—the family room, rumpus room, great room, or whatever they were calling it these days. It was a perfect room, decorated by herself, for herself, the perfect backdrop when she'd been interviewed, which was often, in the early days of her career. Now, though, the interviews were almost nonexistent and the furniture was beginning to show signs of wear even though Dolly, her housekeeper, was meticulous about caring for everything in the house.

"I love this room, I really do," Ariel said as she reached out for the drink Dolly held out to her. "It's so warm with all the earth colors and the soft pastels on the walls. I always thought it was pictureperfect. I hate that word, Dolly. I think I always hated it."

The perfect couch, so deep and comfortable, welcomed her. Ariel settled herself by propping her feet on the coffee table. She reached for her third cigarette.

"Didn't get the part, huh?" Dolly said.

"No. A forty-five-year-old got it. Her face-lift was so new I could see the pink scars. Maybe I should get one. I was perfect for the part, too. But . . . You know, Dolly, and I'm sure you're keeping track, this is the first call I've gone on in three months. I knew this day was coming—I just didn't think it would be this soon. I also thought I was prepared, but I'm not. My agent isn't very hopeful. There just aren't any good supporting roles these days. Each day I'm getting older." She gulped at the drink she usually sipped.

"It sounds to me like you're full of self-pity," Dolly snapped. She twisted the cap off a bottle of Budweiser and took a swig. She was a tiny woman with a single, thick, black braid that hung down to her skinny buttocks. She wore jangly hoop earrings—her arrival was always announced by sound. She wore baggy overalls with colorful shirts and no fewer than seven beaded Mexican necklaces. Her feet were bare and

thickly calloused. On those occasions when guests were expected, she donned a French maid's uniform with a prissy
white apron and stiletto-heeled shoes.

"I deserve to feel pity," Ariel snapped back, her blue eyes
flashing angrily. "I'm getting so sick and tired of this business
I want to quit. The problem is, the business is quitting on me.
I've been thinking more and more about starting up my own
production company. By God, if I do, I'm going to scour this
town for scripts that call for older women. Why is it that as
men get older they're distinguished and women are just older?
Get me another drink. Please. And another thing, I want mashed
potatoes, gravy, and a pot roast for dinner. Make sure you
cook an apple in the gravy and mash it up. Make coleslaw,
fresh rolls, lots and lots of soft butter, no other vegetable, and
I want a peach cobbler with fresh whipped cream for dessert.
Then I want real cream in my coffee, and a brandy, too."

"You'll make yourself sick if you eat all that. You haven't
eaten food like that in years. Your stomach is used to tuna
and salad with lemon juice. I'll have to go to the market."

"I don't care if I get sick. I want it. Will it make you feel
better if I have some red beets in vinegar? So, go to the store
already. Tomorrow I want steak and french fries and the day
after that a leg of lamb. I'll let you know what I want on
Thursday."

"I'll do it, but you need to know we're talking ten pounds
here. Can you live with ten more pounds on that skinny
body? You'll have to go on a diet or buy new clothes. I'm
going, I'm going. Do you want turnips mashed along with
the potatoes?"

Did she? "Of course. With lots of butter and salt and pep-
per. Don't forget my drink. Better yet, bring me two. I need
to unwind."

"Three drinks will put you under the table and you'll sleep
till morning. Then who's going to eat this fancy dinner?"

"Wake me up. Go!"

Her second drink firmly clasped in her left hand, Ariel reached for the portable phone and pressed the memory key. "Sid, it's Ariel. I didn't get the part. They gave it to Wynona Dayton. Her face-lift looks real good. I'm batting zip here. This makes twelve calls, that's an even dozen, that I've lost. I think it's time to sit down and do some serious talking. Today convinced me that I need to . . . . do something. Of course, I realize movies have been my life, but there *is* life after the big screen. There has to be." She heard the desperation in her voice and hated it. God, what would she *do?* Her eye went to the Oscar she'd won four years ago for best supporting actress. Two good movies after that, and then it was all downhill.

Ariel swallowed the rest of her drink and knew immediately that Dolly had watered it down. Damn. "Of course I'm listening. Don't I always listen to you, Sid? I have an idea— why don't you come over for dinner? We're having real food tonight—pot roast and peach cobbler. No, nobody died. This is how I'm going to eat from now on." She listened for a moment to the squawking on the other end of the line. "Of course I'm serious. Today convinced me that Hollywood is finished with me and you know what, Sid? I'm finished with it, too. Acting, that is. This seems as good a time as any to do what I said I was going to do when this day came. I want to form my own production company and maybe take a shot at directing. So, are you coming to dinner or not? Fine, I'll talk to you tomorrow. Maybe I'll talk to you. Then again, maybe I won't." She listened again to the furious squawking on the other end of the line. "I looked perfect. I acted perfectly professional, the way I always act. I read perfectly, too. Maybe you should call the producer and ask him yourself why he chose Wynona over me. I'd like to know myself." She forced herself to take a deep breath and exhaled slowly. None of this was Sid's fault. It was her fault for having the poor judgment to begin the aging process. She gulped at the drink again and wished she had another. "I'm sorry, Sid, it was a bad day. Let's talk tomorrow when I'm not so testy."

The silence hammered at her once she replaced the phone. Had she always lived in a silent house? Didn't she play the stereo? Didn't Dolly have the kitchen television turned to the afternoon talk shows? Where was the noise she was accustomed to? Maybe she should have told Sid about the new lump on her cheek and the one on her forehead.

"Today I feel fifty!" Ariel shouted to the empty room. "I know it's two weeks till my birthday, so technically I'm still forty-nine." She thought about Carla Simmons because she always thought about Carla when things were going bad. Carla Simmons, top model and then Best Actress three years running. And then zip. Nada. Nothing. A face-lift and a boob lift couldn't help the aging actress, but she was hanging in there because she didn't have any kind of backup. Money-hungry husbands had cleaned her out a long time ago. Tina Turner wasn't even a good runner-up where Carla was concerned. Even with all of her cosmetic surgery, Carla *looked* old. How many times Ariel had given the actress money just to help her pay the rent. She'd helped in other ways, too, paying for her health insurance and getting her into a rehab clinic and paying for that, too. Well, if she went through with her plan to form her own production company she might be able to hire Carla for some good character parts. Carla would play any part just to be in front of the cameras.

She'd promised herself a fire. Well, then, by God she was going to have a fire. Just as soon as she changed into her sweats. A shower might not be such a bad idea.

Inside of ten minutes she had a blazing fire with firewood she'd personally lugged from Oregon along with baskets and baskets of pine cones. Just for good measure, and to be sure the fire would still be blazing after her shower, she tossed on an artificial log, something the instructions said not to do.

Before heading upstairs, Ariel picked up her Oscar and stared at it. It was a statue awarded for excellence. She belonged to that select group: the best of the best. Oh, how the mighty have fallen, she mused as she replaced the shiny gold statue on the mantel. She wondered what would happen to it when she died. "Guess I'll have to will it to someone." She was still muttering to herself as she made her way up the winding circular staircase.

At the top of the stairs, she turned and looked down over the railing. Years ago, when she'd refurbished the house, she'd had the old stairs ripped out and installed what she privately referred to as her *Tara* staircase. Oh, how she'd played with it, giving lavish dinner parties, descending the stairs after the guests arrived, just so she could show off. Each time she did any kind of interview she made sure she was photographed on the beautiful stairs. A weary sigh escaped her.

Ariel was a quick-change artist. She was also adept at doing two things at once. She undressed as she selected a CD, then turned up the volume so she could hear it in the shower. *Pretty Woman.* Tears burned her eyes. Too much soap.

The after-shower ritual took twenty-five minutes. Body lotion, elbow and knee lotion, special lanolin hand cream, cuticle cream, facial moisturizer, neck cream, eye cream, hair conditioner that wasn't supposed to be rinsed out, and lastly, foot balm.

Her reflection in the mirror worried her. When was the last time she'd had a facial? About three weeks ago. She was persnickety about her face since she earned her living in front of the camera. She didn't have these bumps on her face three weeks ago. She looked at the offending blemishes in her magnified makeup mirror. Makeup could cover them. In the great scheme of things, she decided, it simply wasn't all that important.

Downstairs, the fire was still blazing. She threw on another log just for something to do before she made herself a fresh drink with more liquor than was good for her. She could hear Dolly banging pots and pans in the kitchen. She switched off the CD player and found herself grinning as she listened to Dolly's soap opera. Two actors grumbled that at least seventeen people knew someone had had a child out of wedlock thirty years ago and the only person who didn't know was the father. By seven o'clock Dolly would have tomorrow's episode down to a science.

Now what should she do? Smoke a cigarette, of course. Who cares if I get those deadly little lines over my upper lip?

Was she over-reacting? Was today just a bad hair day, a bad complexion day? No, she decided. If nothing else, she was always honest with herself. Today marked the beginning of the end of her acting career. Better to quit now. Go on to other things. She could still be a name in this town, provided she wanted to stay in Hollywood. Did she? Of course she did— she'd been here for thirty years. It was home.

Once she'd thought another place was home, but she'd been a kid of sixteen then. Living in Chula Vista, outside San Diego, had been the happiest time of her life. Even now, thirty years later, she still remembered it. Of course, there were reasons for that happiness, but she wasn't going to think about those now. Living with a father who was in the military didn't allow a child to call any one place home because you were never in that place long enough to put down roots. *I wish . . .*

Ariel never finished her wishes, but her wish list was long, taped to the inside of her closet door. Almost fifty pages of "I wish," with nothing following. Why, she didn't know. Maybe she was afraid. She told herself it was better than writing in a diary, better than having some stranger see her private thoughts. She knew what the fifty-page wish list contained: the same wish, over and over and over. Every night before she went to bed she wrote, "I wish . . ."

She could still hear Dolly's TV. The soap stars were battling each other over DNA testing. Life should be that simple, Ariel thought. Life was never simple. People were simple. Life was goddamn complicated.

"Dolly!"

"What?" the housekeeper bellowed from the kitchen.

"I'm going to get a dog! Maybe a cat, too, so they'll be company for each other."

Dolly was breathing like a long distance runner when she skidded over the polished floors to stand over her employer. "Then I quit! I'm not cleaning up after a dog. I have enough to do picking up after you. Dogs chew, cats spray and you never get the smell out of the furniture. I don't have time to walk a dog. You have to pay attention to animals. You're too busy. I quit!" she shrieked.

"So quit," Ariel retaliated. "Who in their right mind would pay you what I pay you, and allow you to watch soap operas all afternoon? Nobody, that's who. We're stuck with each other and we both know it. You aren't getting any younger, you know. Face it, this is one cushy job. I pay your social security, provide a pension plan, give you two days off a week, let you drive my car. I give you smashing Christmas presents. So, quit!"

Ariel and Dolly had discussions like this at least once a week, with one or the other always backing down. Long years of friendship allowed both women to be open, to speak their minds and walk away after these discussions, with head high. *Familiarity does not* always *breed contempt,* Ariel was fond of saying.

"What are you giving me this year?" Dolly asked craftily.

"Nothing—you're quitting because I'm getting a dog and

a cat. What were you going to get *me?*" Her voice sounded just like Dolly's.

"I never shop till the last minute. Something meaningful, as always. Maybe *one* animal would be okay. A dog that doesn't shed. You could go to the SPCA and get one that's already trained. They're free, too—you just pay a small fee like maybe fifteen dollars. No cats!"

"Two dogs."

"This is not negotiable. One!"

"Don't forget to leave a forwarding address. Gee, it's time for me to make your pension contribution, too. Oh, well," Ariel said, throwing her hands in the air. "Goodness, isn't your birthday next week? I was going to take you to Planet Hollywood for dinner and get you a Chanel handbag."

"All RIGHT! Two dogs. That's my final offer."

"I accept your offer. Dolly, I'm scared. No, what I'm feeling goes beyond scared. I'm petrified. Acting is all I know." She was blubbering, tears washing down her cheeks in a mini-waterfall, a luxury she could rarely afford for fear her eyes would be puffy and bloodshot.

"It's okay," Dolly said, dropping to her knees. "Go ahead and cry all you want. And when you're done, I'll peel some cucumbers to put on your eyes. Crying is very therapeutic. It releases all kinds of tensions and toxins. All you have to do is tell yourself it's their loss. And it is. You've had more than most in this town, you have your Oscar, your star, and your footprint. Not too many people can say that. Nothing lasts forever. That's always been one of your favorite sayings." She was crooning as she rocked Ariel back and forth like an indulgent mother. "Okay, a cat, too. Two dogs and a cat. They'll do a writeup on you in *Variety.*"

Ariel hiccupped as her outburst subsided. "In this whole damn town, you're my only true friend, Dolly. Sometimes I think you and I are the only ones who know what the word *loyalty* means. I'm okay now. I am scared, but I'll deal with it in my own way. I'm fortunate enough to have options. Today was . . . the confirmation I needed to know I'm finished as an actress in this town. You're probably right about the animals. Perhaps later when things are more settled.

"Dolly, do you ever want someone to love? Someone to love you? I mean *really love*. Did you ever have that? In the twenty-five years we've been together, I never asked you. I don't even know why I'm asking you now. I had that once, a very long time ago. I didn't have it in either one of my marriages, though. Do you think it's true that you only love once?" Her voice was sounding fretful. Almost whiny.

"Once, a very long time ago," Dolly said softly. "It wasn't meant to be, I guess. I never found anyone after that. The truth is, I didn't look very hard. I'm contented. I would have liked to have children though. It's my only regret. Are we letting our hair down here, Ariel? If we are, then what about you? You had two husbands and several relationships so you know what love is all about. I wish one of them had worked out for you. Is it possible, Ariel, that at one time you lost someone you really loved and no one else measured up?"

"*I wish . . .*"

"How many does that make for today's wish list?"

"Two," Ariel said.

"Two's good. Two's better than the six you logged yesterday. And the five the day before that. Those lists have grown a lot in the past year. Are you aware of that, Ariel?"

"Of course. But wish lists don't mean anything. It's just something I do. Did I answer your question?"

"No."

"Once, a long time ago, I loved someone, but my father called it puppy love. My parents said I was too young and they didn't like the boy. My father got transferred and we moved away. End of story." *No, it isn't the end of the story.*

Someday you're going to have to talk about that little tale. Aloud. I wish . . .

"I'm going to make you a cup of tea. You look peaked, Ariel. I wouldn't be a bit surprised if you aren't coming down with the flu. You could even have some kind of intestinal bug. I think you can use a nap. We won't be having dinner till around eight. The fire will keep you cozy. It's raining out right now and the wind is kicking up. It's going to be an awful night."

"You don't have to be so cheerful about it," Ariel grumbled as she settled herself into the mound of pillows. She was sound asleep when Dolly returned with the tea.

The housekeeper set the tray down on the low table in front of the sofa. She dropped to her knees, her hand going to her employer's forehead. Warm, but not alarmingly so.

Dolly rocked back on her haunches. Ariel was always so in control of her life. She never did anything until she mapped it out, checked it longways, sideways, and up and down the middle. Then she talked the problem to death until she was one hundred percent comfortable. Many a night they sat up talking about a problem, drinking black rum tea and nibbling on dry toast. Ariel shared all her problems with her, valued her opinion. Not only was she a wonderful employer, she was also a marvelous friend.

Dolly struggled to her feet and picked up the tea tray. She shook her head. Rejection had to be the worst thing in the world, especially for an actress. It bothered her that Ariel hadn't confided her worries about losing out these past months to other younger, more glamorous actresses. Actually, it was more like an entire year since Ariel had been offered any kind of serious role. So many scripts, so many readings, and then . . . nothing. Today must have been some kind of invisible deadline for her employer. She wished she could remember exactly how many calls she'd gone on the past year. Sid would know, but she wasn't going to call him. That would be stepping over boundaries. She turned, set the tray back down, bent over, and stared intently at Ariel's face. The little bumps Ariel was so worried about were raised almost like pimples, but they weren't pimples—she was almost sure of it. She could feel her stomach muscles begin to tighten. She almost ran from the room, the tea on the tray splashing over the side, dribbling down to the polished hardwood floors.

Something was really wrong with Ariel's face and it was getting worse every day.

"So, Dolly, what's for breakfast?" Ariel asked.

"You get half a grapefruit and a slice of dry toast. Five minutes. Coffee's ready."

"Today, Dolly, I'll have two scrambled eggs, three slices of toast for dipping in my egg yolk, lots of strawberry jam, and real cream for my coffee. I have a full day ahead of me and I need sustenance. I'm going to take a full page ad out in *Variety* asking for scripts. I have a call in to my attorney and one to Sid. I'm going forward with my plan to form my own production company—and I'm seriously thinking about directing a movie if the right script comes along. After breakfast I'll call my financial advisor to see if he can get me some backing. First rule of business, Dolly: you never play with your own money. If I absolutely have to, that's a different story. I figure I'll be scared for the first two camera set-ups, then I'll be fine. I've learned a lot over the years. Sometimes I even surprise myself with what I've picked up. It stays with you, if you know what I mean. I know I have to wear comfortable shoes, not those spike-heeled numbers I've been wearing every day of my life. Hollywood doesn't take women directors seriously, but they're going to take me seriously. The secret is control. I'll buy the property outright. I can do it. I *feel* it. What do you think, Dolly?"

"If it feels right, I say go for it."

"It feels right," Ariel beamed.

"How long have you been planning this?"

"Since my first turn-down. In my thirty years in the business I always got the part, every time I read for it, until that day. I was right for that part, too; the producer and director thought so, but the money people wanted someone else. When it happened a second and third time I saw the handwriting on the wall. You know me, though, I have to be hit over the head with a hammer before I give in. Even a stupid person would realize the game plan changes after a dozen turn-downs. I'm not a stupid person."

Dolly set Ariel's breakfast in front of her. "You haven't eaten a breakfast like this in ten years. Maybe fifteen. I hope your stomach is up to it. You better buy a girdle along with those comfortable shoes." Her voice was sour sounding, but Ariel was so busy wolfing down her food she didn't notice.

Dolly poured herself a cup of coffee, adding four sugars and enough cream to turn the coffee white. She sat down across the table from Ariel, her eyes sharp. "Ariel, have you ever thought about leaving Hollywood, you know, going somewhere else?"

"And do what?"

"Any number of things. You need to slow down. This . . . whatever it is . . . hasn't really hit you yet. Maybe something to do with fashion. You've got a great eye for color and design. We could start a catering company. Low-fat everything. I could do all the cooking and you would be my best endorsement. That would be interesting. With all your resources maybe you could start up some kind of business where you could utilize the talents of people like Carla. I

guess I'm saying don't rush into anything. Think about it before you jump in with both feet."

"That was wonderful! I'll have another cup of coffee,
Dolly. I have thought about it. For a whole year. Am I missing something here? Are you thinking about going into business for yourself? If you are, I'll back you all the way. This is
all I know, Dolly. It's my life. I have to have something. I
could never just get up and walk away. I bet I could even act
and direct at the same time. Others have done it. The bottom
line is, I believe in me. That's half the battle right there. Now,
to the good stuff. Let's plan a party. This company will be
formed before we know it. Scripts will be arriving by the
truckload. I know Kenneth Lamantia will have our backing
before either one of us can sneeze. It's almost like it's a done
deal. So, let's plan a real gala. Grand announcement. The
whole nine yards. We'll invite the whole town and pray half
of them will be a no-show. This has to top the party we gave
after I won my Oscar. You're going to see some major sucking up. It might feel good for a change to be on the other side
of the fence."

Dolly wrinkled her face into a grimace that was supposed
to be a smile. Her fat pigtail swung from side to side as she
bobbed her head up and down. "No, I do not want to go into
business myself. I was thinking about you. I don't want to see
you get hurt. This town is a killer. You know it and I know it.
I meant us. For whatever good I'll be, I'm with you all the
way. A party it is. I must say, you're taking all this pretty
well. I thought you'd be . . . devastated."

"I was. Don't forget this has been going on by degrees this
whole past year. While I'm not used to it, I can live with it.
It's my choice to walk away. There will be parts offered to
me, but they won't be good and I'll feel like I have to take
them. I don't want that to happen. This is best."

Ariel finished her coffee. "Well, it's off to my office. I'm going to think about redecorating it. I'd like it to look more feminine. We can change the drapes, get some new carpet, get rid of that monster desk and get a white one. Colorful cushions, some new chairs for clients, loads of plants, and maybe some of those crisscross strips for the windows. I want it to be a cozy room. Thank God for the fireplace. Two chairs and a low table will be just the right touch. I think I'm getting excited. Listen, do me a favor and run to the drugstore and get some of that coverup for these spots on my face."

"You could go to the doctor, you know. What's a half hour out of your life? You might need an antibiotic. Makeup is not going to work, I can tell you that."

"We'll try it. If it doesn't work, I'll go to the doctor. It just seems kind of silly to go to a doctor for a few little bumps."

By the time Dolly announced lunch, Ariel had the wheels in motion to start up her own production company. Her ad was placed in *Variety*, she'd rented a post office box in Dolly's name, and opened a business bank account in the name of her new corporation, Perfect Productions. She had a new tax ID, and would shortly receive tons of legal documents, according to Lamantia.

Ariel dusted her hands dramatically as she made her way to the kitchen. A ham and cheese sandwich with side orders of potato salad and coleslaw waited for her. Ariel ate it all, grumbling that it hurt to chew. "I'll bet I'm getting an abscessed tooth and that's why these things are erupting on my face. Five bucks, Dolly. It didn't hurt when I ate breakfast. Maybe I will make an appointment with the dentist tomorrow, just to check it out. Boy, that was a good lunch. It's wonderful to eat again. I'll do the treadmill this afternoon to walk off the calories, so stop fretting. And now," she said, "I'm going to plan my office. I have some papers you have to take to the bank—and you have to go to the post office and sign something, and pay six months' rental. The rest of the afternoon is yours for your soap operas."

"Make the office pretty, Ariel, so we can take an afternoon tea or coffee break like they do on those coffee commercials. You know the ones, where the women are all dressed up, sitting in brocade chairs wearing high heels and there are fresh flowers everywhere. Everything is frilly and pretty."

"I'll do my best. Do you have any Motrin?"

Dolly shook three tablets into her hand from the bottle in the kitchen cabinet. Ariel swallowed them with the remains of her soda.

"Call me when dinner's ready. Let's call the party a soiree. I'll make up the list and you can take it to the printer tomorrow. Three weeks from Saturday. Off the top of my head, how does this sound? 'Ariel Hart requests the honor of your presence at a soiree on November twelfth, nineteen hundred and ninety-four.' I'll spell out the day and the year, makes it look more formal. I'll go on to say something like, 'In Celebration of the Formation of Perfect Productions.' I know it's not worded right, but you get the idea. What do you think?"

"Sounds good. Formal, right?"

"Absolutely. I'm going to wear that beaded dress I had made in Hong Kong. We'll have to go to Rodeo Drive and get you something super fancy. Start thinking about what you want."

"I wouldn't count on wearing that dress if you keep eating the way you are. I looked at it when it was delivered and there aren't any seams to let out."

"Well, I'm not going to worry about it now. I'm so excited, Dolly. I think I can do this. It'll be a real hoot when some of those players who crossed me off their list start sucking up. Guess that's not very nice of me, huh? Who cares? It's my turn now. I do feel good about this. Jeez, it's raining again. Back to my work and my toasty fire. You should build one here in the kitchen fireplace. Do that, Dolly, and we'll eat dinner out here. Let's go to Aspen for Christmas and see some snow. I'll make the reservations. Maybe we should invite Carla. What do you think?"

"What I think is you got a whole lot on your plate. The party, Aspen, the new business. Slow down. You don't have to do everything all at once."

"Yes, I do, Dolly. I have to keep busy so I don't think. I don't want to turn bitter and become one of those unforgiving recluses who abound in Hollywood. I knew what would happen going in, but I was young then and thought this day would never come. Life goes on and I want to go on, too. It's the only way I know."

"Okay, but pace yourself. Promise me."

"I promise. See you at six o'clock."

The afternoon passed quickly for Ariel. The decorator would arrive first thing in the morning. She made reservations for a seven-day stay in Aspen, then called Carla, who said she'd be delighted to make the trip. The dentist was away in Vegas on a convention so she made an appointment for the following week. Before she did her five miles on the treadmill she washed her face, then reapplied the coverup. She wasn't sure, but she thought the bumps were bigger and her entire face ached. The Motrin should have kicked in by now. Maybe she should try another dentist. She finally de-cided if she wasn't any better by morning she'd call Dolly's dentist. She popped two more Motrin from a bottle she kept in her desk.

Ariel was a half-mile into her walk when she had to get off the treadmill because her head started to pound unbearably. Never a worrier by nature, she was now more than a little concerned that something might be seriously wrong. Lord, what if she did have an abscessed tooth and they had to take off all her pricey porcelain? I'm not going to worry about it now, she told herself. They'll fix me some kind of temporary and I'll hide out. It's that simple.

The clock over the mantel said it was four-thirty. Time for a little nap before dinner. Tomorrow she would feel better, she was sure of it. Tomorrow would be the first day of her new career. She crossed her fingers the way she did when she was a child, hoping that this new career would be as successful as the one she was giving up. *I wish . . .*

Chapter Two

It was a celebratory meeting in more ways than one. It was also Halloween and Dolly had decorated the lawn and front door with fake spider webs, goblins, and witches chasing sheet-dad ghosts.

They were all waiting for Ariel to return from town: financial advisor Ken Lamantia; agent Sid Berger; broker Gary Kaplan; actuary Alex Carpenter; and a team of lawyers, Marty Friedman, Ed Grueberger, and Alan Kaufman. Audrey and Mike Bernstein, Ariel's long-time accountants, and Carla Simmons were the last to arrive. They were all talking at once, each offering input and toasting the success of Perfect Productions with fresh apple cider.

"Have all the RSVP's for the party come in yet?" Sid asked.

Dolly nodded. "Two hundred people. Everything's under control. I'm sure Ariel will be home any minute now. She's pretty excited."

A discussion followed about how well Ariel was making the transition from actress to producer and how successful they all knew Perfect Productions was going to be.

"Where'd she go?" Carla asked curiously.

"I believe she had a fitting for her dress. You know how that goes. She probably lost track of time. It's possible she had some last minute details to see to about the party. It's just two weeks away. I think I hear the garage door. If anyone wants to spike the cider, feel free. I'll be back in a minute."

Dolly opened the kitchen door that led to the garage. Ariel was sitting in her car, her head in her arms over the steering wheel. She didn't move when Dolly opened the door. "Everyone's here, Ariel. They're probably spiking the cider as I speak. How did you like the lawn decorations?" When there was no reply, Dolly reached in to the car and tugged at Ariel's arm. "What's wrong?" she asked fearfully.

"Everything is wrong. Dolly, go in there and tell them all to go home. Tell them I'll call them in the morning. I'm not up to . . . I can't face . . . do it, Dolly."

"Not until you tell me why. You went to the dentist, didn't you? I told you not to cancel that appointment, but did you listen? No! You have an abscess and he wants to take off your caps? It's not the end of the world, Ariel. Come on now, you're an actress. Prove it. Your friends have worked night and day to get you to this point. They're excited for you and for themselves. You can't let them down. Are you listening to me, Ariel?"

"I didn't go to the dentist, I went to a doctor. These . . . *things* on my face aren't from an abscessed tooth. They're *growths*, and Doctor Davis wants to operate on them as soon as possible. I have to have a biopsy tomorrow morning. I'm scared, Dolly. I could have . . . I mean I really could have . . . Oh, God!"

"What else did he say?" Dolly demanded. "Tell me everything he said. And don't tell me you don't remember. You can memorize an entire script so I know you can tell me verbatim what he said."

"He said I was a fool to wait so long to make an appointment. He doesn't think they're malignant, but surgery is required. He wants a biopsy. He's going to have a plastic surgeon there tomorrow when they do it. I asked him if I'd be disfigured and he said there was a possibility and that's why he wants the plastic surgeon there. That's all he said, Dolly."

"Okay. We know what to expect now. We'll deal with it. Get out of that car and start acting. We aren't going to fall apart here. There's too much at stake. We're thinking positive. That's an order, Ariel. A doctor wouldn't commit to saying he thinks your bumps are benign if he didn't think so. Come on, you're in perfect health. If you don't get out of that car right now, I'm quitting. For good. I mean it. I want to see that famous smile of yours. You can do this, Ariel." Her tone of voice was so forceful that Ariel climbed from the car.

"We're canceling the party," she said.

"Okay by me. You have to stop being so damn vain, Ariel. And remember something else. God never gives you more than you can handle. Okay, let's go," Dolly said as she held open the door leading to the kitchen.

"What would I do without you, Dolly?"

"You'd do just fine."

It was one of Ariel's best acting jobs. When she said goodby to the last guest, she flopped down on the couch and lit a cigarette. "By God, I did it."

"Yes, you did. I can't believe Ken raised five million in just a few weeks. Somebody has confidence in you. Now, all you need is a good script and actors who can put you over the top. People are standing in line to go on your payroll. You're on a roll, Ariel. I'm going to make us a quick dinner and then I'll get on the invitations. I think I'll just say due to a family emergency we're canceling till after the first of the year. It'll be a one, two, three thing. I can have them in the mail first thing in the morning. By the way, I logged in another 44 scripts this morning. That brings your total to 611. You have to hire some readers, Ariel, and you can't put it off any longer. Carla took a batch home with her. I told her you'd pay her by the script. Was that okay?"

"Sure. You probably should have written her a check."

"I did. I even gave her some extra. I entered it in the checkbook. She ate like a wolf. I gave her a pie, a jug of cider, and those two chickens I roasted for dinner. We're having scrambled eggs since I don't have time to cook now."

"You're a good person, Dolly."

"That's because I had a good teacher. What time is your appointment tomorrow?"

"Eight A.M."

"I'll drive you. Okay, let's do something about these scripts. I'll make us some coffee and we'll work until dinner. You're going to be really surprised at some of the names on those scripts. Fast track, big money writers. They must think you have something going here. I'm impressed, Ariel. I mean that."

"Yeah. Me, too. Dolly, look me in the eye and tell me the truth. Do you think I'll come out of this okay?"

"Absolutely!"

"Okay, get the coffee."

Ariel pushed the thickly padded chair to the farthest corner in the room where she sat down to wait for Dolly. God, she would be so glad to get out of here. All she wanted was to go home and suck her thumb. She should have gone home four days ago, but she'd run a low grade fever that prevented the doctor from discharging her. Now, after three weeks and three operations, she was fit to be sent home.

The doctors and nurses were upset with her because she refused to look in the mirror. Well, guess what, Ariel thought. I don't care if you're upset with me or not. I want to be in the privacy of my own bathroom, with all that glorious lighting, when I see myself for the first time. If I fall apart I don't want anyone to see me. God, what did I ever do to deserve this? Why me? Why now?

Next week her face would be plastered all over the tabloids. Before and after pictures that they would peddle for money. Maybe I'm flattering myself, she thought glumly.

I wish . . . Maybe . . . She closed her eyes and tried to think and remember all the decisions she'd made while lying in her hospital bed. So many of them. One after the other. Give up on the production company. Or, turn it over to Carla, but that probably wouldn't work. Tell Ken Lamantia to return the money to her backers. Send back all the scripts. Close up shop and . . . do what? Put a notice in all the trade papers that she was retiring and moving away? Where? Back to Chula Vista. The only place that ever truly felt like home. And do what? Who knows. She'd be just a person there, not a hasbeen movie star. She'd buy a house, get a few pets, argue and fight with Dolly, do some gardening, get a library card, shop in Wal-Mart, go back to church. I'll write my memoirs, she told herself, put all my scrapbooks in a trunk in the attic. Maybe I can become Agnes Bixby again. Good old Aggie. I'll take long walks with my two dogs, do good deeds. And when I'm done doing that, what will I do? Exist. Try not to think about the past. Maybe I'll learn to cook. Dolly will teach me. Two dogs will keep me busy.

She cried then, because she didn't know what else to do. She thought about the good old days everyone talked about. But, were they really the good old days? Did working like a Trojan six days a week for over thirty years with vacations so few and far apart that she could barely remember them, count as good old days? Did starving herself so the extra pounds wouldn't show up on the camera constitute good old days? Did being so tired at the end of the day with no time for a social life, count? Good old days, my ass.

She thought about Max Winters, her first husband. He

was happily married now with three children. They were friends. He called often to see how she was. Max had wanted children, but she didn't. She hadn't really loved him, either. She'd tried. It didn't work. He'd been more than generous with his divorce settlement. She hadn't wanted anything, but he'd settled two million dollars on her and even told her how to invest it for the best return. Every year at Christmastime she sent champagne and poinsettias to Max and his wife, and toys for the children. He'd sent so many yellow roses, her favorite flower, after her operation, she'd been dizzy with the scent. Every day he sent a card and he called first thing in the morning and again before he retired. *Keep your chin up, kiddo. Nothing's as bad as it seems at first. Just hang in there and if there's anything you want or need, call me.*

"Give me back my old face," she blubbered into a wad of tissues.

And then there was her second husband, Adam Jessup. Adam was an actor—and prettier than she was. A fine man who didn't know the first thing about being a husband. That was okay, too, because she didn't know much about being a wife. Still, they'd stayed married for seven years, and mutually agreed to the divorce. He'd been generous, too, giving her the Malibu beach house, the Bentley, the ski chalet in Aspen, and a cool million dollars. He'd even paid her legal bills. She'd just wanted to walk away and pretend she'd never been married, but Adam said it would look terrible if he wasn't generous. *I have an image to protect, Ariel. You have to take it.* So, she'd taken it and asked Max the best way to invest it. He told her to sell the chalet and the beach house and bank the money. *Keep the Bentley—it'll be worth a lot one of these days.* She was a very wealthy woman. And look at me now. What good is money when you have to hide so people don't see you? She was crying again, and angry with herself for doing it.

Ariel paced the hospital room, her eyes deliberately avoiding the mirror over the dresser. "C'mon, Dolly, where are you? I want to get out of here." The moment the words were out of her mouth the door to her room opened. Dolly and Carla Simmons walked in, pushing a wheelchair.

"I know you don't need this, but hospital rules say you have to ride in it down to the door and then through the door to the car. Hop on, Ariel," Dolly said.

"Well, aren't you going to say something?" Ariel demanded.

"Yep. The turkey's all ready to go in the oven. I just have to stuff it in the morning. I made cranberry sauce and three pies. We're having turnips, candied sweet potatoes, string beans almandine, fresh peas that look like little emeralds, and homemade dinner rolls from scratch. Plum brandy for us and Diet Pepsi for Carla. I got this great White Russian coffee the woman in the store said is all the rage. That's it. Well, we're ready if you are."

"That's not what I meant and you damn well know it, Dolly."

"Oh, no, Ariel. If you want to know how you look, there's a mirror behind you. We'll wait. We have all the time in the world."

"I can't," Ariel whispered.

"Yes, you can. All you have to do is turn around. It's not a big mirror. You have to do it sometime, why not now so you can get it over with? Tomorrow's Thanksgiving. Think about how much you have to be grateful for. Stop being so selfish. It all worked out for you. You don't have that deadly disease you were so worried about. You had plastic surgery and now it's all over. You're going to get on with your life and life is going to be beautiful. Believe that and you're home free."

"Easy for you to say," Ariel snapped. "Carla, how bad is it?"

"You're as beautiful as you ever were. Beauty, Ariel, is in the eye of the beholder. You tell me that three times a week. If you were giving me a snow job I'm going to be mighty upset. You're a kind, generous, caring human being and it shows. Be glad you're alive and well. Think about the people that aren't so lucky. God smiled on you, Ariel, so don't be a shit now. Turn around—let's get it over with so we can go home. And get that damn hair off your face. You look like Cousin It."

"I'll do it . . . look . . . when I get home."

"No. You need to do it now. Do it, Ariel, or I quit and you can make that turkey by yourself. You can get yourself home, too."

"Why are you doing this to me? Don't you have any compassion? I'm firing you as soon as we get home."

"It doesn't work that way. Either you look now or you get home on your own. I quit yesterday so you can't fire me. I'm here now out of the goodness of my heart. I'm leaving right after Thanksgiving. To answer your question, I have bushels of compassion. So does Carla. Do it, Ariel."

"All right!"

Ariel turned, using both hands as she did so, to grasp her thick hair to pull it back from her face. Her gasp was so loud the two women watching her shuddered. When she started to wail they clasped hands, but didn't move.

"So you have a little hole in your forehead," Dolly said. "Bangs will cover it. That little droop by your left eye can be camouflaged with makeup. The one in the middle of your chin can be called a cleft. Actually, it's kind of cute. The hole in your cheek can be considered a rather large dimple. The surgeon said the droop at the corner of your mouth will disappear in about six weeks. The scars will fade in time. You're alive, Ariel. You have so much. Be thankful this is as bad as it gets."

They were right and she knew it. They cared about her. She was being selfish. She knew that, too. It was all going to take some getting used to. She turned around and smiled. She wasn't acting when she said, "I never knew how much you two meant to me until this very minute. Thanks for being here for me. I probably wouldn't have made it without you. I'm sorry about . . . being such a . . ."

"*Snot's* the word you're looking for," Dolly said and grinned.

"It's as good as any I can come up with. C'mon, let's go home and get that turkey ready. Are you really making dinner rolls from scratch, Carla? I thought you didn't know how to cook."

"I don't. It's going to be a first. They'll probably come out like hockey pucks."

"Who cares?"

Ariel sat down on the edge of the bed, weary beyond belief. The performance she'd given for Dolly and Carla's benefit during the preceding hours was worthy of an Oscar. She rolled over and snuggled with her pillow. She was alone now, in her own room, with the door locked. Now she could beat the walls, smash things, howl, swear and curse, do whatever she damn well pleased. Well, it pleased her to cry. Not just for what she was experiencing, but for all the negatives in her life. She could allow herself the luxury of tears now because it didn't matter if her eyes got red and puffy. There would be no cameras tomorrow or the day after tomorrow. There would never be cameras again. *I wish* . . . She was off the bed in a flash. She reached for the pencil hanging on a string next to the batch of wish lists. She scribbled furiously. *I wish I was still married to Felix. I wish I could find Felix. I wish he would remember me, still love me, come looking for me so he can tell me none of this matters. I wish I could recapture*

*those wonderful, special feelings I felt that day when I was
sixteen and we got married in secrecy in Tijuana. I wish . . .
Oh, Felix, where are you?*

Ariel stared at the only entry on her wish list. One entry in
thirty years. How was that possible? Why did she ever begin
the wish list in the first place? So I would never forget Felix,
that's why. He'd promised to start his own wish list. She
wished she knew if he'd followed through.

Ariel slammed the door of the louvered closet with a bang.
She was crying again. The only time you think about Felix
Sanchez is when things aren't going right for you and you
wonder what would have happened if . . . *If.* It's always *if.*
Track it, Ariel, track it to the present. If you have the guts.
Make a list, number it. I dare you. Then get the guts to add it
to the wish list. Go ahead, Ariel. That's why you want to go
back to Chula Vista. It's not that home thing, it's that Felix
thing. Admit it. Make the damn list, Ariel. Now.

1. I am Agnes Bixby. Agnes crossed the border and
married Felix Sanchez in a secret ceremony thirty
years ago.

2. Two days later Daddy got transferred to Germany. There was no time to cross the border to find
Felix. The navy packed us up and we left in thirty-six
hours. I left a note in the mailbox.

3. When I got to Germany I wrote to the school, I
wrote to everyone I could think of. I wrote letters to
Felix in care of General Delivery. I did everything I
could.

4. I dated other boys when I was in Germany. I almost forgot about Felix until I returned to California
four years later.

5. I tried to find Felix. I spent months trying to
track him down. I went to a lawyer. He did a search.

He said there was no marriage license. He said Felix tricked me to get in my pants. He told me to grow up. I think now he hated Felix. He said I was never married. Never, ever.

6. I finished college, majoring in drama. I changed my name from Agnes Bixby to Ariel Hart. I became a movie star. I changed the color of my eyes and my hair as easily as I changed my name. I had my teeth capped. The day of my first screen test Agnes Bixby retired and was never heard from again.

7. After I became a movie star I never tried to find Felix. I would have been dead in the water if I pursued that relationship. I guess he never tried to find me, either.

8. I loved Felix. He's still in my heart somewhere. I dream about him from time to time. It's true. I often think, what if . . . what if . . .

9. I was only sixteen. My parents said Felix wasn't good enough for me. I tried. Germany was so far away. I wrote hundreds of letters. Most of them came back.

10. I'm sorry, Felix. So very sorry.

Ariel walked back to the closet, removed the sheaf of papers, and added the list she'd just finished to the back of the thick pile. She tacked it back up, stared at it a minute, and then closed the door.

Why was she doing this? Because . . . because . . . Felix was always so comforting. Just thinking about him makes me feel calm. Okay, now that you've calmed down, do what you have to do. Go in the bathroom, stare at yourself, and get ready for bed. Tomorrow is another day. A new day. It's going to be whatever you make it.

Never one to follow her own advice, Ariel flopped down on the bed and was asleep within minutes. Her dreams were invaded by a tall, slender, blackeyed boy with a halo of ebony curls and the sweetest smile in the world.

"Don't be scared, Aggie. He's just going to say some words. They're going to be in Spanish. I'll whisper the meaning as he goes along. I have the ring. I made it from fishing wire. I braided it. I made one for me, too. You have to put it on my finger just the way I have to put it on yours. Someday when I'm rich and famous, I'll buy you one that's full of diamonds. What kind will you buy me?"

"A thick, fat, gold one, maybe with a design on it. Our initials on the inside and the date. How long will we have to keep our marriage a secret, Felix?"

"Until your parents start to like me. Maybe that will be soon. How long do you think it will be, Aggie?"

"I don't know, Felix. I think we might have to wait until I'm twenty-one. Then I can do whatever I want. They won't be able to say anything. It makes me mad that my mother used to let your mother clean our house, but says you aren't good enough for me. I wish my father didn't hate you. He's not tolerant at all. He doesn't even care that you have a dual citizenship. I wish your mother hadn't told my mother that you were born on her employer's kitchen floor. I heard my mother talking to my father. She said you told her that after she cleaned you up, she continued to clean the kitchen. She knew she wouldn't get paid if she didn't finish out the day. I cried when I heard her say that."

Felix's face burned crimson. "My mother worked herself into an early grave. She did all she could for us. There's no shame in hard work, Aggie. I wish . . . I wish she was alive so that when I get rich and famous I could buy her a big house and have some Anglo lady clean it for her."

She squeezed Felix's hand. "I love you so much. This is right, what we're doing, but I'm scared. How about you?"

"I'm excited. It's going to be wonderful because we love each other. Don't be scared. I found the perfect place. I fixed it up yesterday. It smells so good, Aggie. I put flowers all around and there's moss all over the place. My people call it a wedding bower. It's perfect, just the way you're perfect."

"Are you sure no one will find out, Felix? My father will kill you if he . . . he will, Felix."

"No one will find out. That's why we're going up to the mountains. The man who will marry us is a very old priest. I've known him since I was a small boy. He will keep our papers safe until we want them. I thought that was best. Do you think so, too, Aggie?"

"I can't keep them at home. My mother goes through my things. She's always looking for something. She shakes out my school books. I always tear up your notes after I memorize them. It's good that the priest is willing to keep them. You can always go back and get them when the time is right. I think I'm getting excited. More excited than scared. At this time tomorrow I'll be Mrs. Felix Sanchez. It sounds nice. Agnes Sanchez. Someday I'm going to get writing paper and have my name at the top. Should I put Aggie or Agnes?"

"I like Aggie best. It's time to go, Aggie. We're going to cross the bridge it's a long walk. Then we'll go through town till I find the path that will take us up to the mountains. It's a three-hour walk. If you get tired I'll carry you. I'm stronger than I look."

"You're perfect, Felix. Two whole days! The most time we've ever spent together. I'm so happy. We wouldn't be able to do this if my friend Helen hadn't agreed to say I was spending the weekend with her. Promise me we'll always be this happy."

"I promise. Promise me you'll love me forever and ever."

"I promise if you promise, too."

It was a long, steep climb and it took all of the three hours Felix said it would take. "I could never find my way up here again. How do you know where you're going?"

"I used to take sacks of food to the padre twice a week. Now, another family in the parish does it. The padre is a very kind man. He won't ask us any questions. I spoke to him three times. The only thing he made me promise was that I would love you in sickness and health and that part about till death do us part. I promised. You have to promise, too. I told you he doesn't speak English, didn't I? It's not a problem. We're almost there. I brought water and a soft cloth so you could freshen up. I made you a present, too," he said shyly.

"A present. Is it a wedding present? I brought something for you, too," Aggie said just as shyly.

"I love you, Aggie."

She believed him because she loved him, too.

Twenty minutes later, Felix said, "We're here." He looked up at the sun. "We have fifteen minutes before we meet the padre. We have to be on time. He takes a long nap and you can't wake him. If we don't get there on time we'll have to wait until tomorrow. Hurry, Aggie."

She wore a simple white dimity dress with a pale satin sash. She'd brought a pair of soft leather slippers to complete her wedding outfit. "I'm ready."

"Oh, Aggie, you look so beautiful. When I close my eyes I'll always remember how you looked at this moment. Here, I made this crown of flowers for your hair and this is your bouquet. I kept them in water so they're still fresh. Do I look okay?"

"Oh, yes," Aggie said. "You look more handsome than a movie star. I like your tie."

"Hurry, Aggie, It's not far, but we can't dilly around. Actually, we should run. Are you up to it?"

"For my wedding, I could fly if I had to. Lead the way, Felix."

They were breathless and flushed when they came to a halt outside a small hut in a nest of lush greenery. There were flowers everywhere, colorful blooms that were so heady, Aggie felt drunk on the scent.

The padre was old and frail, his shoulders bowed from carrying the sins of the world. His hair was a glistening pearl white in the bright sunshine. Later she swore she saw a halo over his head. He was ill, too. She didn't know how she knew, she just knew.

"Pinch me, Felix. I want to be sure I'm not dreaming," Aggie whispered as she held out her left hand. Tears misted in her eyes when she stared at the simple homemade wedding ring. She was so in love she picked up Felix's hand and kissed his ring finger.

"It's over—he just pronounced us man and wife. He's waiting for me to kiss you, and then I have to give him his present. Rich people give the padre money. I'm giving him a pouch of tobacco."

It was the sweetest kiss in all the world.

"I love you, Mrs. Sanchez."

"I love you, Mr. Sanchez.

Ariel woke from her dream, the same dream she'd had many times, her body bathed in sweat. She felt disoriented and her head was pounding. She reached over to turn on the bedside lamp. From the nighttable drawer she withdrew her keepsake box. In the bottom, wrapped in tissue, was the ring Felix had slipped on her finger. She'd looked at it before, but had never put it on her finger. She did so now, and all the memories of what came after flooded through her. That had never happened before. She told herself she'd never been this vulnerable before.

Ariel crawled back into bed. She pressed her left hand against her cheek. She was back in a mossy, flower-laden bower, a gentle smile on her face as she slipped into a dreamless sleep.

Chapter Three

Ariel looked at the Christmas tree with disdain. It was one of those perfect, artificial Hollywood Christmas trees, complete with gilt and plastic. She hated it.

It was January 2, 1995. The second day of the New Year. "I say we just dump this tree and forget about it. There's something really depressing about a white plastic tree with blue ornaments. I must have been out of my mind. It doesn't give off one bit of Christmas cheer, at least none that I've ever noticed. Less to pack, Dolly. Anything that's artificial, get rid of it. If I'm going to move into the real world, I don't want any leftovers from this world. Next Christmas we'll order a real live tree from Oregon and lots and lots of garlands to hang everywhere. Evergreens that smell good. No matter what or where we lived, my mother always insisted on a real Christmas tree. I hope next Christmas is better than this one."

Dolly ripped a strip of packing tape from the roll. "If you're in a better frame of mind than this year, it'll be great. Did you hear anything more on the house?"

"As a matter of fact, I did. Max called me this morning and made an offer. Twice what it's worth. He said he wants it for his wife's mother. I don't know if I believe him or not. I know Max—he wants to make sure I'm taken care of. He's such a decent person. In the end, I'm sure I'll sell to him because it will make life simpler. When we leave at the end of the month we won't look back."

"Are you all right with the move, Ariel? Things have moved so fast, and I worry that you might have regrets. In twenty-nine days we're moving, lock, stock, and barrel, as they say. You've been through a lot these past few months and it isn't too late to change your mind."

How worried she sounds, Ariel thought. As concerned as Max sounded. Didn't they have any faith? Do they think I can't manage my life? "Yes, it's too late, and I have no intention of changing my mind because I realize this is best for me. I'm just sorry I didn't do it two years ago. I do regret getting everyone stirred up about Perfect Productions. The truth is, it wouldn't have worked. Knowing me, I would have run myself into the ground in six months. And I would have used a lot of energy trying to stay away from people so they wouldn't pity me. *That* I couldn't handle. Since my options are limited, I'm looking at this as an adventure. Or, the beginning of the second half of my life."

"Then I say, okay. Let's roll, baby," Dolly said as she bent over to drag the white Christmas tree to the sliding door where she gave it a shove. The casters on the tree stand sped across the flagstone patio. Both women clapped their hands in glee.

"Decision number one. Accomplished! Let's get rid of all these ricky-ticky decorations. We'll get new stuff next year. Stuff that has some meaning to it. You know, things people make. Ken's bringing the pictures of our new house. It has a guest cottage on the premises. Five bedrooms, oversize den, library, Mexican kitchen, whatever that means. An Olympic-size swimming pool, tennis court, Japanese garden. A front porch. Honest, Dolly, a real front porch with rocking chairs and all kinds of green plants. He said it was gorgeous and half the price of this one. Taxes are good, he said. Oh, it has four fireplaces and you know how I love fireplaces. A dual one in the kitchen and dining room, one in the den, one in the family room, and one in my bedroom. We can put one in your room if you like. You know, in case you get the romantic urge to entertain and have a fire going. They do it in the movies all the time."

"Forget the fireplace. If I ever find someone I want to go to bed with I'll use the guest house so I can make him breakfast."

"That's a hoot, Dolly. This is the 90's. He makes breakfast for you, and do you know how I know that? I read that in not one, but two of the scripts that came in."

"I'll bear it in mind. This is the last box for this room. Do you want to start on another room or wait until after Mr. Lamantia leaves? How about if I make some hot pepperoni bread? I think it will go better with the vegetable soup than tuna, and it will be done by the time Mr. Lamantia gets here. There's some ambrosia left from yesterday."

"Sounds good to me. I'll stack these cartons against the wall. All my personal stuff that's going with us in the Range Rover is in the hallway. I don't want it to get mixed up with these cartons. When I'm done, I think I'll go for a walk around the yard."

Outside, Ariel pulled up short and stared at the house she'd lived in for twenty-five long years. Was she going to miss it? Perhaps, for a little while. God, what was she going to do with her life? She touched the holes in her face and wanted to cry. Don't think of them as holes, the surgeon had said; think of them as indentations. He'd also said if she put on some weight they would be even less visible. *They aren't as bad as you think they are, Ariel.* Easy for him to say, it wasn't his face. *Come to terms with it and move on.* "I'm trying, I really am. I'll try harder tomorrow and harder yet the day after tomorrow."

Ariel was by the front gate when a horn sounded. She pressed the release button for Ken Lamantia. His baby blue 560 SEL crept between the gates. "I do like it when my hostess meets me personally at the gate. Hop in, Ariel. I'll park in the back. This way I can go through the kitchen and see what Dolly's making for lunch and maybe filch one of those fat sugar cookies she keeps in the cookie jar."

He was a nice man, a dear man. More than that, he was a good friend of many years. He was tall and thin with dark hair graying at the temples that matched his mustache. His dark eyes twinkled behind wire-rimmed glasses. He was also a monogamous man, something almost unheard of in Hollywood. One of the things Ariel loved about him was his soft, cultured, caring voice. When he spoke, even if he was relaying bad news, you knew he was going to make things better.

Ariel could feel the knots of tension in her shoulders start to loosen. "It's a nice day, isn't it?"

"I see you finally got rid of that ratty Christmas tree. About time. This is the time, Ariel, to get rid of all your old baggage, physically and emotionally. I found you a wonderful house. Dory says it's to die for. She also said she's jealous. I think she was just saying that, don't you, Ariel? We have a beautiful house and she works hard to keep it looking that way. Sometimes I think maybe we should move, too, but my life is here, and Dory has family up in the canyon."

"Dory loves her house and no, I don't think she'd ever leave here. She's the happiest, most well-adjusted person I know, next to you. It's just an expression, Ken. And, she probably said it for my benefit, knowing you'd say something. I still can't believe I let you buy me a house."

"Why? I bought this one for you. And don't tell me I didn't

get you a good deal. Max called me yesterday and told me he's making you an offer today. Snap it up, Ariel, and don't look back."

"He's offering twice what it's worth. That's not right. I don't want or need his charity." Her voice sounded huffy, something she didn't intend.

"Not in today's real estate market. I say take it, and Max will be forever in your debt. If you don't sell to him, his mother-in-law will be living with them and he doesn't want that. You're actually doing him a favor. So, can I call him and tell him it's a deal?"

"Okay. Tell me about the business I'm buying." Ariel linked her arm with Ken's and led him around the side of the house to the kitchen patio.

"Not till you feed me. You have to eat, too, because this is the kind of business you're going to need a full stomach to hear about. Did I say that right?"

"It doesn't matter. I get your point. I think we can handle a catering business with Dolly doing the cooking and me doing the delivering and scheduling. The other possibility we discussed was a kennel you know, grooming, breeding. Jack Russell Terriers, maybe. I'd like that. The only problem is I'd probably want to keep all the puppies. Dolly seems to think a tea room would be nice. Lunch and brunch, that kind of thing. Carla suggested one of those yearround Christmas shops. None of this is right away, of course. I'll need some time to settle in and maybe piddle around with my memoirs. Everyone wants to put it on paper. Why should I be any different? I'll want to set up my house, buy some new things. If I'm going to live there the rest of my life, I want it to reflect me, Aggie Bixby, not Ariel Hart. Do you understand what I mean, Ken?"

"Yep. That's all prissy stuff, Ariel. You have so much to

offer. You need to do something meaningful. You need to make a contribution, to give back a little for all the good in your life. If you think of it in those terms we're going to make this work."

The idea was overwhelming. What did *meaningful* mean? "Dolly, I'm starved," Ariel said, to cover her discomfort. "What's for lunch?"

Dolly grinned. "Your favorite—pepperoni bread and my homemade vegetable soup. The one with the little white beans. Ambrosia for dessert."

"Our cook only makes desserts that have pumpkin in them and the only thing she cooks well is pork chops. My wife likes pork chops. Or a pork loin with potatoes and carrots. Spareribs. Pork. Callandra says pork is the other white meat. She makes wonderful desserts so we don't complain. I'll double whatever Ariel is paying you, Dolly." It was an offer he made every time he came to visit. Neither woman took him seriously.

"Eat, eat! Hurry up, Dolly," Ariel said as they finished the meal. "I can't wait to hear how we're going to earn our living from now on. More coffee? Drink it fast, Ken. Okay, tell us."

Ken leaned over the table, his chin cupped in his hands. A devilish light gleamed in his eyes. "Ariel, you are buying a trucking company, the biggest trucking company in the San Diego area. Aren't you thrilled? It's profitable. The owner thinks he's too old to run it any longer, and his wife wants to move to Hawaii. They have a son, a rock musician, who wants no part of the trucking business. Good price. You can make a fortune if you run it right. Say something, ladies."

"You're out of your mind," Ariel said.

"Now wait a minute, Ariel, think about it," Dolly urged. "I could cook and sell the truckers baskets of food. You're right, he's out of his mind."

"I knew that would be your first reaction. It was my wife's, too. Even our housekeeper said the same thing. Think about it—you're moving produce across the country. Truckers are what makes this country tick. The company is called Able Body Trucking. Mr. Able is the owner. His father and grandfather owned it before him. Very stable company. The offices leave a little to be desired. Great compound. Nine rigs go with the deal. Do you know what those babies go for? A hundred grand, some are two hundred. I signed both of you up for truck driving lessons. Can't you see yourself tooling down the roadway of life? God, this is one of the best deals I've ever put together."

"You signed us up for WHAT?" Ariel screeched.

"Truck driving lessons. You can do short hauls when business is booming. I thought you'd be excited. I spent a lot of time with Mr. Able to get the deal I got. I didn't exactly think you'd jump up and down with joy, but I did think you'd have an open mind. You do, don't you? Have an open mind, I mean. Think about the get-ups you can wear. Tight Levi's, flannel shirts, baseball caps, those yellow work boots that lace up around your ankles. Men, all kinds of men. Provided you're looking. You'll be the talk of the town. Trust me, you are gonna love this. Besides, I bought it. We can't back out now. You told me to go ahead, Ariel. You said whatever would provide a decent living, something you could sink your teeth into. This is it! The rigs have names. You can rename yours and you get to use a CB and get a handle. You know, something like 'Hot Lips' or 'Doll Baby'." He faltered at this last bit when he saw how glazed the women's eyes had become. "C'mon, Ariel, this is going to be the adventure of your life. Dolly, you tell her. I guess it is a bit of a shock. A tea room or a catering company isn't on a par with a trucking company. You need to be open-minded."

"You already said that. Whatever possessed you to buy a *trucking company?* I don't know the first thing about trucks and I don't want to learn, Ken. Neither does Dolly. Truckers are always going on strike. They want more, more, more. Those big, burly men will never accept a woman boss, much less an ex-movie actress with a disfigured face. God, Ken, I can see it *now—hear them* is more like it. Men don't like taking orders from a woman. No, get our money back. I'm not interested in the trucking business."

"It's too late. It's a done deal."

"Then you and Dory run it. This is your chance to hit the open road and take the little woman with you. Those eighteen-wheelers are nothing but penis extensions and you know it. NO!"

"Will you at least sleep on it for a few days? It's so totally unlike anything you've ever done. From the wide screen to the open road is a big change. Ariel, if this wasn't one of those once-in-a-lifetime deals I wouldn't have gone ahead with it. You love challenges. It's the perfect new life for you, in my opinion. You can do it—that's the beauty of it. A very wise investment. All right, I'm leaving now if Dolly will brown bag some of those sugar cookies. It was a delightful lunch, Ariel, and I hope I haven't made you too unhappy. I'll call you at the end of the week."

Dolly winked at Ken as she slid four plump sugar cookies into a plastic bag. "I think it's kind of a neat idea," she whispered. "What do you think about 'Big Doll' for a handle?"

"I love it! When the smoke settles, head for Rodeo Drive and pick up some classy truck driving duds. Those yellow boots will do it. They have a name, but I can't remember what it is. They never wear out, and if they do, the company replaces them. Well, I'll see you in a few days."

"Don't bother, Ken. I'm not driving a truck!" Ariel snapped.

Ken retraced his steps until he was towering over her. His usual smile and the twinkle in his eyes disappeared. "I forgot to tell you the most important thing. You have to get a dog and you need a shotgun and a revolver. The dog goes with you at all times, as do the weapons. I'd suggest a shepherd or a Doberman. I signed up both of you for lessons at a rifle range nearby. Consider it a refresher course. I know you were a crack shot in *Lady Bandit,* but this is real life and you probably forgot everything you learned. A retired police officer will teach you. I also signed you up for a refresher course in karate. You were a star pupil, as I recall, and I know that you kept up with it, but again, this is real life so a few lessons will be good."

"Give me back those cookies," Ariel said, snatching the brown bag. "Go! Go! Out! You've finally lost it, Ken! Dogs, guns, martial arts, trucks! I'm an actress!"

"You *were* an actress. Now it's time to do other things. I wouldn't take those cookies now if you begged me. Those tears aren't going to faze me one damn bit, Ariel, so don't start blubbering. Do you know where I'm going now? I'll tell you where I'm going. Back to the office to buy you a goddamn, fucking tea room. You can serve herbal tea and cucumber sandwiches till you're blue in the face. Now that's a role I know you can play." He snatched the bag of cookies and was out the door before Ariel could come up with a suitable retort.

"Say something, Dolly."

"I hate herbal tea and I never made a cucumber sandwich in my life."

"What's to know? You cut the crust off, spread some stuff on the bread, and layer the cucumbers. Tea makes itself."

"I don't think I want to do that. In fact, I know I don't want to do it. If I were you I'd call Ken before he buys you a tea room. I don't think I ever said I wanted a tea room. If I did, I was temporarily insane. I said catering. Tea rooms have ruffled tablecloths and prissy white curtains. The waitresses wear frilly aprons and the patrons have white hair. My vote is no."

"Oh, shit!" Ariel said.

"That pretty much sums it up," Dolly said. "I'll clean up here. You can start to pack up your room."

"I'm not driving a truck."

"Maybe you shouldn't be so hasty, Ariel. Think about all the mileage you can get in the trades. They'll probably want to make a movie of your life when this gets out. I think Ken's wrong about Rodeo Drive, though. How about if I go to Sears and pick us up some duds, just for the fun of it. We can try them on and kind of get a feel for it. Then I can take them back. I'll get the permit for the guns and pick up some toy ones so we can practice. The dog will have to wait, though. What do you think?"

"I'm not driving a truck! And, you seem to forget I'm no longer a movie star. No one is going to want to make a movie of my life, and if they did, I'd say no."

Dolly turned her back so she wouldn't burst into laughter as Ariel stomped from the room. She held her iced tea glass aloft. "Here's to the trucking business!"

The dishes were dumped willy-nilly in the sink. In seconds Dolly had her feet into scuffed moccasins and was out the door. "Sears, here I come! Bang! Bang! Freeze!"

Thirty-one days later, Ariel Hart walked into the offices of Able Body Trucking and announced herself as the new owner. Her face was grim, her eyes defying any of the office staff to make a move. To the six women she said, "Stop whatever you're doing and write me a paragraph, two if need be, describing what you do for this company. Attach samples, forms, whatever you use, to the paper. I want it within the hour. After you do that, you can go to lunch."

Voices came from everywhere.

"Who will answer the phone?"

"We never all go to lunch at the same time."

"We're short on forms."

"Who's in charge of the office?"

"Is it still Margie?"

"Duke and Chet are due in two hours and we have to have someone here to talk to Lex Sanders when he calls. He's mad as a wet hornet right now."

Ariel's answer was a blasé "Don't worry about it. Just do as I say and we'll all get along just fine. Cross me and you're out the door. Dolly and I will answer the phones until we can get a system worked out. Talking on the phone will be counterproductive."

"Does that mean me, too?" a frizzy redhead with a face full of freckles asked.

"If you work here, it does. Do you have a problem with this?"

"I don't, ma'am, but Lex Sanders might. I take care of all his business. When he calls in, which is sometimes four or five times a day, he doesn't want to be put on hold or any-thing like that. He wants answers the minute he calls. He's our biggest customer. He gets nasty when he has to wait or if we have to call him back."

"Don't worry about Mr. Sanders. I've just relieved you of that responsibility. You can, however, pull his file or whatever you keep for individual accounts, and bring it to me. Tell me exactly what you do for Mr. Sanders in your summary paragraph. I want to know why one person is on call for a single customer. Another thing, do any of you know who decorated this office?"

The women laughed. The redhead said, "Mr. Able thinks . . . thought, that red shades and green carpet would make people think Christmas all the time and keep them in good spirits. I don't know where he got the desks and chairs, maybe the Salvation Army. Wait till you see his office. Your office, I mean."

Ariel's, "Oh, my God!" rang through the entire five-thousand-square-foot office building. She started to bellow. "Where's the maintence man? Get him in here! Now!"

"We don't have one. Mr. Able took care of his office. We take care of the outer office," someone responded.

"It smells in here," Ariel said, breathing through her mouth.

"Cat urine," Dolly said, taking a deep breath, "and there's the offender." She pointed to a mangy yellow cat sitting in a hole in the middle of a ratty leather sofa full of patches.

"Obviously the cat goes with the deal. Make a list, Dolly: cat bed, litter box, and food. How old do you think this carpet is? I don't think I ever saw a mustard yellow carpet before, even in the prop room back in L.A. Those stains defy description." Ariel dropped to her knees as she held her nose. "Coffee, soda, tomato sauce, ground-in tobacco, cat urine, ink. Do you think I missed anything?"

"A hundred years of dirt," Dolly sniffed. "I say we rip it out right now. We have six able-bodied women out there. They might help us."

"And they might not. We can do it ourselves," Ariel said. "Look at those chairs—they're full of cat hair, stains, and fuzz balls. The couch is worse—you can see the springs sticking out. I don't believe this," she said, pulling a chunk of material out of one of the holes. "It's the leg from a pair of jeans. I bet there are *things* living in this furniture and the cat eats the things and that's why there's no cat food. God!"

Of the five windows in the office, one had a venetian blind

that hung askew, one window had a brown plaid curtain, one had a pull-down shade that was tattered and ripped, and the fourth and fifth windows were bare and dirty, making it impossible to see outside. Ariel snapped the shade and was rewarded with a cloud of dust in her face.

The desk was an old dining room table that had probably been beautiful at one time. Now it was littered, cigarette-scarred, and filthy dirty. Something that looked like green beans and corn had mildew and mold growing around it in the cracks and grooves. An ancient Underwood typewriter sat square in the middle of the desk. Ariel sat down in the burgundy swivel chair. "This is comfortable, but it has to go. I think the cat spent a lot of time here. He might have a home inside the safe, too," Ariel said as she pointed to a large Wells Fargo safe whose door was hanging on one hinge. Aside from the stacks of boxes lined up against the walls, there was no other furniture. The walls, however, were a different story. They were the same mustard color and were peppered with pictures of Teddy Roosevelt: on his horse, in a chair, standing by a railing, at ease under a tree smoking a cigar, and shaking hands with Asa Able. All were signed, *To my friend, Asa*. The signature was simple . . . *T.R.*

"Asa must be Mr. Able's father. I wonder why he didn't take them. They could be valuable. If he doesn't want them, maybe we can donate them to a museum."

The phone rang—a froggy, low-pitched gurgle. Dolly giggled as Ariel reached across the dining room table to pick up the black plastic phone. "Able Body Trucking," she said sweetly. She winked at Dolly, who rolled her eyes. Ariel listened a moment before she spoke. "Bernice is busy right now. Ethel is busy, too. No, Helen is occupied. Well, you could tell me what you want. To whom am I speaking? Lex Sanders. Yes, Mr. Sanders, what can I do for you?" She listened a moment and then said, "I'll have to get back to you, Mr. Sanders. My name? My name is Ariel Hart. No, Mr. Able isn't here. Mr. Able sold the company to me, Mr. Sanders. He told me he was sending out letters to all his clients. I'm sorry you didn't get yours. I could make up a copy and Fax it to you as soon as I get a Fax. Actually, we're in the process of cleaning up these offices and installing a computer system. Things will run so much more smoothly. No, Bernice is still busy." Ariel held the phone away from her ear so Dolly could hear the sputtering and squawking on the other end of the phone. "Late this afternoon or first thing in the morning. It's the best I can do at the moment. Yes, Mr. Sanders, I'll get right on it. Oh, you bet. Uh-huh. No problem."

"Bernice!"

The freckled redhead poked her head into the office. "Yes, ma'am?"

"That was Mr. Sanders on the phone. He says our truck is ninety minutes late and he sounded rather hostile. Did the driver call in? Can't Mr. Sanders call him on the CB or something?"

"He wasn't ninety minutes late, he was forty-five minutes late. One of his hoses broke and he hit three radar traps. He made his delivery. We're ahead of the game if we make delivery within an hour's time frame."

"Is Mr. Sanders insecure?" Ariel asked curiously.

"Mr. Sanders calls his concern 'taking care of business.' He's the biggest rancher in the area. About a year ago the 'Lifetime' section of the newspaper did a writeup on Mr. Sanders. They said he was a multimillionaire. He's got hundreds of employees and he's Able Body Trucking's biggest customer. Mr. Able always . . . what he did was . . . cater to Mr. Sanders because he knew he could count on his money. That's another way of saying Mr Sanders is our bread and butter. Our other accounts aren't as steady as he is. Sometimes Mr. Able would send some of our customers to other, smaller truckers to accommodate Mr. Sanders and at the same time, create good will with the other companies."

"I see." To Dolly she said, "I guess this isn't any different from Hollywood. It isn't *what* you know, it's *who* you know. I had to play that game for too many years. No more. If this is a business, then we're going to run it like a business. If we make mistakes we'll learn from them. We have to establish the ground rules now at the outset. The first thing I want to find out is how much business Mr. Sanders gives us compared to our other customers. Since Mr. Sanders's immediate problem has been taken care of, I suggest we get on with our demolition plans. C'mon, let's start carrying this junk outside."

It was late in the day when a trash hauler pulled his truck up to the loading area and dumped all of Mr. Able's furnishings into the back. Ariel gasped when he handed her a check for five hundred dollars. "For the safe—we can fix it—and for the antique dining room table," the man said.

The trash collector was no sooner out of the compound when the decorator swerved into the lot in a sunny yellow Ford Mustang convertible. A bespectacled man emerged, carrying samples and a heavy case. It took exactly ninety minutes to select the carpeting, tile for the entryway, and fabric for the vertical blinds. Chairs, desk, oak filing cabinets, and lamps were chosen from a catalog of furniture that was in stock. Delivery was promised in five days, time that would be spent having the offices cleaned and painted by a subcontractor on the decorator's list. A florist promised delivery of live plants and agreed to maintain them on a ten-day basis. Another subcontractor was hired to replace the straggly flowers and shrubbery on the outside of the building. A third was to install awnings over the front windows and entrance. Still another agreed to have a new stove, dishwasher, and top-of-the-line refrigerator installed as soon as the new floor was down in the kitchen. A double stainless steel sink was a must, the decorator said, along with ready-made cabinets. He also said he had just the right oak table, inlaid with patterned tile. The kitchen, he said, could easily hold six chairs. A colorful valance was selected for the massive kitchen window.

Ariel dusted her hands dramatically after she signed the contract and only winced slightly when she wrote out the check.

"It's done, Dolly. The telephone and computer people will be here tomorrow while we have our first driving lesson. Do you have everything we need for our work session tonight?"

"I got it right here. Insurance, payroll, the whole ball of wax. Didn't you forget something, Ariel?"

"No. Why?"

"Weren't you supposed to call Mr. Sanders?"

"You're right. Guess what—you packed up the Rolodex. We'll do it when we go home. And if we don't, what's he going to do to us? I don't have time for prima donnas. What do they call a male prima donna?"

"Probably something like jerk." Dolly grinned, then Ariel giggled. Dolly couldn't remember the last time she'd heard Ariel laugh, much less giggle. This new plan was going to work out—she was sure of it.

As Ariel and Dolly carried the boxes and bags into the house, Lex Sanders was bellowing at the top of his lungs to be admitted to the Able Body Trucking offices. When he realized no one was going to open the door, he gave it a vicious kick. Then he stormed over to the loading dock where Stan Petrie was checking in a load of paper products. "Where is everyone, Stan? It's only four o'clock."

"They closed up and left around three. It's been real busy here today. Something wrong, Lex?"

"Hell, yes, something's wrong. I must have called here a dozen times today and got nowhere. This sellout happened rather quickly, don't you think?"

"Not for me to say, Lex. Mrs. Able, she wanted to go to Hawaii, is all I know. They left three days ago. The new lady owner said things would stay the same with a few changes for the betterment of the company. She was real busy today throwing away all of Mr. Able's office stuff. A decorator come by. I hear computer and telephone people will be here tomorrow. A locksmith was here, security alarms are going in all over the place. And an electrified fence."

"Okay, Zack, that does it. See you tomorrow," Stan said. He waved the trucker off before he fired up an evil-smelling cigar.

"Why?" The one word was like an explosion.

A look of disgust washed over Stan's face. "Like I know? The only reason I know this much is because Bernice wanted me to put some air in her tires and she talked to me while she waited. She said the new owner is a movie star. A looker, from what I could see," the older man said slyly.

"Jesus Christ! Does she know anything about the trucking business?"

"Don't know. Bernice says she knows how to decorate and is spending a fortune on that. Wouldn't be surprised if she don't go and hang curtains in the cabs of the trucks. Now wouldn't that be somethin'?" He guffawed, slapping his knees at the same time.

Lex Sanders pushed his Padres baseball cap back on his head. His gray eyes narrowed. "Yeah, that would be something, Stan. Maybe it's time for me to look for another trucking company. You can pass the word along tomorrow."

"You best be doin' that yourself, Lex. I only got five years to go for retirement. I don't like sticking my nose where it don't belong. Now if you want to leave a note or a letter, I can slide it under the door."

"That won't be necessary. I don't suppose you have a home phone number for the lady, do you?"

"Does the Pope wear roller skates? No, I don't have a home phone number. Maybe the night watchman has it. He don't come on till six. You can try calling him then."

"Yeah, maybe I'll do that."

"Now, there goes one wet hornet," Stan muttered as Lex Sanders drove off in a grinding blast of gravel.

On the drive home to Bonsall, Lex tried to shift his angry mind into a neutral zone. He hated losing his cool, because when he got angry, the Arabians sensed it and reacted. A movie star! Damn. And Asa, going off without so much as a goodbye, go to hell, or drop dead. Letters my foot. He'd always gotten mail from Asa—why wouldn't this last notice reach him if one was even sent? It wasn't that he couldn't handle the new sale, it wasn't that at all. Asa was a friend, a surrogate father of sorts. Hell, he'd made him rich. "God-dammit, Asa, I deserve better than this."

Lex slouched down in the seat of his battered pickup, settled his aviator glasses more firmly on the bridge of his nose, and let his mind wander the way it always did when he came to Chula Vista. The drive down was exciting because he always hoped that somewhere along the way, or at the end of the drive, he would see Aggie Bixby. In thirty years it had never happened, but he still hoped. The trip home was always, like now, a real downer.

He wished Aggie could see him now, rich and successful and in a position to give her everything he'd ever promised. All he had left of Aggie were his memories and a tattered marriage certificate. Maybe he should have gotten a divorce. If he wasn't a practicing Catholic, maybe he would have. It no longer mattered. At this stage in his life he wasn't about to get married and share everything he'd busted his ass to get working twenty hours a day, seven days a week, fifty-two weeks a year. And he wasn't about to share his dark secret. No one needed to know he was once a rail-thin Mexican kid born on a gringo's kitchen floor. No one needed to know that after giving birth his mother went back to scrubbing and polishing. No one needed to know that Arnold Sanders sent him to agriculture school and left him his tiny eleven-acre avocado ranch, providing it was always known as the Sanders Ranch. He'd agreed and even took the name Sanders to make life easier. And why not? His father had moved the whole family to Bonsall to work for Sanders. They'd all lived in two cramped trailers tending to the groves and to the Sanders family. His sisters and aunts had cleaned their houses and his brothers and father had maintained the ranch and the animals. He was the only one who had benefited directly. He'd gotten a fine education and now owned over ten thousand acres of avocado groves. He grew lettuce and broccoli on another ten thousand acres and raised Arabian horses. He wished his parents were alive to reap the benefits of all his hard work. He wished Aggie was here so he could shower her with everything he'd promised. He closed his eyes for one brief moment. A vision of Aggie in her white dress and the flower crown he'd woven for her made his eyes water. So long ago. Another life. Why hadn't she ever tried to find him the way he'd tried to find her? He couldn't remember the exact time he'd finally given up. He just knew it was a very long time ago. In his mind, he tried to picture the way she'd look today. She'd had such glorious long, brown hair that curled at the ends and soft, dark eyes. He'd seen dolls later in life who had complexions like Aggie's. He'd even bought some of the dolls for his nieces, but they weren't half as pretty as Aggie had been. He'd asked the salesgirl if she'd put pink hair ribbons in the dolls' hair because Aggie always wore pink ribbons.

Damn, thirty years was too long to carry a torch for a teenage love affair. "Guess that makes me a one-woman man. You need to say goodbye to Aggie Bixby the way you said goodbye to Felix Sanchez. Easier said than done," he muttered.

A long time later, his thoughts in a turmoil, Lex headed for the nearest restaurant for a quick bite before heading back to Bonsall. It was a steak house known for its charbroiled New York rib eyes and twice-baked potatoes. He usually ordered two of everything. The waitress, a coy blonde, flirted openly as she ignored the two women sitting across from him in a dim corner. To Lex's experienced eye, the waitress looked like she'd been rode hard and hung up wet. He did his best to be polite without being rude. "Two bottles of Bud Ice."

Across the room, Ariel Hart seethed as she tried unsuccessfully to get the waitress's attention. "Five more minutes and I'm getting the manager. I know how busy a waitress can be and how they have to hustle, but when said waitress is flirting with a guy, that makes me mad. The man doesn't seem to be responding, so what's her problem?"

"Why don't *we* flirt with him? He's handsome enough," Dolly said. "He's looking at us and his eyes are apologetic. Did you see that little thing he did with his eyebrows? He's flirting with you, Ariel. Flirt back. He looks rugged. Get a gander at those boots and jeans. Working man. Wears a baseball cap. You love men with dark, curly hair. So it has a little gray in it. So does yours under that Clairol stuff you put on it. Look how much you already have in common."

"Stop it, Dolly. We came in here to eat so you wouldn't have to cook this evening."

"Miss! Miss!" Ariel had never snapped her fingers at anyone, but she did so now. When she had the waitress's attention, she said, "We've been sitting here for almost twenty minutes and we were here before that gentleman. If you're too busy, we can go somewhere else or I can call your manager and see what he can do."

"Ladies, I'm sorry, please accept my apology. My food can wait. Serve the ladies and give me their check. I insist," Lex said to the waitress.

"That's not necessary," Ariel demurred. Dolly was right, he was handsome as sin.

"Oh, but it is. If I was in your position, and I have been, I'd be mad as a hornet. I insist."

Ariel smiled. "Thank you, you're very generous."

Lex turned back to his newspaper, but his mind wasn't on the front page, it was on the pretty woman with the waterfall of blond hair sitting in the corner. He should have gotten up and joined them. The only problem was, he wasn't much on casual conversation and they might think he was trying to pick them up. He felt his neck grow warm. He could have gotten at least fifteen minutes worth of conversation with the Padres baseball cap. He was wearing one and there was one on the table, which meant one of the women was wearing it. Probably the blonde, since her hair was mashed down on the top of her head. The lady with the pigtail probably didn't wear a hat. For someone who doesn't know much about women you certainly are observant, he chided himself.

He liked the sound of her voice when she ordered her meal. "Porterhouse steak, charred but medium rare, large, twice-baked potato, corn, string beans, applesauce, and we'll have two bottles of Coors Light. Chips and salsa with the beer. My friend will have the same." A woman after his own heart. He smiled and wished there was someone in the steak house who knew both of them so he could wangle an introduction. Always the last one out of the gate, Sanders. He tried to concentrate on the problems in the Middle East. Maybe they'd stop by his table when they left. He lit a cigarette and noticed they were smoking, too. That made things easier. This was, after all, the smoking section, one of the few restaurants in California that still allowed smoking. It was one of the reasons he ate here from time to time. He grinned when he noticed, out of the corner of his eye, that both women drank from the bottle. He tried again to concentrate on the front page of the paper. His feet itched to move closer to their table.

Across the room, the women covertly watched the man with the newspaper as they munched on chips and salsa. They ordered a second beer. "He reminds me of someone, but I don't know who," Ariel whispered.

"If you knew someone like that, I'd remember. Unless, of course, you don't tell me everything. That's a *man*. Back in Hollywood the actors looked like that, but off the screen they were *wusses*. I think we should stop by his table and thank him on the way out. You know, hold out your hand, introduce yourself, and thank him for dinner."

"I can't do that. Besides, I already thanked him. Stop matchmaking. He'll think we're trying to pick him up like that waitress. There's two of us. God, he might think . . . No, one thank-you is enough. Here's our food. Look, she's got his on the tray, too. That means he'll probably finish when we do. If we leave at the same time we can say something casual then. Eat," Ariel ordered, clearly frustrated with the scenario she'd just created.

"Who do you think he reminds you of?"

"I don't know. Someone who's passed through my life. I'm pretty good with faces, but I'm not good with names. It doesn't matter. I'm really tired, Dolly. I can't wait to get out of here and home to a hot bath."

"Me, too. I'm almost too tired to eat. Am I going to give you a computer lesson tonight or do you want to get up early tomorrow? Guess what I learned today. We got an order to pick up twenty thousand Coke bottles. But, they aren't the real bottles you see in the store, they're like test tubes and our driver takes them to where they get blown into bottles. Interesting, huh? And a pickup came in for us to haul forty-two thousand pounds of butter cookies. Pickups come in all the time. Tomorrow we have to pick up a load of Guess? jeans and take them to the place where they get stonewashed. The things you learn. I say we skip dessert."

"Okay, I'm ready, but I have to use the ladies' room. Where is it?"

"Over there," Dolly said, pointing to Ariel's left. "Guess we can leave by that entrance. Which means we either walk over to that guy's table or we forget it."

"Let's decide after we use the ladies' room. Two beers don't allow me to stand around and chitchat."

"He's gone," Dolly said.

Outside, in the darkness, a dark pickup backed up, turned, and crawled past them. "It's him," Dolly said. "Do something. His window looks like it's down."

"Thanks for dinner," Ariel shouted. "That was very kind of you."

"My pleasure," the man said as he drove off.

"I know that voice or one that sounds like it. When I least expect it, it'll come to me. Time to go home, Dolly."

"Bet you dream about that guy tonight," Dolly said.

"Bet I don't."

"Bet you do!"

"That's a sucker bet and you know it," Ariel giggled, "but I'll take it."

"You're on, Miz Ariel Hart."

It was almost like old times, when Ariel was one of the prettiest actresses in Hollywood.

Almost.

"The morning will be fine."

Lex saddled up one of his Arabians, a stallion named KO for King Omar. He cantered away from the barn before giving the stallion his head. The horse pounded over the hard ground, his hooves spewing up clumps of dark brown sod. Go, KO, drive these demons from my head. "Go, boy, go!"

Chapter Four

The grand unveiling of Able Body Trucking's new offices was scheduled, ironically, for Valentine's Day. "It's probably an omen of some kind and I'm too stupid to see it," Ariel said as she fit the key into the brand new lock on the office door. It was six o'clock in the morning and she was shivering, as was Dolly. "Maybe we should have stayed yesterday, but it was ten o'clock and I was too tired. I'm still tired." She was grumbling, and she hated herself for acting this way. "The carpet people promised to place all the furniture. I paid extra for that little contribution. The florist said she'd be here a little before five, or as soon as she can after she gets back from the wholesale market. So . . . I say let's open this door and hope everything is the way I want it to be."

It was everything she wanted it to be and more. The meadow green carpet seemed thicker and more lush than she'd remembered. The vertical blinds, with a thread of meadow green running lengthwise, were a perfect complement to the luxurious carpet. The light oak desk and hunter green leather chair brought the room together. The deep, comfortable client chairs in front of the desk were covered in a nubby green fabric that felt silky to the touch. Feathery green ferns nestled on oak pedestals in all the corners. A shiny-leaf plant in a red clay pot sat on the corner of Ariel's desk, right next to the brand new computer she didn't know how to use. A smaller room, next to Ariel's office, was Dolly's office. The furnishings were identical, right down to the computer and plant on her desk.

Dolly's braid swished back and forth as she bounced up and down on her ergonomic chair. "This is all pretty nice, but neither of us knows diddly-squat about computers. Those women in the outer office don't know anything, either. We could probably run this company into the ground with very little effort."

"We'll be computer literate inside of a week. We're going to . . . to . . . input all that stuff in those boxes into the computer. We can do this, Dolly. Think positive."

"I *am* thinking. When are we going to fit this into our schedule? We have truck driving lessons every morning. We have firearms in the afternoon and martial arts lessons. We'll be too tired in the evenings to absorb anything. You have to pay attention when you're on a computer. One of the characters on my soap opera erased a whole folder full of numbered Swiss bank accounts. *'Gone'!*" she said dramatically. *"'Millions down the drain'!"*

"That's not going to happen to us. We'll schedule the computer lessons for early in the morning at my house. We'll pay the girls for their travel time and the time they spend on the class. I think that's fair. The lessons can start at seven, after we have breakfast. Nothing fancy, whatever you feel in the mood to make. Supper's leftovers."

"Who's going to be in the office? Somebody needs to be here. Think about this—I make breakfast and then I go to the office. Maybe they have another teacher who can train me there. See if you can find one with a lot of patience who won't mind interruptions. Phone's ringing, Ariel."

"I know. I just don't know which buttons to press. There should be a manual here someplace."

"By the time you find it, we'll have lost an account. Press all of them and see what happens."

Ariel did as instructed. She pressed button after button and said "Able Body Trucking" six times before she heard a voice on the other end of the line. "Yes, Mr. Sanders." She listened politely. "It's ten minutes past six, Mr. Sanders. We don't open until seven. I think it's wonderful that Mr. Able was in the office at five in the morning. I'm not Mr. Able. The schedule is on the door. I believe Mr. Able put it there him-self. Our hours are seven to seven. The dispatcher's office is open twenty-four hours a day. It's commendable that you rise at four in the morning. I get up at six the way most people do and I'll be here at seven. Now, what is it you want? I'm prob-ably not going to be able to help you, anyway. We're under-going renovations here and all the paperwork is . . . is being . . . fed into a computer. You can, however, check with Stanley or the dispatcher. Yes, he is a bit of a curmudgeon, but he's a loyal curmudgeon and it's my understanding that he knows everything there is to know about Able Body Trucking. Lunch? I can't. I'm too busy. I'm booked up until the middle of June, lunchwise that is. No, I'm not putting you on. Of course we can accommodate you on delivery. Tell me what you want. I can't make arrangements unless you're specific. Yes, I have a pencil."

"As usual, his problem is not earth-shattering and he could have called the dispatcher. You know something, Dolly? He has this strange voice—it reminds me of someone, but I can't think who. Actually, it's kind of sexy." Her hand flew to her cheek in a purely reflex motion. Dolly turned away. "He in-vited me to lunch. I said no. He probably wants preferential treatment and wants to butter me up. Not likely." Her thumb caressed the indentation in her cheek and then moved down to the cleft in her chin. "Not likely."

"You know, Ariel, he *is* this company's biggest client. You should give this man a little more consideration. What if he takes his business elsewhere?"

"And do you think another company will put up with him?"

"Money's money. People shape up real good when greenbacks are involved. A smaller company might have the time to coddle him."

"That's like paying a maître d' for a table in a restaurant."

"And you've never done that? Get real, Ariel. I say you should meet him for lunch or coffee the next time he's in town and lay down the ground rules. When he understands, he might fall into line. If he doesn't, you tried. Unless, of course, you're afraid to meet him." Her voice was sly sounding, her eyes just as sly looking. She watched as Ariel continued to massage the pink scars on her face.

"I'll give it some thought. Don't get any matchmaking ideas, Dolly. The first rule of business, as anyone knows, is don't mix business with pleasure. Let's make some coffee and get the inventory started."

They worked steadily until the office staff arrived. They were rewarded with exclamations of delight that sent shivers up and down their spines. "I guess that means we did good," Ariel said, and smiled.

"This can't be the same place I've worked in for ten years," the freckle-faced Bernice said "That computer looks like a machine from hell. I'm getting nervous just looking at it."

"Not to worry," Ariel said blithely. "Here's the plan. But, first I want to ask all of you something. Do any of you want to learn how to drive these rigs? If you do, the company will pay for the course. Even if you never drive on the open road, having the license will be a plus. If the truckers ever go on strike we'll have it covered to a degree. This is in no way mandatory. The course starts today at nine o'clock. We can call in a temporary agency to work here mornings until we get through it. Inventory is a bitch, as you well know. And, putting all this stuff into these computers is going to take some expertise. I say we go for it."

"Okay, count us in," Bernice said, speaking for the others.

"Will the guys start calling us 'the good old girls'?" someone asked.

"Will we have to learn how to park those rigs? I can't even parallel park my car," another said.

"Guess we'll find all that out this morning. Dolly's going to call the temp office so each of you get out your work for the day and have it ready. The computer people loaded your program so a knowledgeable person shouldn't have any trouble."

"Who's our boss?" Bernice asked. "What I mean is, if we ever go out on the road, who do we answer to?"

"Me!" Ariel said smartly. Her heart was pounding so furiously she thought it would jump right out of her chest. She was taking charge, and she was damn well going to make all of this work. She gave herself a mental shake when she saw an eighteen-wheeler glide past the wide double windows. It looked like an untamed monster. She remembered a trucking movie with Jan Michael Vincent called *White Line Fever.* She also remembered rooting for the actor and cursing the bad guys, who just happened to be other truckers. That was a movie. This was real life. Things like that didn't happen in real life. Maybe she'd call Jan and ask him where he did his research for the role. When she had time.

Promptly at 8:45, the women piled into the company van and headed for their instruction course five miles away. As they were exiting the lot, Bernice shouted from the back seat, "Lordy, lordy, there goes Mr. Sanders. Bet he gives that temporary an Excedrin headache. Do you want to hear something funny?" Not bothering to wait for a reply, she continued, "Mr. Sanders rarely comes down here, but he's been here several times recently. He does call all the time and he did go to Mr. Able's for dinners and such, but he hardly ever came here. It seems strange to me. Maybe he's frightened of you, Miss Hart. A big guy like him, frightened of a little slip of a thing like you. It's just too funny."

Ariel adjusted the brim of her Padres baseball cap lower over her forehead. She found herself tugging at a lock of hair over her ear so that it would partially cover her cheek. Her heart was pounding again and she didn't know why. In the whole of her life, to her knowledge, no one had ever been frightened of her. Bernice was being silly. Too silly to even think about.

"Stop doing that," Dolly hissed. "People tend to stare more, trying to figure out what you're hiding. Stick that hair back under your cap. That's an order, Ariel."

"Nag, nag, nag." But Ariel did as instructed.

"And stop touching your face. Every time I see you doing it from now on, I'm giving you a good swat. It's there, it isn't going away. Life goes on, Ariel. Live with it. End of sermon."

"Thank you. As usual, you're right. He was rather handsome, wasn't he? Reminds me of that guy who paid for our dinner the other night. He was driving a truck, too. Maybe it's him."

"You noticed."

"I would notice anyone doing eighty miles an hour over a stop ramp."

"Jeez, we're among the living again. Thank you, God," Dolly said.

"Thank *you*, Dolly," Ariel whispered under her breath.

Ariel swerved the van into the trucking lot. "This is it, ladies. Take a good look, but make it quick because in less than ten minutes you'll be behind the wheel of that mother. Looking at these trucks from our window is one thing, sitting behind the wheel is something else. Are we ready?"

God, she was enjoying this. She felt really alive for the first time in years. How much the feeling had to do with returning to Chula Vista and how much it had to do with a man named Lex Sanders, she didn't know.

"We're ready!"

"Hmmmnn," Lex Sanders mused as he brought his pickup to a stop outside the dispatcher's office. "Tell me something, Bucky," he said to the gravelly-voiced dispatcher. "Was that the new owner in the van?"

"Sure was. Strange lady. But a nice lady. I just got done sneakin' a look at the new office decorations. I ain't no expert, but my wife buys furniture from time to time and we don't have nothin' as good as that lady put in them offices. Shiny green plants, colored ashtrays, fine pictures on the wall. You can see out of them windows now. She tossed out Asa's safe and had a spiffy new one put in the wall. There's an alarm system, computers, a fancy-dancy telephone with all kinds of buttons. Chairs look comfortable. There's a person in there now, bangin' away at the computer. Wait till you see that carpet. Makes you want to take off your shoes and wiggle your toes. Real pretty." He spit a wad of tobacco juice out the door before he reached for his cup of coffee that was so dirty and cruddy, Lex knew it had never seen soap or water.

"Who's operating the office?" Lex's expression was baffled.

The dispatcher grinned. "A machine answers the phone and a lady's doing somethin' with that computer."

"I'll be damned! Is she really a movie star?"

"That's what they say. I ain't never seen her up close.

Spoke to her on the phone. Seemed real nice. Asked me if I needed anythin'. Her assistant brought me a real nice lunch the other day. Good cook. This ain't my business, but seein' as how Mr. Able thought so much of you as a friend and customer, you should know Chet's stirrin' up trouble. I heard—and I ain't sure I should even be mentionin' this, but I'm gonna do it anyway—I heard he's goin' after the rancher's workers, stirrin' them up, too. Best keep your eyes and ears open. Ain't nothin' worse than a wildcat walkout. Don't even matter what the reason is."

"Maybe the new owner will fire him. Asa seemed to think he needed him. He's trouble and I think Chet is one of the reasons Asa sold out. He didn't want to be hassled anymore."

"Asa left this letter for you. I been holdin' it till you got here. Asa felt real bad."

Lex sighed. Suddenly he no longer felt betrayed. Asa hadn't turned on him and gone off without saying good-by. He now regretted his surly attitude with the new owner. He could make that right on his way back to the ranch. He'd stop and have some flowers sent to Ms. Ariel Hart. Small white orchids mixed with those little popcorn balls, the kind of flowers Aggie used to like. Hang it up already, Lex. Stop living in the past. Send the lady a dozen roses and be done with it, he admonished himself. Invite her out to a nice dinner and make peace. You need her trucking company. You might even like her. Better yet, she might like you.

Highly unlikely. He was talking to himself something he hated doing, yet he did it almost every day of his life. He was his own best friend, his only confidant. Why, he didn't know. On the other hand, maybe he did know and didn't want to deal with it. It was that old Mexican thing. The old mores: you Mexican, me gringo. Know your place, Mex. Don't step out of line. He'd worked his ass off and gotten his degree and then, because a very kind man believed in him, he'd stepped over the line. Because . . . because he'd received an American inheritance and an American name.

Damn, he'd almost missed the flower shop. He ground to a halt, his tires smoking on the asphalt. For a moment he felt befuddled. The windows of the flower shop were covered with red hearts, cupids with arrows, and trailing ribbons. "Valentine's Day!" He groaned. A bell tinkled over the door as he walked through. A day for lovers. He felt like groaning again.

"I'd like an arrangement of small white orchids and those . . . no, no, that's not what I want. Roses, pink or yellow. White's okay. No red."

"I'm sorry, sir, we're all out of roses. We do have orchids. I could make you a lovely arrangement."

"Okay." It *was* okay; he'd followed his own advice and there were no roses. Orchids didn't mean he was living in the past, orchids meant he had a choice. Huge pompoms, big as grapefruits, or delicate, hybrid orchids. He rather thought the huge blooms were for grandmothers and aunts. He handed over seventy-five dollars after he winced from the shock, gave the address, and filled out the little card. He apologized for his surly attitude, suggested dinner, and promised to be more considerate of her employees.

That done, Lex climbed into his truck. The letter from Asa Able was on the seat. He ripped it open and read the short note, feeling his eyes mist over.

Dear Lex,

I'm sorry that you have to hear about the sale of the business this way. Forgive an old man who can't bear to cry in front of a man I respect. This way seemed best, at least for me and Maggie. She seems to think we'll be happy in Hawaii living in one of those high-rise condo-

miniums. No grass to mow, no flowers to tend, no truck fumes. I hope she's right.

The deal was too good to pass up, Lex. Miss Hart appears to be a very nice lady. She'll learn the business in her own good time. You can be a real help to her, son. I know the others will be real hard on her. This business, as you know, is hard on us, and we're grown men. A lady, now, she might want to quit once some of those hellions get on her case. They could be her undoing. She's got guts. Her business manager said she's aces. She's fifty years old and pretty as a picture. Her manager said she lived in these parts once and that's why she chose this place to come home to. She's rich, too. You ain't getting any younger, Lex. Maybe you two will hit it off. If you do, honeymoon here in Hawaii and we can kick around old times.

I'm going to miss you, Lex. I'll probably be calling you from time to time. I'm sending off a letter to Miss Hart telling her I want you to have my Teddy Roosevelt pictures. Take care of them—they're valuable. Maggie said they won't go with our condo furnishings.

Maggie and I both send you our love.

Your friends,
Maggie and Asa

Lex blew his nose lustily. Damn, he was really going to miss Asa. He was upset now, nostalgic, and when he was like this he knew he shouldn't be around people.

He drove like a robot over familiar terrain until he was at the bridge, at which point he headed over to Tijuana, parked his truck, and got out and walked to the base of the mountains. He stopped at the little house he'd lived in with his family, felt his heart thud in his chest. It looked the same— there seemed to be just as many children, just as many chickens, dogs, and cats. It looked neat and clean, just the way his mother had kept the house. So long ago. So many memories. What the hell was he doing here? And why now? He hadn't been up the mountain in twenty years. Maybe he should go back. He didn't belong here. This was another time, another place. He turned to follow his own advice and return to his truck, but something seemed to pull at him, something strange that he couldn't explain. He turned again and headed up the grassy slope that led to the padre's retreat that he was sure was now empty.

He remembered another time when his legs had been skinny and his feet had been bare, a time when he'd made this climb with a girl in a soft white dress.

As Lex made his way up, he thought about all the women he'd been with over the years. He couldn't remember their names now. There should have been one that stood out more than the others, but there wasn't. Only Aggie, his first love. His only love.

Valentine's Day.

He continued his climb. Maybe when he reached the fern bower he'd take a nap and dream about a brown-eyed, brown-haired girl who promised to love, honor, and obey until death drove them apart. Then he could climb back down the mountain and get on with his life. He'd be able to put this maudlin day behind him and face the reality of his world.

"Now that was an experience! I thought my heart was going to leap right out of my chest! Did you really feel like you could take on anything? That truck was massive. *Massive* isn't even the right word. Humongous. Gigantic. It was absolutely awesome," Ariel said. "I loved it! I have to call Kenneth and tell him he was right. I came down on him so hard. Oh, my, what's this? Dolly, look at these flowers. I bet they're from Max. He's the only person I know who will spring for more than twenty bucks on flowers. Miniature orchids! Ooohhh, let's see what the card says. Max is so romantic and this is Valentine's Day. You're not going to believe this, Dolly," Ariel said, handing the card over.

As Dolly reached for the card she noticed Ariel's hand go to her face. "Stop that!"

"Habit."

"Get a new one. Chew your nails, suck your thumb, twirl your hair the way you did when you were little. Don't touch your face. He's a romantic. Baby orchids. That cost him. This is nice, Ariel. He apologized and invited you to dinner. You're going, aren't you? This might turn into something. The girls said he's handsome as sin. Say something, Ariel."

"Look at me, Dolly. He's just being polite. Obviously he needs Able Body Trucking. It's a package deal. I'm sure he's a very nice man, but that doesn't mean he's going to be interested in me. No one is going to be interested in me. I've accepted that and I can live with it. I'll call him and thank him for the flowers. Don't worry, I'll be nice. See if Bernice has his home phone number. I'll do it right now and you can listen."

Ariel mouthed the words, "He's not home—his answering machine is picking up."

This is Lex Sanders. Please leave a message. If this is an emergency, call 425-9698. Thanks for calling.

"Mr. Sanders, this is Ariel Hart. Thank you for the lovely flowers. They've been my favorite since childhood. It was very nice of you to send them. I would love to have dinner with you soon, but not right now. My schedule is so full I'm like an accident waiting to happen. Again, thank you for the beautiful flowers."

"That was nice, Ariel, until you got to that accident part. Oh, well, he'll call again and invite you. If he does, say yes. The world won't come to an end. He might turn out to be a good friend like Ken and Max. If there's one thing I've learned, Ariel, it's that you can never have enough friends. Next time, okay?"

"Sure. Next time."

"I suggest Burger King on our way to firearms class and let's do Chinese after martial arts."

"Sounds good to me. Whatever makes life easier," Ariel said. "You know what, Dolly? Life is good. I feel great! We did the right thing coming here. I can't tell you how excited I am. It's not something I can put into words—it's a feeling that something wonderful is going to happen. I feel at peace here—I can't explain that feeling, either. Promise you won't laugh if I tell you something?"

"I promise."

"I feel . . . feel like there's some invisible hand guiding me here. That hand . . . is comforting, making me feel safe, a presence. I never felt anything like this before. I'm afraid I might get spooked and ruin everything. I like to understand things. This move . . . this business . . . Ken finding it at just the right time . . . that hand . . . forget it, I'm just imagining things. Think about it—why would God send me here?"

"I guess you're the only one who can answer that question. He did send you—the rest is up to you. Maybe you're supposed to do something meaningful while you're here. You know, make a difference, maybe right old wrongs, that kind of thing. I seem to remember a conversation we had once where we both agreed that everything in life is preordained." This last was said so slyly, Ariel jerked around to stare at her friend's guileless expression.

The rest of the day passed in a blur of activity. More than once Ariel had an eerie feeling that someone, somewhere, was thinking about her. More than once she looked over her shoulder, but there was no one around who seemed to be paying attention to her.

"I'm exhausted. I really enjoyed that Chinese dinner."

"No mess to clean," Dolly said tiredly. "I'm for bed. I'm surprised we lasted this long. Actually, I could have fallen asleep at nine o'clock."

"Are you kidding? I was ready at seven-thirty. See you in the morning." She hugged her best friend in the whole world, the way she did every night. "Thanks for coming here with me. I've been thinking, Dolly, if we get this business to the point where we can run it successfully, I'm going to make you a partner. We'll hire a housekeeper. You shouldn't be doing all this anymore."

"It's all I know, Ariel. Not for nothing you won't. If that time comes, I'll buy in with whatever savings I have. I won't allow you just to give it to me."

"We'll talk about it when the time comes. 'Night, Dolly."

"Sleep tight, Ariel."

As Ariel prepared for bed, her thoughts drifted back to the past, to a happier time. She'd give anything to be young again and in love. She had so many longings and desires that had never been fulfilled. You should have tried harder to find Felix, she scolded herself. It's entirely possible that that lawyer took your money and lied to you. Maybe you really were married. Maybe that attorney was wrong when he said Felix tricked you. He was a priest—he wore a white collar. Priests don't lie. Then why wasn't the marriage recorded? Why couldn't Mr. Anthony find any records? "I don't know," Ariel whispered to her reflection in the mirror. She continued to massage cocoa butter up and around the scars on her face. Disgusted with her reflection, she tossed the medicated stick into the sink.

She sat cross-legged in the middle of the bed, the wish list in her lap. She flipped the pages to her last entry. She wrote haltingly. *I wish I knew what was happening to me. I wish I knew what it was that brought me here. I know it wasn't just the business. I wish . . . I wish I could find Felix. I wish . . . so*

*many things. I wish I knew if he was happy . . . I wish I knew
if he was married with children . . . I wish I was beautiful
again. I wish he would think about me. Maybe that's why I
feel the way I do . . . Maybe all my wishing is making Felix
think about me. Maybe he's close by. I wish . . . Oh, God, I
wish . . . for happiness. For myself and for Felix. I wish . . .*

With tears dripping down her cheeks, Ariel shoved the
wish list under her pillow. "Tomorrow I'll set the wheels in
motion. I'll try to find Felix. I want to know if he's happy. I
won't invade his life or try to rekindle anything. Perhaps I
can make his life better—I certainly have the money to do
that. If he's doing all right, maybe I can help his family out in
some way. Anonymously, of course. Thirty-five years isn't so
long. I'm here. I was meant to come here. Everything happens for a reason, I truly believe that.

A moment later she was asleep.

Twenty-five miles away, in Bonsall, Lex Sanders was pulling off his boots. He debated half a minute about whether or
not to shower. He decided to go for it even though he was exhausted. He padded naked to the bathroom, taking a second
to press the message unit on his private answering machine.
He smiled at a garbled message from one of his nieces and
then one from his sister that was just as bad. When he heard
Ariel Hart's voice he stopped and listened. His eyebrows shot
upward in surprise. He pressed the Save button and rewound
the tape. He didn't know why.

Lex danced beneath the cold, needle-sharp spray. When he
was sure he was about to turn blue he switched to Hot, then
did another jig before leaping from the shower. He pulled on
a pair of pajama bottoms and settled down in bed. Ten minutes earlier he'd been tired to the bone. Now he was wide
awake, elated and yet confused; how could a sweet
sounding voice confuse and elate him at the same time?

A soft knock sounded on the door. "Senor Sanders, I have

the sandwich and milk for you. An enchilada just the way you like it. Corona beer in case you don't wish the milk. Good night, Senor."

"Good night, Tiki."

He was wide awake with no one to call and nothing to do but watch television. And no *TV Guide*. He flipped the channels the way he did every night. Reruns, late-night talk shows, infomercials. Surely there was a movie somewhere. More commercials. And then he saw her. A young Ariel Hart—but not that young. Maybe late thirties. All golden and warm with a sunny smile to match. She had the bluest eyes he'd ever seen. Cornflower blue. Now, where did that come from? Because the male actor had just said her eyes reminded him of a field of cornflowers? What the hell were cornflowers, anyway? How corny can you get? He snorted his displeasure before he swigged from the beer bottle.

Lex settled deeper into the pillows. Here was his chance to get to know Ariel Hart, super sleuth. A female private dick. He snorted again. She looked believable, even appeared believable. She packed a gun, a sizeable looking gun. She was pointing it, threatening to shoot. He leaned forward for a better look when he noticed the angle of the gun. The man's lower extremities. Lex groaned. Pure Hollywood. At its worst.

"You won't shoot," the man said.

"You don't know that for a fact. If you don't give me Annabelle's passport you'll find out if I will or won't. Hand it over. Now!"

"You probably don't even know how to shoot that toy," the man snarled.

"Really?" Ariel drawled. Lex watched, fascinated, as her clasped hands moved ever so slightly. A second later a chandelier hanging from a slim brass chain crashed to the floor. In the time it took his heart to beat once, the gun was pointed in its former position. "The passport."

"Jesus," Lex sputtered before he bit into his enchilada.

The passport was tossed on the table. Still wearing his sneer, the man back-stepped toward the front door.

"Michael, listen to me and listen good. If you ever so much as look at Annabelle Lee again, I won't be so accommodating the next time."

"The next time I'll be packing my own piece, bitch!"

Bang! Bang! Bang!

Lex roared with laughter as the man danced backward to avoid the bullets splintering the hardwood floor in front of his feet.

"Way to go, lady," Lex chortled.

The camera panned in for a closeup. He heard Ariel say, "You're my only friend," as she stroked the gun.

Lex fell back into his nest of pillows. Once, an eternity ago, Aggie Bixby had stared into his eyes and said, "You're my only friend." She'd followed that up with, "You're my lover and my husband."

Lex continued to watch the movie until it ended at midnight. When he switched the set off, he made a mental note to stop by the video store to see if Ariel Hart's other movies could be rented. He wanted to see them all.

There was a smile on his face when he drifted into a sleep filled with mannequins, all dressed in cornflower blue. They were chasing him up the mountain, their dresses billowing behind them in the gentle breeze.

"You aren't real, this is a bad dream," he shouted, his bare feet slipping and sliding in the soft, brown loam. He looked behind him, and all but one of the mannequins had given up. He risked a second glance and was horrified to see a shiny black revolver pointed at the middle of his back. He blinked in fear and tried to call out—to the padre, to anyone who could hear him, but it was no use. The mannequin was gaining on him, her artificial wig askew, the blue dress swishing angrily about her knees. She looked maniacal and for the

first time he felt fear wash through his body. "What do you want?" *he pleaded.* "Who are you? Why are you following me to this special place? Go away, I don't want you here. This place belongs to me and Aggie. Not you, never you."

He ran faster, his toes digging into the brown earth. He heard birds crying shrilly as he invaded their world. He mumbled and muttered words he made up as he went along. He thought he was praying, he wanted to pray, but he couldn't remember the words the padre had taught him. He stopped to catch his breath. "Wait for me, Felix. I hurt my ankle. Let me lean on your arm."

"Aggie! Aggie, is it really you? Where's your blue dress? The one that looks like cornflowers. What did you do with the gun?"

"I killed them all, Felix. All those plastic people who were chasing you. Their hair fell off. They weren't real like us. I want our marriage certificate, Felix. The girl is supposed to keep it. I didn't know that before. I should keep it. Please, Felix, can I keep it? I promise to treasure it the way you have."

"Do you still want it even if your name is spelled wrong? That's why I kept it. You left me and I didn't know how to find you. I tried and tried. I didn't get the certificate changed because I was afraid someone would find out. You said we had to keep our marriage a secret."

"Why did the padre spell my name wrong, Felix?"

"Because he was old and couldn't see well. He didn't mean to make a mistake. I think his pen slipped. When I noticed the mistake and went back up the mountain he was dead. His family buried him on the little hill where he married us. The bishop blessed the ground. I was afraid to tell anyone. Please, don't be mad at me, Aggie."

"I'm not mad at you, Felix. How did the padre spell my name?"

"*He spelled it* Bivby. *It was an honest mistake. We're still married. You signed your name and I signed mine. Do you remember signing the padre's book after the ceremony?*"

"*Of course. I signed it Agnes Marie Bixby Sanchez. I was so proud. It was the first time I signed my new name. I will always be Agnes Marie Bixby Sanchez. Forever and ever.*

"*You're going to kill me, aren't you?*"

"*Yes. I'm sorry.*"

"*Why?*"

"*Because you spelled my name wrong on my passport. It was okay for the padre to make a mistake, but I'm your wife. You shouldn't have spelled my name wrong. Say hello to the padre and tell him I forgive him.*"

"*No! No! Wait!*"

Lex tumbled from the bed, his body drenched in sweat. "Jesus!"

Trembling from the nightmare and his memories, he marched down the hall to the kitchen where he loaded four bottles of beer onto a tray. If he wanted to sleep he knew he'd have to drink all four. He'd been down this road before, too many times. He wasn't about to give up another night's sleep.

And this is your life, Lex Sanders.

For now anyway.

Tomorrow is another day.

Maybe it'll be better.

Don't count on it.

I never have.

He thought about Ariel Hart and how pretty she was in the movie. Maybe tomorrow *would* be a better day.

Chapter Five

*I*t was a glorious place, a fairyland, and it smelled better than fifty Christmases combined. A special place, so special only she and Felix knew about it. Special because it was their honeymoon suite. She curled herself into a little ball next to her new husband. "Isn't it wonderful, Felix? You were my only true friend in the whole world and now you're my husband and my friend. I wish we could tell everyone. I wish we never had to leave. I wish . . ."

"You can't wish your life away Aggie. Wishes are nice. I made a list once and called it my wish list. I pretended I had a fairy godmother and she told me to write down everything I wanted. She said I should call it my wish list and when one of my wishes came true I should put a gold star next to it. I didn't have any money to buy gold stars so I colored one in with my little sister's crayons. My first wish was that you would like me. My wish turned out better than the one I wrote down. You love me. Maybe I'll put two stars next to the wish. I'm going to keep it forever and ever."

"I'll do the same, " she whispered. "Will we look at each other's lists?"

"They should be secret. You can see mine if you want.

Maybe we should make a pact not to show each other until we're old in rocking chairs."

"Okay. Are you going to kiss me? Are you going to touch me all over?" *How breathless her voice was.*

"I want to touch you all over. Will you touch me?"

"All over?"

"I want you to."

"Then I will. I'll do whatever you want me to do."

"Will you always love me, Aggie?"

"Forever and ever. Will you always love me, too?"

"Until the day I die. I'm going to get a good job and give you everything. I'm going to love you so much. Every day I'll tell you how much I love you. You're so beautiful. I wish I had a picture of you. Will you give me one?"

"My parents don't take pictures anymore. They used to take a lot of them when I was little. Do you want one when I started school? I think I was six. Do you have any pictures of yourself?"

"No. We don't even have a camera. We should have a wedding picture. You might be sad when we get older and you don't have a picture to show our children. I can go back to the padre and ask him for some paper and a pencil and we can draw ourselves. Would you like me to do that, Aggie?"

"Yes," *she whispered.*

When Felix returned with the paper and pencil, they sat cross-legged in the fern bower like the children they were. They stared solemnly at one another as their fingers traced each other's likeness. When they had every contour memorized, they took pencil in hand.

"I want to keep this, but my mother goes through my things. You have to keep it, Felix. Do we get a marriage certificate? You should keep it, too."

"All right. Our marriage certificate is in Spanish. I have a *safe place where I can keep it. No one will ever know until we want them to know."*

"I want you to kiss me, Felix. Now, here in this wonderful place you've made for us. It smells better than Christmas and Easter all rolled into one. Mmmm."

"Rise and shine, Ariel, it's a quarter to five!"

Dolly's voice was so cheerful Ariel groaned and then tossed her pillow in Dolly's general direction. "I was having such a nice dream. Now I have to get up and drive an eighteen-wheeler around a parking lot. Then I have to shoot a gun for hours and after that I have to kick the hell out of someone and bow and say what fun it was. Does that instructor really expect me to be a pro in three weeks? Double clutch, oh yeah, and when does he think I'm going to get the hang of that satellite computer screen? Not today, that's for sure. And that log book . . . how are you supposed to drive, type messages, receive messages, talk on the CB, and keep your eyes on the road? Trucking is not an easy job. I have to get certified on doubles, triples, and tankers. It's going to take me a year to get my CDL. I can't remember if that's the federal license or what it is. How am I supposed to remember all of this?"

"The same way you memorize a script," Dolly retorted.

"It's the practical application I'm having trouble with. That double clutching is what's getting to me. Push clutch in, transmission is disconnected, go to first gear, let clutch up, move slowly, push clutch in, move to neutral, take foot off clutch. It's like neutral is a gear itself.

"What's for breakfast? I'd like French toast with lots of butter and warm syrup," Ariel called on her way to the bathroom.

"I'd like that, too. Unfortunately, we're eating donuts and drinking coffee on the way. Shake it, Ariel, we're already running late. It's pretty raw out, so dress warm."

Forty-five minutes later, Ariel climbed into the tractor. When she exited the cab three hours later she felt like she'd done double duty with a gila monster. Her stomach was in knots as she eyed the instructor warily. "I will do this. I've got it down, but if you keep talking to me about trucking, I'm going to make mistakes. If you have to talk to me, talk about something else. Okay?"

"Well, sure, Miss Hart, if that's what you want. What would you like to talk about?" Not waiting for her response, he rambled on. "Looks like you might have a fight on your hands with a few of those renegade truckers Asa kept on the payroll. My advice to you, and I know you're new to this business, is get rid of them now before they really brew up a batch of stuff you won't be able to deal with. This is just scuttlebutt, but sooner or later it all filters down here. That Chet, he's all set to stir up the workers at the different ranches. He's got a hate on for Lex Sanders that goes way back. He blames Sanders for his two brothers' deaths. It wasn't Sanders' fault those guys were drinking behind the wheel and drove down into the ravine. All old Chet would say was it was Sanders' fault and he had to pay. The insurance paid damages, but because they were drinking, there was a problem. Sanders is a decent guy and he treats his wetbacks better than anyone around."

Ariel's right arm shot out, knocking the instructor against the door. "Don't you ever refer to those workers in that manner again. If you do, none of my people will take these lessons and I'll cancel the program. Refer to them as workers or laborers. Do you understand me?"

"Yes, ma'am. It's just a term. Everyone uses it. My wife is always on my case about it. Sometimes I forget. When you're around men who talk like that all day, you tend to do the same thing."

"That's just an excuse, Mr. Norbert. I said what I had to

say and you said what you had to say. Now, why is Chet stirring up the workers? What does he hope to gain?"

"He's got a top dog mentality. Asa kept him on because he's one of the best drivers around. He likes to drive hazardous materials because the pay is better. The other guys, they don't like to drive chemicals. He has his own rig and he's got a partner so he makes his run pretty much non-stop. I've heard, and this is just a rumor, that he keeps two log books. Him and his partner don't pay no nevermind to the 70-hour driving schedule. He was money in the bank for Asa. Heard he got fined a few weeks back. He was carrying two skids of cigarette lighters and he took it through a tunnel in Pennsylvania. He got fined and had to pay out twelve hundred big ones. Out of his own pocket. It's not the first time, either. Sometimes, rumor had it, Asa bailed him out. He might be worried you won't do the same. You did okay today. If you keep up the good work you should be able to take your test in a few weeks."

In spite of herself, Ariel was pleased. "See you tomorrow, Mr. Norbert."

Ariel was back at Able Body Trucking in less than twenty minutes to pick up Dolly. On the way to the shooting range she swigged from a bottle of Diet Pepsi and wolfed down a Hot Pocket sandwich. "It's illegal to carry a gun in the rig, but all the truckers do it. Most times the cops look the other way. I found that out today. I bought a gun ten days ago, picked it up two days ago. It's a Glock 9 millimeter. Norbert said it's light and made out of some kind of special porcelain. We're getting you one, too."

Dolly groaned in dismay. "I don't think I could shoot anyone."

"You could if your life was in danger. Trust me on that one. Remember that picture I made a long time ago called *The Lady and the Thief*? I really got into that part and when he was about to toss me over the roof, I pulled out my prop gun and shot him dead. I remember how real the feeling was. I guess you have to experience something like that to understand what I'm talking about. Let's just hope neither one of us has to use it. How are the computer lessons going?"

"Terrible. There's this thing called a mouse. You move it around. I moved it all right, and erased a whole file. The teacher said not to worry because it was on the C Drive and I was working on the A Drive. The instruction book is absolute Greek to me. I don't know, Ariel, maybe the only thing I'm good at is keeping house and cooking. I don't want to let you down, but I'm not capable of driving a truck and my bones are too brittle for martial arts. Guns petrify me. I'm game to go along with you on all of this, but if I flub it I don't want you to be angry."

"Would you rather stay at the office and forget all this other stuff?"

"Oh, yes. I'll stick with the computer because the teacher said kids in the first grade know how to use computers. I'm viewing it as the ultimate challenge. Ariel do you know you have 900 tractors and 3000 vans? It's time to buy more and sell off some of the ones we have. Seems Mr. Able bought 150 cabs, or tractors, as they're called in the business, at one time. He got a good deal on them. Then when they get 200,000 miles on them, instead of assigning the cab to a team he gives it to one guy, gets another hundred thousand miles out of it, and turns around and sells it for almost as much as he paid for it. Now, even I know that's sharp business. My point is, it's time to buy 150 new cabs. This company will run itself once we get it all on a computer. I learned something else this morning. Those hookers that hang out on the fringe of the property are called 'lot lizards' and they charge twenty bucks. That guy Chet is their best customer. You need to run them off. Mr. Able wouldn't allow them on the property. I guess it's up to you now."

Ariel told her about her conversation with Norbert. "Bring Chet's file home with you tonight. After firearms class I'll drive you back to the office and do the martial arts class myself. It's basically a refresher course for me, anyway. My teacher said he thinks I can qualify for a brown belt if I want to. I'm better than anyone in the class," she said proudly. "I had an edge, though."

Ten minutes later Ariel said, "It's all coming together, Dolly. I didn't think it would happen for months, maybe even years, but it is. I even think I'm beginning to enjoy this new life."

"I'm happy for you, Ariel. You know what they say— life's a stage and we're all actors."

"Yes, Dolly, but I'm not acting. I'm living. For the first time in a very long time."

"I knew that would happen," Dolly said smugly.

Ariel smiled in her sleep, stretched luxuriously, then remembered where she was and how many times she'd had the same dream. She also remembered her resolution to do something about finding Felix Sanchez. She wondered if there was such a thing as a twenty-four hour detective agency.

Why now, why after all these years? Because . . . I had a different life. Oh, he wasn't good enough for you then. Now, maybe he is. That's terrible, Ariel. Damn, she had to stop talking to herself. I tried, I really tried. Maybe he should have tried, too. It wasn't meant to be. That's the bottom line. This is a new time now. The rules have changed. All I'm going to do is make sure he's happy. If he needs anything, or if his family does, I'll help. I'll go to one of the parish priests and have him do it. I won't interfere with Felix's life. That's a promise I'm making to myself.

Ariel showered, dressed, and was ready for the day within

fifteen minutes. She spent another five minutes going downstairs for coffee and carrying it back up along with the phone
book. In the yellow pages she wasn't at all surprised to find
that more than one detective agency was open around the
clock, but she *was* surprised to hear a human voice so early
in the morning. A woman, no less. She jotted down notes as
the woman spoke. Detectives didn't come cheap. She should
have known that. It wasn't that long ago that she'd played a
female detective in a very successful movie. In fact, she'd
played the same role four times. And everyone said sequels
wouldn't fly. They had, all four of them. In the movie, the
character she was playing got two hundred a day plus
expenses, which was exactly what Beverly Leroy was quot-
ing now.

Ariel told the woman her story, finishing up with "And
that was the last time I saw him. I realize it's thirty-four years
later, but maybe you can turn something up. Mail me your
reports in care of Able Body Trucking and mark them 'Personal.' I'll send out a check today. Of course, I want it in a
plain brown envelope with no return address. I'll look forward to hearing from you."

And now a new day was staring her in the face. It was
hard to believe she'd been in the trucking business for six
weeks.

The new day started off badly and quickly worsened.

The moment Ariel swerved into the lot she was over-
whelmed with noise from the truckers milling about while
their engines idled ominously. "This looks like it could be
trouble," Ariel said, hopping out of her Range Rover. "Is
there a problem? You're wasting fuel. Since I pay for that
fuel, I suggest you cut those engines now. I'll give you three
minutes and if you don't follow orders, draw your pay and
get out of this yard. I don't care if you have families or not."
This is a role, Ariel. Play it out. Don't let that pack of wolves

dictate to you. She turned on her heel and marched into the office.

"Is this going to be one of those wildcat strikes? What do they want? Do I call the police? The teamsters? Or do they do that? Get Stan in here." She was flustered, the way she used to get doing a scene with one of Hollywood's top male stars. Take a deep breath, then another. Whatever this is, to-morrow it will be over. Get through it the best you can. You can do this. You can do whatever you have to do. The silent pep talk had the desired effect; her breathing returned to normal.

"They want to push your buttons to see how tough you are," Dolly said. "They're expecting you to back down. Find out how many of those trucks are owner-operated. Call the police to make them leave. Stan must have extra keys. Get them, and we can all turn off the engines. Don't say anything you don't plan to back up. If you want to fire them, then fire them. I don't know anything about unions or if there can be ramifications. Stan will know. Here he comes. Maybe he knows what the hell they want."

"Ma'am," the older man said respectfully.

"Stan, do you know what's going on out there? We have spare keys, don't we?"

"They're testing you because you're a woman. They don't like taking orders from a female. That's the long and short of it. We have spare keys, yes, ma'am."

"I haven't given them any orders. Yet. It's been business as usual so far. Until I know more about the management end of things, it'll stay the same. I'm not saying I'll change things and I'm not saying I won't. Call the police, Dolly, and get the owner-operators off this lot. They're fired from this com-pany."

"Even Chet?" There was dismay on the older man's face.

"Definitely Chet. Do you have a problem with that, Stan?"

"Lord, no. I been praying I'd be around long enough to see that buzzard get his. He don't think you mean it, ma'am. Mr. Sanders is going to be mighty pleased. He won't let Chet haul anything for him. Even his trash. He pays two cents more a mile to the truckers he uses from here. He's a good man, a fair man. Demanding at times, but he has to be. I'm sure he'll come right down here if you need him."

"Let's wait. What are the chances of this man getting violent?"

"Pretty good."

Ariel opened her shoulder satchel that doubled as a purse and withdrew the Glock. Stan's breath hissed inward. It hissed again when she shoved in the clip. "Get the keys, Stan. The engines are still running." She shoved the Glock into the back of her jeans. Then she opened the door and stood aside for Stan to go to his office for the keys.

Ariel's stance was pure Hollywood. Her right hand went to the brim of the Padres cap, moving it back slightly. Her feet planted firmly on the ground, she drew a deep breath and shouted, "All right, what do you want? I'm asking so I can tell the police when they get here. This is an unauthorized strike. I gave you an order and you disobeyed it. I also told you to pick up your pay. Get those rigs out of here or I'll shoot out the tires. That will cost you some bucks to repair." Damn, this was almost like a movie role. Hands on hips, Ariel advanced close enough to Chet to smell his sour breath. *Don't show any fear—play it out. You can yell CUT! your-self.* She neatly sidestepped the man until she was less than a foot from his rig. She noticed the painted sign on the side. Big Red. She'd bet five dollars it was his CB handle.

The roar was deafening, but started to lessen the minute Stan cut the engines one by one. When the last Able Body truck became silent, Chet strolled around the lot like he owned it. "So where's the cops you said you called?" His face was so mean and ugly, Ariel winced. Then she remembered the Glock stuck in the back of her jeans.

"They're on their way. You still haven't told me what this is all about."

"What it's about, lady, is, the old man promised me five hauls a week. It ain't been happening. A man's only as good as his word. We had a deal. I got payments on this rig and kids to support. If I ain't making any money I can't do that, now, can I?"

"I don't know anything about your deal. Mr. Able didn't say anything to me about a deal when the company changed hands. You haul when we tell you to haul. If you don't like it, get yourself another job. Don't think you're going to bully me. Take your cronies and get off my property. Now!"

"You owe me some money, Miss Movie Star, and I want it."

"You get what's on the books. No more, no less. You men, you're willing to give up your jobs for this man? Jobs aren't that plentiful, in case you're interested. You're entitled to apply for health benefits. COBRA says you can keep the benefits for eighteen months, but you'll be paying for them. After that you're on your own. The paymaster has your pay—pick it up," she said, addressing the men, her eyes everywhere but on Chet. "Otherwise, we'll mail your checks."

Chet's face turned uglier still. He raised his fist and advanced a step. The others backed off. Suddenly the Glock was in her hand. She didn't stop to think; she pulled back the hammer and fired into the ground at Chet's feet one, two, three, four shots. Bits and chunks of concrete shot upward. Too stunned to move, Chet froze in his tracks. "Not bad for a movie star, huh, Mr. Truck Driver? This is the last time I'm going to tell you to get the hell off my property. If you come back, my aim will be somewhat higher, like right there," she said, pointing the barrel of the gun at his groin. "Well, here come the police. Goodbye, Mr. Truck Driver."

Behind the police was a blue pickup. She whirled and was halfway through the door when she heard the police officer say, "Lex, how's it going?" To Stan he said, "What's going on here?" Ariel watched from the window as the toe of the officer's polished black shoe scuffed at the holes she'd shot in the concrete. "You want to tell me what this is all about?"

"Wildcat strike. Sort of. Chet Andrews was acting like a horse's patoot. The owner settled him right down. She fired the lot of them. Good riddance, I say."

"The lot of them? How many constitutes *the lot of them?*"

"About an even dozen. No great loss. We got a waiting list of drivers who want to work for this company. They won't have any trouble working for a woman. It's under control, officer," Stan said. "I think Miss Hart handled it just right. Chet was starting to get ugly."

"If you have any more trouble, call the station. I'll have to file a report. It's best that things like this go on record, Stan. I'll keep my eyes open and double the patrols out this way. Nice seeing you again, Lex."

"You too, Stoney. The next time I'm down this way, let's have a beer."

"Give me a call. Just out of curiosity, who shot up this concrete?"

A wicked grin on his face, Stan said, "The new owner. She scared the bejesus out of Chet when she said if he ever came back, her aim would be a little higher. He knew what she meant. She might have been scared, but old Chet, he didn't see it. She's a tough little lady. She's going to be okay. She handled that gun like a pro. It was a Glock, 9 millimeter. Can you beat that? You got business or are you visiting, Mr. Sanders?"

"Business. You got a driver in Seattle who's deadheading? If so, you got my business. You got anybody bobtailing in

Oklahoma? If so, have him pick up my load." Lex handed over a slip of paper.

"Thirty-two cents a mile, Mr. Sanders?"

"Yep. I think I'll go see the new owner."

"You're gonna have to follow her then. There she goes. She's taking lessons on how to drive these rigs. She'll be back around noon. Miss Dolly's still inside, though. She's Miss Hart's assistant. She's learning the computer."

"Commendable. Where is everyone?"

"Taking driving lessons. After today, I'm beginning to think it's a good idea."

"You might have a point, Stan. If there's a problem with my loads, call me at the house. I gotta get back—I have a mare about to foal. She's going to be a beauty. Good bloodlines."

Then Lex Sanders did something he thought he'd never do. He chased a woman, burning rubber as he barrelled down the road in pursuit of Ariel Hart. He couldn't explain his actions, he just knew it was something he wanted to do. No, he *needed* to do it. He saw the dark green Rover three cars ahead. He did a reckless thing and cursed himself as he skirted one sedan and then a small sports car until he was directly behind Ariel. He blew his horn, three short blasts, his arm waving wildly for her to pull over. "This, Lex Sanders, is probably the stupidest thing you've ever done." He was muttering to himself, something he seemed to be doing a lot since Asa sold Able Body.

Ariel looked in her rearview mirror, saw the blue pickup and the man waving for her to pull over. Lex Sanders! "Oh, God!" Did she put makeup on this morning? If her life depended on it, she couldn't remember. She wanted to look in the mirror to see how visible her scars were, but she was afraid. Could she inch the hair out from under the Padres baseball cap? She slowed and pulled over to the shoulder of the road, then sucked in her breath as she waited for Lex to come alongside. This is just one more role, Ariel. There was a time when you could charm the birds right out of their trees.

"I thought it was you. I remember your truck that night at the restaurant. The waitress let you sit there for a long time."

"And you bought Dolly and me dinner. I was going to stop by your table, but you'd left. I'm not usually that impolite." He was staring at her as though there was nothing wrong with her face. Maybe he was a frustrated actor and he was playing a role, too.

"I stopped you for a reason. Stan told me you were on your way to take a lesson, but I was wondering . . . if you might consider . . . what I mean is . . . have you ever played hookey? The reason I'm asking is, I breed Arabians and my prize mare is about to foal. It's such a wonderful experience, I was . . . ah . . . wondering if you'd like to come up to Bonsall with me. You'll never forget it. I'd also like you to see and hear for yourself what's going on with my workers. Chet Andrews has been stirring them up and I'm damn good to my employees. Will you come?"

The role was taking on deeper dimensions. "Actually, Mr. Sanders, the last time I played hookey I was in the fifth grade. I got my fanny whipped that night and I never did it again. I'd like to see your new foal. Shall I follow you?"

"You will? Yeah, yeah, follow me. Unless you want me to bring you back. It won't be a problem. We can stop at a service station and leave your truck and pick it up on the way back. Either way is okay with me." He waited for her reply.

Ariel's mind raced. He'd followed her, flagged her down, invited her to his ranch to share something with him. If she went in his truck, she'd have to make small talk, and he'd be able to stare at her more. Better to follow him. "I'll follow you, then you won't have to come all the way back down here. You could do me a favor, though. Call the office and tell Dolly where I'll be. I've been meaning to get a phone in the truck, but just haven't gotten around to it. Actually, it's scheduled to be hooked up tomorrow." She was babbling.

"Good. That's good. I'll call her for you. I've seen all your movies," he blurted. "I tried to rent them at the video store, but every time I asked for them they were out so I bought them."

"All of them?"

"All fifty-six. I watched them, too."

She was flustered. "Thank you. Did you like them?" She nodded and smiled when his head bobbed up and down.

"You're a fine actress—I enjoyed all of them. The one I liked best is the one I saw late one night on cable. After that I was hooked. It was the one with Annabelle's passport. You shot up the floor the way you did back there in the lot."

"I guess you could call it a repeat performance."

"We better get off this shoulder before some cop comes along who has to fill his quota. Just follow me."

"Okay. Don't forget to call Dolly."

She followed him, her thoughts in a turmoil. What was she doing? Dolly would say she was going with her instincts. No, she was following him because . . . because . . . he didn't seem to . . . he didn't stare at her . . . she didn't see pity in his eyes. Maybe he would turn out to be a good friend the way Ken and Gary and Max were friends. Maybe he would be more than a friend someday. He was single. She was single. She remembered how angry she'd been the day Bernice told her she was his personal office contact. Obviously, there were two sides to everything. Now she was going to have to start thinking about Lex Sanders as a person, not an account. Suddenly she felt giddy.

Forty minutes later, Ariel parked the Rover alongside Lex's Ford pickup.

"You should buy American," Lex said.

"I know. A friend got this for me and it was too good a

deal to pass up. Maybe I'll trade it in on a Jeep." Damn, she
was flustered again.

"No, you won't. A Range Rover is too good a truck to
trade in on a Jeep. It's the Cadillac of trucks. It will last you
forever. You should buy American, though."

"Point taken." She looked around, her jaw dropping in
awe. "This is beautiful. Is all of this yours? I never saw iron
gates like these. Are they twelve feet? You must have had a
real craftsman make them up. It seems," she said, looking
around, "like you're self-contained."

"I am. I have a hundred people working this ranch. That
doesn't count the ones who work with the horses. They
pretty much leave at the end of the day and return in the
morning. The other workers live here. They go across the
border a few months out of the year and then come back. We
even have a school at the back end of the property. It's not
much—three classrooms and three great teachers. Most of
the children can't speak English when they get here. The
older ones take the bus to the school in town. We give them a
good start here with their English so they won't be ridiculed
when they enter the public school. I'm happy to report we
can take credit for twelve teachers, nine lawyers, three female
doctors, four male doctors, two priests, and three nuns. You
should see this place at Christmastime when they all come
back. We also have two guys serving time in the federal pen
for drug dealing. Sometimes doing your best just isn't
enough. Peer pressure is an awful thing."

"What's that building over there?"

"The store. Food, clothing, anything my people need. We
sell it at cost and it comes out of their pay. We even have a
bank of sorts. Actually, I'm the bank. I keep their money if
they want me to. I even pay them interest." He chuckled.
"This young man came up to me about a month ago and said
I made a mistake in his father's account and from now on he

would be in charge of auditing all the bank accounts. He's studying to take the CPA exam. I gladly paid up and turned it all over to him. Over there is a tennis court and swimming pool. For some reason no one uses it, not even the children. It's that boundary thing—there's an invisible line they won't cross."

"How many families do you have here?"

"Right now, about thirty. It changes, goes up, goes down. When we pick a harvest it goes way up. The apartments are behind the house—come on, I'll show them to you. It's on the way to the stable."

"What do you think?" Lex asked as he pointed to a row of tidy, pink brick buildings.

"I think it's wonderful. The flowers are so pretty. It's so . . . so neat and tidy. Can I look inside, or would that be an invasion of their privacy? Of course it would be—forget I asked."

"No, that's okay, the unit on the end is empty. Miguel went back to his home because his elderly brother needed some work done. He took his family with him, but they'll be back right after Easter."

Ariel opened the old-fashioned screen door, smiling when it squeaked. It was a small apartment—two bedrooms, a living room, an eat-in kitchen, a pretty tile bathroom, and a back porch with a portable grill. "Where's the washer and dryer?"

"What?"

"The washer and dryer—where are they? There's two sets of bunk beds, so they must have four children. Right? Where do they do their laundry? Going to school is one set of clothes, working the fields is another, Sundays another. So, where do they do their washing?"

"Jesus, I don't know. The . . . bathtub, I guess. I never thought about it."

"I see," Ariel said.

She was frowning. Suddenly Lex wanted to run out and buy washers and dryers by the truckload. "There's no room in the kitchen for extra appliances."

"I see that. Don't you have an empty building somewhere? You could make a laundromat. You wouldn't have to give each family a set. Six or eight would probably do it. You use well water, so the only cost would be the electricity and the units themselves. If you had to, you could charge, but I think that would be tacky."

"Tacky," Lex said, a stupid look on his face.

"Cheap. A man in your position charging to use washers and dryers? Cheap."

"Cheap. I see your point. How soon do you think I should do this?" There was humor in his voice.

Ariel laughed. "I'd get right on it. There's nothing worse than rinsing out sweaty underwear in the sink. Think about it."

"Okay, it's a done deal. I'll call a plumber and the appliance store. You call your company and have them bring them up here as soon as possible. We'll put them in the garage. That means I have to keep my truck outside."

Ariel sniffed. "That truck looks like it got caught in a hurricane. When was the last time you garaged it?"

"The first day I got it. Too much trouble to open and close the doors." He stomped ahead of her, his shoulders stiff with embarrassment.

"Lex."

He turned, his face pink with something she couldn't define.

"I didn't mean to come on so strong. It's just that I know what it's like to be poor. Even when I was just a child, I knew how difficult it was. The same clothes, day after day, but always clean and pressed. When God gives you the power to help make things better, you can't stop in midstream. You have to keep on doing everything you can. I wasn't criticizing you. If it seemed that way, I'm sorry."

"No apology necessary. When you're right, you're right. I was stupid for not thinking of it myself. Why didn't they ask? Damn, it's that boundary thing. Did I miss anything else?"

"Do the children have bicycles, roller skates, wagons, games and toys?"

"Their parents don't have money for things like that."

"I see."

"Okay. I'll call the bike store. And the toy store. Maybe you could go with me to pick them out. Or are you too busy?" He held her gaze, waiting for her reply.

"I'll make the time. Why don't we do it after you show me your horses? If you pay them, they'll assemble everything. For some reason I don't think you have the patience to put a bunch of bikes together."

"You're right about that. I never had a bike when I was a kid. I think I would have killed for one. Well, probably not. Even if I had one I would have felt guilty and I wouldn't have been able to enjoy it knowing the money could be used for food and clothes." He reached for her hand. "Thanks for bringing me up short."

"Any time." She squeezed his hand. It felt wonderful, *right* somehow.

"This is Cleo," Lex said as he led her over to a stall in the clean-smelling barn. "Ariel Hart, this is Dr. Lomez."

Ariel shook hands with the vet. "What a beautiful animal."

"That she is. It won't be long now. She's doing fine, Lex. Relax or Cleo will pick up on your panic; you *are* feeling panic—don't deny it. Get down here and talk to her. Honest to God, Lex, I think she's been waiting for you to get here. Just like a woman, wants to please her man. Softly, Lex."

Ariel backed off and watched as this strange man who had been holding her hand dropped to his knees and started to croon softly to the horse on the ground. How gentle his hands must be. She felt a sense of awe when the big horse quieted almost immediately at Lex's touch. Who was this man who was touching her life? Why did she feel so drawn to him, and she *was* drawn to him—she couldn't deny it. She'd been with men who hadn't talked to her as gently and kindly as this man was talking to his horse. It was obvious how much he loved the animal. She couldn't help but wonder if he would love a woman the same way. Suddenly she felt warm all over as she imagined what it would be like to make love to this man.

Who was Lex Sanders? He spoke about being poor in his youth. He seemed to have a special affinity for the Mexicans he employed or else he was just a kind, generous man. Where had that compassion come from? She couldn't tell.

"She's ready. Hold her head, Lex. Talk to her, stroke her head. That's it, that's it. Here it comes. Oh, Lex, it's . . . he's beautiful."

Ariel watched, mesmerized, as Lex continued to stroke the hard-breathing animal. She'd expected him to turn around, to stare at the foal, but he didn't. Cleo was the only thing that mattered to him at the moment. "I know he's beautiful, Cleo. He's going to be strong and healthy like his mother. Shhhh, it's okay, just a few more minutes. She wants to get up, Frankie. She wants to see her son. Easy, girl, just a few more minutes. Okay, now." He backed up as Cleo struggled to her feet. She snorted happily and her head reared back as she pawed the ground, to Lex's delight. The vet clapped her hands.

"He's a beauty, Cleo," Lex said, careful not to touch the wobbly foal. The first contact belonged to Cleo and both Lex and the mare knew it. The vet backed off, too, as Cleo nuzzled her offspring. When she was satisfied all was right with her son, she nudged him toward Lex.

Tears misted Ariel's eyes. How wonderful motherhood was. She watched breathlessly as Lex went cheek to cheek with the foal. "He's handsome, Cleo, as good lookin' as his mama. We're not selling this one. He's staying with us. We have to think about a proper name for him. Something that sounds majestic. By tomorrow I'll come up with the perfect name. Thanks, Frankie. I don't know why, but I sweated this one."

"That's because you love Cleo. Hey, it was the least I could do. You put me through vet school, after all. They're doing fine. I'll stop back this evening. Leave mother and son to get acquainted. Don't go fussing over her, Lex. She knows what to do and she's damn tired. Nice meeting you, Miss Hart. Is there any chance you might want a dog? I have this gorgeous shepherd that the Seeing Eye rejected because she was too playful. Her name is Snookie and she's wonderful. Guess not, huh?"

"She'll take it," Lex said smartly. "Miss Hart is one of those people who have the capability to take on any project and turn it into a positive experience. If you're capable, then you should act on that capability. Isn't that right, Ariel?"

"Absolutely. I'd love a dog. I've been wanting one for a long time. But I have to admit I know nothing about them."

"Not much to know with this one. She's perfect. She's trained and she's obedient. She likes women better than men. Sometimes she thinks she's a lapdog. Best watchdog I've ever seen. She's in perfect health, had all her shots. She even comes with her own bag of dog food. And, get this—she's got a Gucci collar and leash."

"You don't have to convince me. I'll take her."

"Great. I'll drop her off around six when I come back. Will you be here then?"

"She'll be here. We're going out to buy some bicycles for

the kids. Frankie, when you were growing up here, did you want a bike?"

"So damn bad I could taste it. Why?"

"Why didn't you say something? Why didn't you ask for one?" The look Frankie gave him was so scathing, Ariel looked away. "Hey, wait a minute, where did your mother wash clothes?"

"In the bathtub."

"I'm putting a laundromat in the garage. Twelve units," he said airily.

"That's great, Lex. That's really great. Bet it was Miss Hart's idea, huh? I know it was her idea to get bikes." She blew him a kiss and was out the door before he could say anything.

"They're like an extended family."

"I see," Ariel said.

"What now?"

"Nothing. Well, maybe swimming lessons and maybe tennis lessons. Little kids shouldn't be working in the fields. Pay their parents more money. Pretend you're a guardian angel. I'm hungry."

Lex reached for her hand again. She let him take it because it felt like the most natural thing in the world. She liked this man.

"Come on, I'll show you the house. Tiki will make us some lunch. We eat pretty simple around here. Mostly Tex-Mex. Then we can go get the bikes and other things. I'll have Tiki make us a list of the children's ages. God forbid I should screw this up. This is it," Lex said, waving his arm about. "My humble abode. I'm going to open the door, but step aside or you'll get mowed down. Okay, here goes."

They came from everywhere, puppies by the dozen, all colors. They slipped and slid down the tiled hallway in their hurry to get Lex's attention. "My dog had a litter of twelve.

I'm keeping them all. The kids love them. You're getting your own dog so don't go getting attached to mine."

"Oh, they're wonderful." Ariel laughed as she got down on the floor with the pups. They were all over her, crawling up her legs, bouncing on her stomach, licking her face. She continued to laugh as she cuddled and squeezed the fat puppies.

"You should do that more often," Lex said quietly.

"Do what?" Ariel shrieked as one of the puppies crawled up to the top of her head and plopped down. Another one peed on her leg. She shrieked again in pure delight.

"Laugh," Lex said softly.

"Tiki! Let's put them on the sunporch. Can you make us some lunch? I need you to make me a list of the children female, male, and their ages. We're going shopping after lunch."

"Si, Señor Lex. One little momento."

"Come along, I'll show you the house. I added on to it. I lived so long in cramped quarters, brothers and sisters, all in the same two rooms. I . . . I wanted a little walking around room. It's called mission style, lots of terra cotta and stucco. A decorator added all the bright colors. Comfort and color, that's all I care about. And lots and lots of bathrooms. Seven in all. Six fireplaces. I hate to be cold. They say being poor builds character. Do you believe that, Ariel?" How anxious his voice sounded. As if her opinion really mattered.

"I suppose it does. Poor is poor. I don't think people tend to think about building character if they're cold or hungry. At least I don't think I would. However, look at you now. You're obviously successful. You appear to be a kind, decent person. You love animals and the people who work for you even if you *are* a little shortsighted. You never married?"

"Once. It didn't . . . work out. What about you?"

"It didn't work out."

"How do you deal with the loneliness? Everyone needs someone to be with."

"I know. Sometimes I cry. I have friends. I figured if God wanted me to spend my life with one certain person, it would happen. For a long time, I've thought I was in a holding pattern, waiting for it to happen. I just met you—why are we having this conversation?"

"I pretty much feel the same way. Isn't that strange?"

"Guess so."

"I really meant it—you should laugh more often. You're pretty. You try to hide those little things on your face, don't you?"

He sounded like he was discussing the weather, not her deformity. "Wouldn't you?"

"Hell no, I wouldn't. Obviously, it's something you can't change. If someone didn't like me because I had a pimple on my nose, then I say the hell with them. It's what's inside that counts. Guess women don't see things the same way men do."

"Easy for you to say since you aren't sporting any 'pimples'. I had to have major surgery. The doctors say it will get better with time. I hope they're right."

Lex snorted. "You can hardly tell. If you'd stop calling attention to whatever you want to call it, you'd be better off. It's there, so live with it. We're getting along pretty good, don't you think? You tell me off and I tell you off. Nicely, of course. C'mon, I bet Tiki has vegetable enchiladas for lunch."

"How do you know?"

"Because that's what she makes for lunch every day. And I like them."

"I do, too. I can eat four," Ariel said proudly.

"No!"

"Yep. And a side order of refried beans. How many can you eat?"

"Six, and a fajita. So there."

He was holding her hand again and it felt just as right as it had before. She felt like singing, but she couldn't think of a song. Instead she laughed, a sound of pure delight.

Lunch was delicious, and fun, the conversation consisting of Lex's questions about her movies. Impressed with his memory, Ariel said, "I can't believe you watched all of them and remember so much. Why? You didn't even know me."

"That's the point. I thought I could get some insight where you were concerned. I needed to know, or at least I wanted to know, how you were going to run Able Body. I've been doing business with them for years and years. Selfishly, I wanted things to continue the way they were. I'm sorry if I behaved less than professionally."

"I saw your actions as a threat. Either I did what you wanted—and the girls *said* you were demanding—or you were going to pull your business. I couldn't allow you to intimidate me. You can't, you know."

"Look, business is business. I'm sure we'll have words from time to time. I need your company and your company needs my business. That's a given. We'll go on from there. We'll discuss one more thing and then finish playing hookey. Chet Andrews is not a man you want to tangle with. You came out on top today, but he's ugly. There isn't another trucking company that will touch him. Able Body was his last shot. The last time I talked to Asa, he expressed concern about Chet. Actually, I believe Asa was afraid of him. I know his wife was frightened. She told me so, and wanted me to talk to Asa. I never got the chance. I was out of town when he made his snap decision to sell the business."

"What can he do? Scare me? Get the others to fall into line

behind him? If anything goes wrong, the police will go straight to him. As far as I can tell, Mr. Able ran a very clean operation. I'm the first to admit I don't understand a lot of the business, but I'm not stupid. My financial advisor, Ken Lamantia, did extensive research on Able Body and it all checked out."

"A lot of things can go wrong. The decent truckers won't have anything to do with him. There are others who will, though. Maybe sixteen or seventeen. Renegades, the ones who live in their trucks and shower at the truck stops. No families, no ties to anything or anyone. Chet is divorced. Asa told me his ex-wife came by the offices a couple of times to see if there was a way she could get some of Chet's money legally. Asa called in the welfare people and Chet's child support was taken out of his pay automatically. He's been in jail so many times I've lost track. A lot of things have happened these past years. The police, Asa, and I pretty much know Chet was involved in a lot of strange things, but we had no hard proof. Trundle Trucking burned to the ground, Mathison Trucking had the Feds come down on them so hard that Jack Mathison said to hell with it and sold out. The smaller companies are just getting by. Then there's the hijackings. All Chet and his cronies have to do is get on the CB and listen. If Chet can't make the payments on his rig he loses it. We're talking a hundred and seventy grand. Chet has a top-of-the-line rig, a Peterbilt—that's the Cadillac of trucks. Some of those rigs go for two hundred grand. Asa said Chet paid one hundred and seventy for his. He's one of those 'I got the best so I *am* the best' guys. The mentality of his friends is like his. Believe it. You're going to have to be real careful."

Ariel shivered. "There's talk he's stirring up the farm workers. To what end? What will that get him?"

"That's the whole point. He's a spiteful bastard. He gets

his kicks out of stirring up trouble. He's got a personal hate on for me that I don't want to go into right now. He stirs up the workers, has them make demands, gets them to walk off their jobs. The ranchers can't operate. They don't have anything to take to market. Then Chet steps in, bullies the workers into going back; then he shows up with his Peterbilt, and for a handsome sum, agrees to haul their loads. Blackmail, pure and simple, but when your back is to the wall, you don't have many options. It's not just the ranchers like myself. He does the same thing with small companies, too. I'm about the only one left who hasn't been intimidated. My gut tells me I'm next on his list because he blames me for Asa's attitude. But that's the least of it."

"And you're telling *me* to be careful? What about you?"

"I've been taking care of me for a long time. I have good, loyal people working for me. I've seen a truckload of Chets in my lifetime, and I'll deal with him when the time comes. Plus, I know how to drive one of those eighteen-wheelers so I can take my avocados to market myself if I have to."

"You are worried, I can see it on your face—and I think you just frightened me. Not so much for myself, but for the others who depend on Able Body for their livelihood."

"Not worried, concerned. I have Chet's M.O. down pat. He's not going to do anything right away. He bides his time, sponges off other truckers, and then when he thinks things have quieted down, he strikes. He's like a rattlesnake. How do you like this deep-fried ice cream?"

"It's delicious. I'm partial to coconut ice cream. It's my favorite."

"Mine, too. Imagine that!"

"I'm stuffed," Ariel said, pushing back her chair. "I never eat this much for lunch."

"I don't either. I was trying to impress you."

"Why?"

"Because I find myself liking you. I want you to like me. I like being up front."

"That's a very nice compliment." She felt shy suddenly, out of her depth. Was he expecting her to say something? She clamped her lips shut.

"Did I embarrass you? If I did, it wasn't my intention."

"No. No, not at all." She'd never felt this flustered in her life. Her fingers automatically went to her cheek. When she realized what she was doing, she stuffed her hands in her pockets. "I'm ready whenever you are. If we're lucky we might be able to get the bikes here by the time the kids get out of school."

"Should we take two vehicles or just one?"

"One. You can pay for delivery. Hey, I own a trucking company, remember? I can have Dolly send up a truck if I call now." She looked at him expectantly. He grinned and nodded, pointing to the phone on the wall.

"We're in luck. Dolly says there's one on the way down from Rancho California. What's the name of the store?"

"Maynards. They sell all kinds of toys, the kind you say we need."

"Maynards, Dolly. Of course you send Mr. Sanders a bill." She winked at Lex, who winked back. "Wait till you see what I'm bringing home. Probably around seven, maybe a little later. I'm having a very nice time. Uh-huh. Oh, yes. Certainly. I'll ask him. Now? Wait a minute. Dolly wants to know if you know a nice man around sixty or so who has his own money. He has to have a sense of humor, his own car, and his clothes have to match." She waited for Lex's answer.

"Not offhand, but I can check around." He was laughing, the sound so reminiscent of . . . of . . .

"Yes, I'll see you later."

"Is something wrong? You looked . . . strange, there for a minute."

"For a second you reminded me of someone. When you laughed. It was the sound. You should laugh more often, too. My acting coach told me once that it takes twenty-one facial muscles to frown and only nineteen to smile. An actress has to be aware of things like that." She was giggling like a schoolgirl, and Lex Sanders was flirting with her, and she was flirting with him.

Oh, life was good.

Chapter Six

Lex didn't know who was more excited, Ariel or himself. Everything was lined up in a row—forty-seven two-wheel bicycles, four with training wheels, eight three-wheelers, fourteen red wagons with collapsible sides, roller skates and roller blades, their boxes stacked neatly inside the red wagons, tennis rackets, cartons of tennis balls, and a wild assortment of inflatable pool toys. Doll babies in gingham outfits, doll buggies, swings, and beds waited for young hands to embrace them.

"Here comes the school bus. I hear the little ones singing. They always sing on their way home. Jesus, I haven't been this excited since I got a new shirt for Christmas when I was a kid. I had this girlfriend and I couldn't wait to show it off. She knew it was new and she said it was lovely and that I looked handsome in it. Do you have memories like that?" Lex asked.

"All the time," Ariel said softly. "Here they come. Are you going to give a speech or something?"

"Speech?"

"Yeah, you know, I got these things for you because . . . They're going to wonder what it's all about. I think you need to say something."

"Guess you're right. Hey, kids, c'mere. I've got a surprise for you. This is all for you. Look for your name." He rattled off something in rapid fire Spanish that Ariel couldn't grasp.

The children beelined for the row of bikes. Pink and purple for the girls, blue and red for the boys. Metal baskets on the backs of the boys' bikes, white wicker on the front of the girls'. All of the bikes, even the trikes, had either a bell or a horn. The sound was suddenly deafening. But, it was the dark-eyed wonder in the children's eyes that tugged at Ariel's heart.

"You did good, Mr. Sanders," she said, poking his arm. "Don't tell me you don't have a good feeling about what you've just done. Sometimes you have to give back for your good fortune. Otherwise good fortune means nothing. Here come the mothers and their faces are full of questions. This might be a good time to tell them about the washers and dryers."

"I hope they don't take this the wrong way. They can be funny sometimes about accepting gifts. Charity, stuff like that. However, they themselves are big givers, usually things they make with their hands. Oh, shit, I knew they would think these things were going on their bills at the store." Using his hands, he gestured wildly and kept shaking his head no, no, no. "Gifts. From my heart." He thumped his chest, his voice quivering until Ariel heard the words, *washers and dryers.* Then he pointed to her, his arm reaching for hers.

"Ah, sí. Si, señor." They smiled as one, the children laughed, and Lex heaved a sigh of relief.

"What did you tell them?" Ariel asked suspiciously.

"That we were getting married. Someday. I didn't say right away. I said it was your idea."

"You didn't! How could you do that? I don't even know you. Tell them you were joking. Lex!"

"I'm going to let you get to know me. I told you, I didn't say right away. *Someday* covers a lot of territory. I can't tell them I was joking. What kind of boss will that make me? I'm only as good as my word. Oh, Jesus, they want to see your ring."

"Let me see you get out of that one, Mr. Smart Ass," Ariel hissed.

Lex mopped at his forehead. He babbled on for five minutes, then mopped at his brow again.

"Ah, si, Senor Lex."

"What'd you say?" Ariel demanded.

"I said you were skinny, as they can see, and the ring was too big so we had to send it away to get sized."

"What are they saying?"

"They want to know how big the wedding is going to be." Lex guffawed.

"Boy, are they going to be surprised when you're standing at the altar all alone," Ariel jibed. "I'm not saying anything right now because I understand that bit about losing face in front of your people, but I'm not marrying you. I just met you today."

"Let's go for a walk so you can get to know me. I'm pretty much an open book. Ask me anything. After all, you just spent close to five thousand dollars of my money and I have yet to get the bill for transport. So, what do you want to know?" He reached for her hand.

Ariel felt pleased. She wanted to be angry with this man, but she couldn't work up one ounce of anger. He was simply too nice a person. They walked along, their hands and arms swinging freely. "Why don't you stay for dinner? Frankie won't get here till six or so. You could spend the night and go back early in the morning."

"No, I can't do that. Perhaps another time."

"When?"

Ariel smiled. "Whenever you ask me. You know, a date. You ring my doorbell, Dolly answers it, she grills you, tells you to have me home by midnight. A date."

"How about Saturday?

"Saturday's fine. Pick me up at seven."

"Great. Do you ride?"

"Yes. Rather well, as a matter of fact. I had to learn for a role. It took some getting used to. My backside was sore for a year. I like to ride at least once a month."

"Is there anything you can't do?" Lex marveled.

"Yes. I can't cook. I don't plan to learn, either."

Lex threw his head back and roared with laughter.

Ariel's heart skipped a beat at the sound.

"You said you were poor as a child. How did you get all this?" she asked, waving her arm about.

"My family worked the avocado groves for the owner. He took a liking to me and sent me off to agricultural school. When I graduated from college I came back here to oversee the groves and work off my education. The owner died and left me the ranch. It was a little over eleven acres and there was another parcel of three or four. I busted my hump, saved all my money, bought up land a little at a time. I also have property in Mexico where I raise avocados. It was a hard life for a long time, and then things started to go right. Several of the other ranches fell on hard times and I bought them up at auction. I own about a hundred thousand acres. I did all the work on the house myself. It was just five rooms when I got it. It took me ten years to get it to where it is now. There were times when I didn't think I would ever finish. I was going to hire a contractor a couple of times, but decided against it. I wanted to do it."

Ariel's voice was curious. "Why?"

"Remember that girlfriend I told you I wanted to impress with my new shirt? Well, I promised her the moon and the stars and a big house. The moon and the stars are bigger and brighter here than any place I've ever seen. Sometimes I think I can reach up and pluck them right out of the sky. I've got the house, but the girl got away."

Ariel thought she'd never heard a sadder voice in her life. "What happened to her? Never mind, that's none of my business. I'm sorry, I shouldn't have asked."

"That's all right. I don't know what happened to her."

Ariel looked at her watch. "I think we should start back. Is that a van pulling into your driveway?"

"That's Frankie. She's early. C'mon, I'll race you to the barn.

"A real gentleman would have let me win," Ariel said five minutes later.

"You should have said you wanted me to cheat."

"I didn't say you should cheat. How would you like it if I beat you at, say, tennis?"

"If you're a better player, that's good. I could handle it."

"I like to win."

"So do I," Lex said.

"Hey, you two, come here. I've got someone sitting here who wants to meet you. See how nice she sits with her seat belt. She's one smart dog, Miss Hart. Okay, girl, out. Time to meet your new owner. Let her come to you. She loves Fig Newtons. Put this in your pocket. When she warms up to you, give it to her. If you tell her she's a good girl she'll lick you to death. This dog has so much love it constantly amazes me. She needs to get your scent."

"Oh, my God. How much does she weigh?" Ariel gasped.

"Ninety-six pounds and not an ounce of fat on her."

"She's gorgeous. And huge. Do you think she will . . . you know, protect me? If she's gentle and shy, how will that work?"

"It's instinct. If she thinks you're being threatened, she'll do whatever has to be done. She'll realize you're her mistress when you start to feed her and give her treats. Praise her often. She needs to belong to someone. Let her sleep in your room with you at night. For some reason dogs get very territorial when their master is asleep. You're at your most vulnerable then and they know it. I have a dog, too, and when I take a shower, he lies outside the door until I'm finished. He's my eyes and ears at that time. It took me a while to catch on."

The shepherd started to circle Ariel, sniffing her pant legs and boots. She let out a soft woof and then a second. Ariel withdrew the Fig Newton from her pocket and held it out. The huge dog took it daintily. When she finished the cookie, Ariel scratched behind her ears.

Dropping to her haunches, Ariel put her face close to the dog's face and whispered, "I think we're going to get along just fine. On my way home I'm going to stock up on Fig Newtons." Snookie lowered her huge body and rolled over on her back, a sign that she wanted her belly rubbed. Ariel obliged. "I wonder if I can teach her to scratch *my* back," she giggled.

"I wouldn't be surprised. She likes you," Frankie said. "Well, I have to leave you now. I want to check on Cleo and her baby. It was nice meeting you, Miss Hart. Thanks for taking Snookie. I feel so much better knowing she's going to a good home."

"Thank you. Do you have a business card? I'll bring her to you for her checkups."

Frankie handed over a card. Ariel pocketed it.

"Well, I should be going if I'm stopping for Snookie's cookies. It was a nice day, Lex. Thanks for inviting me. I guess I'll see you on Saturday."

"It was nice, wasn't it? I hope we have lots of nice days together. Like Frankie, I feel better knowing you have a dog.

Drive carefully." He shut the door and watched as Snookie pawed at the seat belt, waiting for Ariel to snap it shut.

Lex watched the Rover until he heard the iron gates squeal shut. He squelched the urge to run after her. He wanted to be with her when she walked into her house with the German shepherd. He wanted to be part of her life. He shook his head to clear his thoughts. Why this woman, after all this time? What was so special about Ariel Hart? Finding no answers to his silent questions, he headed for the barn to the other female in his life.

"It's a beautiful evening, Snookie," Ariel said as she unsnapped the dog's seat belt. The shepherd waited patiently until Ariel exited the car and walked around to open the passenger side of the Rover. She leaped down gracefully, waiting again for a command. Instead, Ariel gave her a cookie which she munched happily. "This is your new home, girl. Let's take a walk so you can sniff everything. Feel free to lift your leg. Ooops, I forgot—you're a girl, you squat." Snookie took that moment to do just that. Ariel remembered Frankie's words—*praise her often.* "Good girl, Snookie. C'mon, let's meander down the garden path." The huge dog walked obediently at her side. She stopped several times, for bare seconds, to sniff a bush or shrub, and immediately increased her gait to keep up with Ariel. "Sometimes, back in L.A., I used to think I could smell orange blossoms. But, the scent I like best is that woodsy smell. Fresh earth, lush green plants. It's so pungent. They even make a cologne for men that smells sort of like it. Not really, though." She was talking to this dog, expecting her to understand. "They call it Wood Glen," Ariel said, not feeling stupid at all. The shepherd tilted her head, listening to every word.

"C'mon, I'll race you to the back door." The dog looked at her expectantly, not understanding if it was a command or not. "Run, Snookie," Ariel said as she sprinted ahead of the dog. "This is a fun thing," she called over her shoulder. The shepherd zipped past her like a streak of lightning and was sitting on the brick steps waiting when Ariel careened around the corner, gasping for breath. "We'll have to find other fun things to do." She handed out another cookie from the grocery bag on the steps. "We're going to meet Dolly now. She's going to love you. Trust me."

Ariel opened the door to the mud room, then she stepped aside as Snookie walked past her. Dolly's feet left the floor when she saw the huge black dog in her kitchen. "What is it?" she squeaked.

"This is Snookie. Lex Sanders' vet gave her to me. She was too playful for the Seeing Eye Program. She's completely trained and she's all mine. I want you to cook up something special for her. Steak, potatoes, hamburger, something wonderful. Maybe some vegetables. She came with a bag of dog food that looks like rabbit poop. What are we having to eat? She loves Fig Newtons so we can't run out. Always put them on the list. Her name is Snookie. Isn't she gorgeous? She weighs ninety-six pounds and doesn't have an ounce of fat. Boy, you should see her run! Say something, Dolly."

"She's pretty, Ariel. I like the way her ears are at attention. We're having pot roast and mashed potatoes. Can she eat a little of that with her dog food?"

"If it's good enough for us, it's good enough for Snookie," Ariel said smartly. "This dog is going to protect us, Dolly. I feel better already. You will, too, once you get the hang of having an animal in the house. We're going to take her with us to the office when we start going in every day. She'll be our mascot. What kind of vegetables are we having?"

"Fresh baby carrots and fresh snow peas."

"That's good. We'll cut them up in her mashed potatoes. I'm going to take a shower. Come along, Snookie, I'll show you the house. Do you think I should get her a bed? They make them, you know," she called over her shoulder.

"Make sure you get her a satin comforter from Bullocks and maybe some 320-thread sheets," Dolly shouted.

"Okay," Ariel shouted back.

Dolly burst out laughing. It was wonderful to see Ariel so happy, and it wasn't just the dog. Lex Sanders had something to do with the light in her friend's eyes. She started to set the table, her thoughts on the good-looking man who had just entered Ariel's life. She looked at the three places she'd set at the table. "No way, the dog eats on the floor." She removed the third plate and set it on a place mat next to Ariel's chair.

With Snookie's arrival life settled into more of a routine for the two women. The dog had needs that needed to be taken care of. Lex Sanders invaded their life with a gusto that neither woman had ever experienced. The days passed swiftly and literally leaped into weeks that soon led into months.

"I feel like life is zipping by. I need more hours in the day," Ariel grumbled on a bright sunny day in early April. Today I take my driving test, Wednesday evening is the martial arts exhibition, and Friday night we face off against the men in the shoot-off. Saturday I'm having dinner at Lex's and I know he's going to want to . . . I think . . . maybe I should cancel . . . I don't think I'm ready . . . men are . . . what they do is . . . it's been a long time." Her voice sounded lame.

"It's like riding a bike—it'll all come back. Providing you're interested. I had the impression you were more than ready. Let's face it, Ariel, you need to get laid."

"Dolly!"

"Well, you do. Who do you think is responsible for that smile on your face? Who's putting that sparkle in your eyes? How come you ordered all those new clothes? Don't insult me by saying it's because of Snookie. Face it, Ariel, you're falling in love and I think it's wonderful. You deserve everything good that life has to offer. Lex Sanders seems to be that rare, one-in-a-million guy. I don't think you should let him get away. I believe he's already in love with you. Now, what are you going to do about it?"

"If it's meant to be, it will be. It's that simple. That's another way of saying if the moment is right it will happen. Stop worrying about my sex life. That's a damn order, Dolly."

"You're flustered and your face is flaming. Okay, I was teasing. I just want you to be happy, Ariel. Did you invite him to the dojo to see you do your routine?"

"No, and I'm not going to, either. I've only gone up a degree on my brown belt. Lex might . . . sometimes men get intimidated when women can do things like that. I'm going to miss going to the dojo, but I'll start up again when Master Mitsu comes back from Japan. Don't say anything, Dolly. And, no, I did not invite him to the shooting range. Same thing. Promise me?"

"I promise. He'd be proud of you, Ariel. That's the kind of man he is. I personally don't think the person's been born yet who could intimidate Lex Sanders."

"I think you're right, Dolly. He is his own person, a one-of-a-kind guy. I like him a lot," Ariel blurted.

"I knew it, I knew it! We have the perfect backyard for a wedding. I'll cook everything. I'll absolutely outdo myself. I want to be matron of honor and I'll bet we can train Snookie to be the ring bearer. I knew it, I just knew it!" Dolly chortled.

Ariel threw the dishtowel at her, her cheeks pink, her eyes sparkling.

Lex Sanders looked as uncomfortable as he felt. Dressed in one of his six dark suits that he'd had custom made in Hong

Kong, he looked every bit as professional as a Wall Street broker. He only dressed in what he referred to as his "Sunday-go-to-meetin'" clothes for weddings and funerals. Today he'd gone to the funeral of one of the ranchers who'd been a good neighbor and friend. He'd stayed just long enough to pay his respects and sample the carefully prepared luncheon.

Saddened that a good friend had gone on to that other place, Lex headed for his car. The car, also his "Sunday-go-to-meetin'" vehicle, was never used more than the suits hanging in his closet. For one thing, the Mercedes-Benz embarrassed him, and he should have known better than to buy it. But the purchase had been made at a time when he thought he needed expensive things to make up for a host of other things he hadn't come to terms with. He'd come to learn that trappings of any kind did not measure a man's worth. He felt even more guilty sitting in the luxurious sedan now that he'd chastised Ariel Hart for buying foreign im-ports. Damn, he couldn't do anything right. He jerked at his tie that cost more than some men earned in a week, and tossed it in the back seat. He yanked at the top button on his shirt and when it wouldn't give, he pulled down and then across, the button sailing out the open car window. He stretched his chafed neck and swore at Tiki for putting so much starch in the pristine white shirt. He rolled up his sleeves and stretched his neck one more time before he put the car into gear.

Within minutes he was on Interstate 5 heading home. In-stead of taking his exit, he kept on driving when he remem-bered Ariel was taking her driving test on the Able Body rig. He risked a quick glance at his watch. If he drove like hell, he could probably be on hand to see if she passed or not. He wanted to be the first to congratulate her if she did. If she didn't, he'd stay in the background and try to be invisible. His heart started to flutter at the thought of seeing Ariel in the middle of the day. He wondered if he was falling in love. If these strange feelings meant he was in love, he had to attend to some serious legal matters. The thought made his neck grow warm.

Lex continued to drive as his mind conjured up one fantasy after another. Before he knew it, he was opposite the driving school where Ariel and the other employees of Able Body Trucking were taking their test. He maneuvered the silver Mercedes into the lot of a Taco Bell and parked. He got out, ordered food he didn't want, and sat down at one of the outdoor tables that afforded him a good view of the driving course across the street. He saw Ariel the moment he sat down. He immediately got to his feet to watch as she swung herself into the cab like a pro. He crossed his fingers, his eyes glued to the eighteen-wheeler as Ariel put the rig through her paces. Twice he sucked in his breath and grinned when she did something better than he himself had done during his own test years ago. He didn't realize he was holding his breath until it exploded from his mouth like a gunshot. What the hell was he doing here? Spying. He hated the word. If Ariel spotted him she would . . . what? He knew he should leave, but his feet felt rooted to the concrete.

Twenty minutes later, when Ariel brought the huge truck to a complete stop, Lex felt like he'd run a marathon. He stood up when she opened the door of the cab, her clenched fist shooting in the air. At that moment he felt capable of selling his soul just to be there with her. Ariel jumped down, slapped Dolly's open palm in a high-five, and grinned from ear to ear. She did a little jig, twirling about in a dizzying circle. Lex's eyes widened and then narrowed. He sat back down on the spindly chair, his breathing suddenly harsh and raspy. Once before, years and years ago, he'd seen a young girl do exactly the same little jig when she made the cheerleading squad.

Five seconds later he was in the silver Mercedes. Super-spy

Lex Sanders was going home where he belonged, to a world he was comfortable with. Memories were always comfortable.

Thirty minutes later, Lex roared through the iron gates the moment they swung open with the use of his remote control. He parked the car next to an ancient Joshua tree. He was ripping at the buttons on his white shirt and kicking his Brooks Brothers shoes off as he reeled up the steps. He stepped into clean, ironed jeans, but not before he peeled off his dress socks. A freshly ironed Banana Republic oversize T-shirt was yanked over his head. He heaved a mighty sigh of relief when he pulled on thick white socks and his worn work boots. This was who he was. He smoothed back his dark, curly hair and was stunned at what he saw in the mirror. Surely this wild-eyed person wasn't himself. But it was. And all because he'd seen a woman do a silly little dance that reminded him of someone he used to know. Not just someone; his wife.

Lex walked back to his bedroom and sat down on the edge of the bed. By God, he was not going to pep talk himself again. *You goddamn well need a psychiatrist, Lex Sanders. You should have gone to one years ago or else you should have hired a private detective to find Aggie. You could afford therapy and a private dick, so why didn't you do it?* "Shut up," he muttered to his conscience. The words hissed from his lips. But his conscience refused to be silent. *Because you were ashamed. That's it. You didn't want to see the ridicule in the gringo's eyes when you said you married an Anglo girl. You knew what they'd say behind your back Even now you don't want to believe it will be any different. You like being Lex Sanders. You buried Felix Sanchez. And now you're worried about Ariel Hart. What if she wants to share confidences and you blurt out something? How will she take that? Until you bury Aggie Bixby, you won't be able to love anyone else, not even Ariel Hart. Today was all the proof you need.*

Lex's head dropped to his hands. His shoulders started to

shake. Suddenly he wanted to be Felix Sanchez again. He longed for his smiling mother and his weary father who'd worked so hard to make sure their family survived the hardships of being poor. He cried then, because he needed to cry, needed to cleanse his spirit. And when he couldn't cry any more he washed his face and combed his unruly hair that was becoming stiff and wiry now that it was turning gray. The moment he finished, he marched, with grim determination, to his study where he picked up the yellow pages. He called the first detective agency listed. In a cool, emotionless voice, he outlined what he wanted, gave a timetable, and then rattled off his credit card number. Until he could lay Aggie Bixby to rest, he was putting his fast-moving friendship with Ariel Hart on hold. To continue to see her when a simple thing like a little dance could throw him into a funk wasn't fair. He could console himself by watching her old movies. He felt as if a truckload of cow manure had fallen on top of him.

Lex's fist crashed down on the top of his desk. If someone came to him with a story like his own, he knew what he'd say. *What do you mean you're still in love with a girl you met and married thirty-four years ago? Get real, man. That only happens in the movies. And, after an hour and forty-five minutes the star-crossed lovers fall into each other's arms, right?* Yep, that's what he'd say. And, that's why he never told anyone about his past. He didn't want to see the pity and disgust in their eyes. Better to keep it to himself in the darkness of his own room.

He looked around at the comfortable room he'd built with his own hands. The solid oak bookshelves were filled with thousands of books, and he'd read every single one of them. The furniture was burgundy, a man's color, deep and extremely comfortable. Oftentimes he slept on the couch if he was too tired to go up to the second floor. He'd chosen the burlap fabric for the draperies and Mrs. Estrada had sewn and hung them, a perfect match for the wheat-colored carpeting. He'd made the desk, too; since childhood, he'd been good with his hands. The lamps were solid brass with burgundy shades that cast a warm, mellow glow to the room. His housekeeper, Tiki, had contributed flowering plants and ferns that she kept trimmed and watered. But it was the watercolors painted by the children of his workers that gave the room life. An exquisite gold frame adorned a cow—he knew it was a cow because the five-year-old artist used a red crayon to print the word *cow* above the animal—-jumping over a yellow moon that had a point at the top. Brilliant stars shone down on tents, fluffy green clouds floated above a blue meadow filled with red daisies. His favorite was a train with nineteen box cars drawn on butcher paper. The elaborate custom-carved frame was worth every cent he paid for it. This was the room where he spent most of his spare time, a room that was his, built by him, for him. The only things missing were the Wurlitzer jukebox, Coke machine, and gumball machine. For years now he'd been trying to get originals, but no one wanted to part with their treasures. They were part of his youth, a youth he'd never really experienced. He'd placed orders up and down the coast, sent out letters all over the country. Just recently a dealer in Las Vegas who handled memorabilia had called and said he had a lead on all three items, but the price was astronomical. He'd decided that the word *astronomical* meant different things to different people. When you were trying to fill in missing pieces of your life, cost took a back seat.

His plan, if he was successful in acquiring the treasures, was to sit here in this room and play all the old records from that time in his life. He'd pop a dime into the Coke machine and drink the sweet drink until he was dizzy. Then he'd put a penny or a nickel into the bubble gum machine and chew until his jaws ached. In the basement he had sixty-four cases of long-neck Coca-Cola. Sitting next to the soda were four cartons of bubble gum, the bright little balls every color of the rainbow. Upstairs in his closet he had stacks and stacks of records that he was going to play by the hour, records he'd bought from collectors from all over the country. He wondered what Ariel Hart would think about his obsession—and it *was* an obsession—if he ever confided in her. "You have a screw loose, Lex Sanders," he muttered. "You can't go home again—some writer said that, and you know it's true. Memories are just that, memories. That's why they're called memories. They happen once and then life moves on. But I want . . . need to know what it feels like to sip a Coke and listen to a jukebox. I want pennies in my pocket to pop into the machine, I want to chew those little suckers and blow bubbles. I want to experience that part of my life. Just once. It won't be the same, he argued with himself. I don't care, I want to try. I need to try. I goddamn will try. Then I'll close that chapter of my life.

"Tiki," Lex bellowed.

"Sí, Señor Lex," Tiki said, waddling into the room.

"I won't be home for dinner. I'm going across the border. Do you want me to take any messages or bring anything back?"

"Sí. I will make the list. Two baskets for the padre, Señor Lex?"

"As many as you want. Pack up some candies for the children and some of those picture books that were delivered the other day. Get Manny to load the truck. We might as well fill it up."

Tiki twisted the hem of her snowy white apron between her fingers. "Señor Lex, the house telephone rings many times today. No one speaks. I say, hello, hello. No one says hello back. Many times yesterday, too."

Lex frowned. "Has that ever happened before? Sometimes

people dial the wrong number and hang up when they don't recognize the voice on the other end."

Tiki shook her head. "I say, 'Señor Sanders telephone' when I say hello."

"If it happens again tomorrow, tell me and I'll call the telephone company. They might be able to trace the call. Are you frightened, Tiki?"

"No, señor. The gates are closed. Manny is here as well as Jesus. I don't want a problem for you, señor."

Lex hugged the elderly woman. "Don't worry about me, Tiki. Did the ice cream for the children come today?"

"Sí. Early this morning. It's in the freezer. Tonight I will call the children and give them chocolate. Tomorrow strawberry, and the day after, vanilla. Little Toro doesn't like chocolate. He says it's mud. I will give him strawberry."

Lex smiled. "Mud, huh? He's only four—how does he know what mud tastes like?"

Tiki shrugged. Lex smiled again. He was still smiling when he climbed behind the wheel of his truck. As always, before he turned on the ignition, he let his eyes scan the vast acreage that made up the Sanders ranch. "Thank you, God, for all that you have given me, and allowed me to do for others."

Chapter Seven

"Dolly, can you believe it's almost the end of April? Where has the time gone?"

"Is that another way of saying it's been almost a month since Lex Sanders called?"

"I guess that's what I'm saying. I must have done something wrong. Was it wrong to call him and brag about passing my driving test? He didn't call after that. He faxes everything to the office. He's been paying his bills in seven days like always. I just wish I knew what, if anything, I did. I guess," Ariel said, her eyes misting, "he realized how bad my face really is. Don't say it, Dolly. We were getting along so well. We actually had fun together and I was looking forward to the date that never materialized the Saturday after my test. He said he'd call on Friday and he never did."

"You could have called him. This is the 90's, Ariel. He might be busy—you don't know what's going on in his life. He could very well be having some kind of family crisis. Things like this happen all the time. And, as my old mother used to say, if it's meant to be, it will be. But, I always tended to believe that was baloney. Think, Ariel, of a reason, a business reason, to call him. There's nothing wrong with that. You might get some kind of clue as to what's wrong."

"Not in a million years. This is not a shy man. He stopped me on the highway and convinced me to go to his ranch. We've had six dates—dinner, movies, and a picnic. Then, nothing. Somewhere along the way, something happened. What ticks me off is I had myself convinced I was going to go to bed with him if the opportunity presented itself. Now, I'm glad I didn't. Damn it, he even told his workers he was marrying me. Yes, I took it as sort of a joke, but his eyes were serious. He meant it. I've never been dumped before. I damn well don't like the feeling."

"Call him," Dolly said.

"Not in this lifetime."

"Then you're never going to know."

"I'll live with it."

"You're always going to wonder. Aren't you the one who always said, 'look it in the eye, deal with it, and get on with it'?"

"Yes, of course, I did say that. However, I was referring to other types of problems. This is emotional. It's different. I can forget he exists. You can take care of his business at the office or assign his account to one of the other girls. From this moment on, Lex Sanders is someone I knew briefly." Her voice was lofty, airy, as she fastened Snookie's leash to her collar.

"That's about the biggest lie I've ever heard you tell, Ariel Hart," Dolly muttered as she went back to paring vegetables for dinner.

Outside, the early evening closed around Ariel like a soft cloak. She sprinted with Snookie and then settled down for a brisk walk around her three-acre estate. She felt like crying. She wanted to cry, but what good would that do her? Besides, her bad eye would puff up and made her look lopsided. She was falling for Lex Sanders. At the age of fifty, no less. Did people still use that term, *falling for,* she wondered.

Snookie woofed softly, her signal that she wanted the leash removed so she could have her own private run. Ariel obliged.

"Make sure you get back here in five minutes. I don't want to lose you, too." Her voice was hoarse, her eyes tear-filled. The shepherd nuzzled Ariel's leg, but didn't go off on her private nightly run. Ariel crouched down to wrap her arms around the dog's neck. "It's important to believe things will get better," she whispered. "You know what, Snook? Upstairs is my very first report on Felix. I'm going to read it tonight before I go to bed. I was so excited when I got it, I couldn't bear to open it up. I wanted to be by myself, in my own room, with the door locked. Now, isn't that silly?" The dog inched closer to her legs, her long snout searching out her petting hand. "I wonder if Beverly what's-her-name found out anything important. I think I need to put that time in my life to a final rest, if you get my drift. It's always been there, hanging over my head. There was no closure. We all need closure. Like with Lex. Damn it, maybe I will call him. Maybe I'll tell him to take his business somewhere else. I deserve better than this. We're adults, for God's sake. He's hanging me out in the wind like a sheet off his bed. I would never do that to someone. I hate men. I really do, Snookie. C'mon, Dolly probably has our dinner ready and here I sit moaning and groaning. Tomorrow the sun is going to shine and it will be a whole new day for everyone. You can do a lot with a brand new day if you really want to." She heaved herself to her feet, the dog sprinting ahead of her. The urge to cry again was so strong, Ariel could feel her throat start to burn. "No tears for you, Lex Sanders."

The moment Ariel entered the kitchen she knew something was wrong. Dolly's dark eyes were wide with shock as she handed over the phone. "This is Ariel Hart," Ariel said quietly, her eyes questioning Dolly who just stared at her helplessly.

"This is Stan, Miss Hart. I just got a call from the State

Troopers. One of our trucks was hijacked about an hour ago. Ten John Deere tractors scheduled for delivery to Lex Sanders' ranch. The driver was making a stop in Las Vegas to pick up a $50,000 reconditioned Wurlitzer jukebox, a reconditioned Coke machine, and a special one-of-a-kind bubble gum machine. Just those three items are worth over $150,000. It's a federal matter so Mike called it in over the CB and reported it right away. Is there anything else I can do, Miss Hart?"

"Is our driver okay?"

"A little rocky, but that's to be expected. He's a family man so you can imagine what he was going through. Mike Wheeler was bobtailing so he picked him up at the state line where the troopers dropped him off. The feds will be here first thing in the morning to talk to you."

"Who's the driver?"

"Dave Dolan. He's been with us for twenty-three years. He's one of the best. Two kids in college and two in high school. Sweet little wife. Nice family."

"Pay him for the run as though he completed it, and give him a five-hundred-dollar bonus. No man deserves to be put in a position where he has to fear for his life. I'll want to talk to him in the morning. Did he see the people who did this?"

"Nope. They wore stocking masks and didn't talk at all. Dave said they had it down pat. There were four guys; each one had a job, and did it in complete silence. Do you want to call Mr. Sanders or should I?"

"I'll do it, Stan. I think, and this is just my opinion, that this is the beginning of some bad times. Call a meeting tomorrow of all the truckers. We can have the guys on the road call in from truck stops. I don't want any conversations going out over the CB."

"I'll take care of it, Miss Hart. And for whatever it's worth, I'm of the same opinion as you are."

"We've been hijacked, Dolly," Ariel said. "It was one of Lex Sanders' loads. Ten John Deere tractors, a genuine, reconditioned Wurlitzer jukebox and some kind of super-duper bubble gum machine that the driver picked up from an antiques store in Las Vegas. Real collector's items. I have to call Lex . . . Mr. Sanders. Get me his number, please, and Dave Dolan's home number. I want to talk to Mrs. Dolan personally. Maybe I should call Mr. Able in Hawaii and see what he has to say. We have his number, don't we?"

"Ariel, do you think Chet Andrews had anything to do with this?" Dolly asked as she riffled through a thick book that held all the truckers' home phone numbers and Lex Sanders' private number at the ranch. She copied down the three numbers and handed the slip of paper to Ariel.

"It wouldn't surprise me, but we can't accuse anyone without proof."

Her heart pounding at the thought of talking to Lex Sanders, Ariel dialed the number with shaking hands. "Tiki, this is Ariel Hart from Able Body Trucking. I need to speak with Mr. Sanders. This is an emergency."

"Sí, Señora, I fetch him. He's in the barn. One momento."

Ariel's fingers drummed on the kitchen counter as she tried to imagine Lex's reaction to her news.

"Sanders here," Lex said.

"Lex, this is Ariel. Stan just called and said your load was hijacked outside of Las Vegas by four men. They . . . they took your . . . collectibles and the John Deere tractors. The feds will be at the office in the morning. I'm sorry. We're insured. I don't know what to say." Damn, she was babbling. This wasn't her fault, but she knew in her gut he was going to blame her. She waited for the explosion she knew was coming.

"What?" The one word was a barrage of sound.

"What part didn't you understand? Or is that just a rhetorical question?"

"I understand everything you just said. I don't give a hoot about those tractors. They can be replaced. I've waited thirty goddamn years for the rest of the load. I'm holding you personally responsible. I want them back. Do you hear me, Miss Hart?"

"You don't need to bellow in my ear, Mr. Sanders. Is it possible you think I should have ridden shotgun with that load? If you're stupid enough to believe that, then you're an idiot. You know it's against the law to carry a firearm on a run. It's also against the law to interfere in a federal investigation. The feds will handle it. You are, of course, within your rights to be at the office when they arrive in the morning. Now that you've ruined my evening, I want to tell you what I think of a man who stands a lady up for a date and doesn't call her to explain why. I guess I thought you were a gentleman. My mistake." Ariel slammed the phone down so hard, Snookie took the time to lift her head from her food dish to growl menacingly.

Ariel dusted her hands together. "He's holding me personally responsible. How could he say such a thing? He'll collect from the insurance. He has a right to be upset, but not to blame me. He said he doesn't care about the tractors. It's the collectibles. He said he's waited thirty years for them. I feel lower than a snake's belly, Dolly. You should have heard him. His voice was like chipped ice. I hate men. I mean, I *really* hate men. My fault!" Ariel snorted.

She dialed the Dolans' number, reassured Mrs. Dolan as much as she could, and promised that extra security would be added to the runs to protect the drivers. "If there's anything I can do, call me. If you have a pencil I'll give you my home phone number. You or your husband can call me any time of the day or night. Thank you for talking to me,

Mrs. Dolan. I'll speak with Dave myself tomorrow. Good night, Mrs. Dolan."

"There's a two- or three-hour difference between here and Hawaii. I'll try Mr. Able and see what kind of advice he can offer. I just don't feel qualified, Dolly. God, what if the drivers walk out on me? A hijacking has to be a pretty scary thing. I'm sitting here safe and sound in my kitchen and I'm frightened. Imagine what those truckers feel like."

The phone rang. Ariel looked at Dolly. "Don't answer it. It might be . . . answer it . . . no, don't . . ."

Ariel picked up the phone. "Hello."

"Ariel, it's Lex Sanders. I'm calling to apologize. I had no right to talk to you like that. It was inexcusable. I also want to apologize for standing you up that Saturday night. I had to cross the border for a family funeral. There have been a lot of pressures here at the ranch and I have a few . . . ah . . . personal problems consuming my time. I'll be at the office tomorrow when the authorities arrive. Aren't you going to say something, Ariel?"

"I think you need to get yourself another trucking company. Goodbye, Mr. Sanders." She slammed the phone down again.

"That's really telling him," Dolly snorted. "But aren't you cutting off your nose to spite your face?"

"Probably. My gut tells me I'm going to have more than I can handle, and I don't need Lex Sanders, his personal problems, or his on again, off again personality." Ariel dialed the area code for Hawaii. She was still drumming her fingers on the countertop, and tapping her foot at the same time.

When the phone was finally picked up on the other end, a gravelly voice said, "This is Asa Able. What can I do for you?"

She heaved a sigh of relief. "Mr. Able, this is Ariel Hart. I hope I'm not calling you at a bad time."

"Not a bad time. Just so much sunshine a body can tolerate. I'm having my afternoon beer out on the lanai. It's Hawaii talk for a patio. Must be a problem or you wouldn't be calling me. Bet you want to try and sell me back the business." His voice sounded so hopeful, Ariel hated to disappoint him.

"Not exactly. One of the trucks was hijacked this afternoon in broad daylight. The feds are coming tomorrow morning. It was a load for Lex Sanders—some personal things and ten John Deere tractors. He's pretty upset."

"That personal stuff, that wouldn't be one of those old jukeboxes, a Coke machine, and a bubble gum machine, would it?"

"All three. Stan said the collectibles alone are worth over $150,000. Lex is coming to the office tomorrow when the feds arrive. I told him to find himself another trucking company. My question to you is, has this ever happened before? I had a pretty serious run-in with Chet Andrews and I fired him. He made a lot of threats. I'm calling for advice."

"Had one hijacking about twenty years ago. They got themselves caught in the next town. Lots of wildcat strikes, that sort of thing. Chet was giving me a bad time right before I sold the business to you. He's having a hard time making the payments on his rig. I was the only fool who'd hire him, and I only used him because I was afraid of him. I'm too old to lie and make up stories about why I kept him on. Fear, pure and simple. My missus was petrified. Now, why would you go and do a silly thing like telling Lex to go someplace else? He probably will, and then where will you be? He's my bread and butter. I mean, *your* bread and butter. He's a good man, an honest man. You don't find many like him nowadays. You best straighten up your back and apologize. That's my advice, and it's for free. Chet Andrews is one ugly man. He gave me many a sleepless night. Wouldn't surprise me to find he's behind the hijacking. The man don't have no conscience. Why'd you say you told Lex to go somewheres else?"

"Because he . . . pissed me off," Ariel said smartly. "I don't want to talk about Lex Sanders." The laughter on the other end of the phone brought a deep flush to Ariel's face.

"This ain't no time to be gettin' on your high horse, little lady. You might be needin' some help and Lex Sanders is the man to help you. A fine lady like yourself is no match for Chet Andrews. Would you by any chance want me to fly back there to help out? I could bunk with Lex. I'd be glad to do it." Again, his voice sounded so hopeful, Ariel hated to disappoint him.

"Can I take a raincheck, Mr. Able? I want to talk to the authorities first. If I feel I'm in over my head, I'll call you. Do you like Hawaii?" she asked politely.

"I hate it. My missus loves it. She shops all day long. Buys me flowered shirts I won't wear. Everything she cooks has pineapple in it. Don't like pineapple. Never liked pineapple. Am never going to learn to like pineapple. You gonna be calling Lex? Maybe I should call him. Sometimes he needs to be reminded how to talk to a lady. Is he smitten with you yet? That might be what his problem is. He's not real good with women. Better'n a son, I can tell you that."

"I'll let you know, Mr. Able. Thank you for talking to me. It's very reassuring to know I can count on you. Have a nice evening.

"He's going to call Lex Sanders this very minute," Ariel told Dolly. "I just know it. He's one cranky curmudgeon. Wouldn't surprise me to find out he takes the next plane. To bunk with Lex Sanders. The two of them are going to invade my life and try to take over. I can feel it in my gut. Well, it ain't gonna happen," Ariel said, sitting down at the table. "Let's eat and let's not talk about business."

"Want to talk about the movies?"

"No!"

"Finances?"

"Absolutely not," Ariel said.

"Friends?"

"What friends? Nobody's called me in over a month. Out of sight, out of mind." she sniffed.

"Why don't we talk about what you're dying to talk about? Lex Sanders. Remember when you had those bumps on your face and you didn't want to be bothered with anyone or anything? Well, maybe he's got a personal problem like that. Cut him a little slack, for heaven's sake. Business relationships and personal relationships are separate things. C'mon, Ariel, you're a professional. Don't let him get to you. If you need him, ignore your pride, and if you have to suck up, do it. That's my advice."

"I think it's going to rain this evening. My face is starting to ache and that always means rain," Ariel said, ignoring Dolly's advice. "I can't wait to take a long, hot bath and just sit and relax this evening. I might even make a fire to take the chill off my bedroom. I've got a couple of good books I've been meaning to start. What are you going to do?"

"Iron. I might make some of that marshmallow pecan fudge that neither of us can live without. A double batch. My sweet tooth has been acting up all day. We can take some into the office for the girls tomorrow."

"Dolly, load the shotgun and put it near the mantel. Just in case." This last was said so casually, Dolly gulped her coffee and then yelped when it scalded her tongue.

"I can load it, but I don't think I could shoot anyone. We've been through this a hundred times, Ariel. I went to the firing range with you, I learned to shoot so you would have a companion, but I know if the time came to . . . to . . . you know, I wouldn't be able to do it. Maybe you should keep it upstairs."

"We need to be prepared, Dolly. This is no time to play Pollyanna. I have my gun upstairs, but what good is it going to do you if you're down here and there's a break-in? I didn't say you had to shoot. Usually the threat of a gun is all you need. You did well in the class, Dolly. You're an expert marksman. I don't know if this is any consolation, but I think men—you know, crooks and burglars—might be a little nervous if they see a woman with a shotgun. Any kind of gun, for that matter. Remember what that instructor said: *wave it around below belt level.* Picture this, Dolly. You shoot between some guy's legs—how much damage and blood do you think there would be?"

"Buckets. I hate the sight of blood. We'd have to move out—I couldn't clean it up."

"And on that thought, I'm going to retire for the evening. I locked up when I came in. Great dinner, Dolly. The alarm system is activated. If you get nervous, come upstairs. 'Night, Dolly." She hugged her lifelong friend and whispered, "Chet Andrews would have to be a fool to tangle with us. For one thing, he doesn't even know where we live. Sweet dreams."

Upstairs in her room, Ariel shed her clothes in preparation for the long, leisurely bath she'd promised herself. As she moved, clicking on the gas-driven fireplace, turning down her bed, fluffing her pillows, the shepherd paced. When the dog was satisfied that Ariel was safe in the tub, she leaped on the bed, tugged at the two pillows that were hers, squirmed, and circled the bed until she had a satisfactory nest. The moment the scent of Ariel's gardenia bath salts wafted into the bedroom, Snookie closed her eyes, one ear at attention, the other flat against her head.

Ariel sighed as she settled herself in the hot, steamy water. This is bliss, she thought. A bath, like a cup of fragrant tea, always made things bearable. She'd promised herself a leisurely soak with a good book. She cracked the spine before she started the first chapter of the best-selling espionage novel. Twice she extended her big toe to release hot water to which she added more bath salts. She was in the middle of chapter three when she felt the tension leave her neck and shoulders. Her toe worked the gizmo that opened the drain.

Snug in a cherry-red terry robe, she padded out to the bedroom, kicked at a mound of colorful cushions she kept near the hearth, and plopped down, the wish list from the closet and the private detective's report in hand. At some point during her long soak, Dolly had brought up a tray with a pot of hot chocolate and several chunks of her famous marshmallow pecan fudge. Ariel devoured them immediately. She was licking her lips, wishing she had another piece, when the phone on the little stand by the hearth rang. She stretched, almost missing the antique French phone. "Hello." Silence. She spoke again and then a third time before she hung up. She looked at Snookie, who was staring at her. She shrugged. "Wrong number."

Ten minutes later the phone rang again with the same results. Five minutes later it rang again. It rang seven more times in the space of fifteen minutes. The moment her shoulders started to tense, Snookie was off the bed, circling the phone, the hair on the back of her neck straight in the air. She growled deep in her throat. "I guess we both know it's not someone dialing a wrong number," Ariel whispered.

Snookie nuzzled Ariel's neck as she tried to crawl onto her lap, her huge front paws circling her shoulders. Ariel crooned to her as the dog tried to match the sounds her mistress was making. "C'mon, you can have the rest of this hot chocolate that is now only lukewarm. Do you want to go out on the deck?" The shepherd ignored the chocolate drink and didn't run toward the French doors the way she usually did at the mention of the word *deck*. Ariel shrugged. "It stopped ringing. I'm going to unplug the phone. It's probably some kid

playing a trick. This is an unlisted number—Chet Andrews
can't possibly get this number. It's okay, Snookie." The dog
settled down immediately.

Ariel sat for a long time, staring into space as she stroked
the shepherd's sleek body, her thoughts chaotic as she tried to
make sense of what was happening in her life.

The small clock on the mantel chimed ten times. Ariel
heaved herself erect, calling Snookie to the French doors. The
shepherd liked the cool evening air. Ariel took that time to
read the report from the private detective. She fully expected
to see an address and telephone number for Felix Sanchez.
She was so disappointed she wanted to cry and wasn't sure
why. With a cigarette clutched between her teeth, she read
through the report, the smoke spiraling upward making her
eyes water.

According to the report there were 67 males named Felix
Sanchez ranging in age from ten months to 89 years. There
were an additional 33 males named Felix Sanchez who no
longer lived in either Mexico or California. Of the hundred
males named Felix Sanchez, 17 had a dual citizenship. Nine
of the 17 no longer lived in either Mexico or California. Eleven
of the males' birthdays, schools, and the parents' domestic
jobs fit the profile supplied. However, the report went on to
say, the school burned and all records were destroyed. Several teachers in San Diego vaguely recall a student named
Felix Sanchez. One elderly teacher in a retirement home said
the boy she was thinking of returned to school in Mexico
after his girlfriend's military parents were transferred to Germany. Many years later, she said, the boy came back to tell
her he was going off to college. She cannot remember where.
She was the most promising lead. There is no record of a U.S.
driver's license. A social security number is essential to continue this investigation. A postscript was added in longhand
at the close of the report. *I personally went to Mexico City to
check the divorce and marriage records. I did the same thing*

here in California with no success. Please advise by phone as to how you wish me to proceed, if at all.

Ariel stuffed the pages back into the brown envelope. She'd known it was going to end like this. "Damn."

Snookie scratched the glass on the door to be allowed in. Ariel opened the door, slamming it shut quickly and bolting it. Now what was she to do? She was wide awake, and she was angry. Really angry. Do what you always do, Ariel, when you get mad. Eat. She headed for the kitchen. She wasn't surprised to see Dolly sitting at the kitchen table smoking a cigarette. "Couldn't sleep, huh? I thought I'd make myself a fried egg sandwich. With bacon and lots of ketchup. I'll make it—I need to do something with my hands."

"Oh, no, you make too much of a mess. Extra crisp, right?"

"Snap-in-two bacon. Nuke it."

"So who was calling you all night? Bet it was rancher Sanders. Wants to kiss and make up, I bet."

"Wrong. There wasn't anyone on the other end of the line. I finally unplugged the phone. Probably some jerk getting his jollies thinking he's scaring me."

"More like Chet Andrews. Scare tactics."

"If it was him, where did he get my unlisted number? It's not even on file at the office, just the house phone. Now, if he did manage to get it somehow, that's scary."

Dolly covered the bacon with five layers of paper towels and slapped it into the microwave oven. "I read somewhere that the only people who can get through to an unlisted number is the fire department, and only in an emergency. I can't remember where I read it, though. If you think about it, it makes sense. It's possible that scum knows someone in the fire department."

"Now, why doesn't that reassure me?" Ariel snapped. "God, does that mean I have to hassle the fire department?"

"Unless you have a better idea. Make a list of people you've given the number to, and don't leave anyone out."

"I don't need to make a list. I've given it to seven people. You make eight. Everyone else has the house number. Not one of those seven people knows Chet Andrews, and even if they did, they wouldn't give him my private number."

"Lex Sanders?"

"He hates Chet. Look what that scumbag has us doing. Blaming him, and talking about him at the same time. It's a fear tactic, and we're falling for it."

The buzzer on the microwave sounded. "You could swat a fly with this bacon," Dolly muttered.

"Terrorists prey on people like this. Make my yolk runny so it mixes with the ketchup. I think we're over-reacting."

"I've been making you fried egg sandwiches for thirty years. I know you like the yolk all messy and I know just how much ketchup to put on. And, I know you then like to dip the whole mess into black coffee. Tell me again why we took those shooting classes and why I had to take the basic course in martial arts. I already know why, even after I said I didn't want to take those trucking lessons, I did. Tell me again, Ariel." Dolly slapped the fried egg sandwich down in front of her boss and then plopped a cup of leftover dinner coffee next to the plate. She cut up Snookie's egg and set it on the floor.

"We own a trucking company. It makes sense that the owner and her assistant know how to drive a truck. We might be needed in a pinch for short hauls. Who knows, there could be an epidemic of something or other and the drivers might get sick and then we'd have to pitch in. There could be a union strike or one of those wildcat things. It's up to the owner to step in.

"Ooohhh, this is a good sandwich," Ariel said as she wiped dripping egg yolk from her chin. "When I was a kid my mother used to make me eggs all nice and yellow in the middle with what I called brown lace around the edges. There are a lot of low-lifes and jerks out there. Every woman should know self-defense. You never know when you'll need it. I have to admit, I'm pretty good at it, and so are you. Think of it as an insurance policy. You hate paying the premiums, but you're damn glad you have it when it's time to make a claim. That's what self-defense is all about. C'mon, you can admit you liked pounding on those guys. It's wonderful self-control, and it's an image booster. If we ever come up against the bad guys, we can take them on and come out on top. Trust me on this, Dolly."

"Which brings me to the gun part. I hate guns. Guns kill people."

"People kill people, Dolly. A gun is not a plaything. A gun owner needs to know that going in. It's not like we're packing weapons in our everyday life, although there are times when I think we should. Again, they're like insurance. If someone breaks in here, I'll be damn glad I paid the premium. And if the time ever comes when we have to make a run, even though it's against the law, we'll be glad we have it. You do what you have to do in this life, Dolly. I could really go for a piece of blackberry pie. If you aren't too busy, let's have some this weekend. I say we go to bed now. Five-thirty will be here before we know it."

Before she climbed into her turned-down bed and settled Snookie at the foot of it, Ariel hung her wish list back in the closet. Wishes were for children. Adults made their own dreams and were able to recognize the fact that no amount of wishing could take the place of hard work.

" 'Night, Snookie."

The shepherd woofed softly, her snoot buried in her own pillow.

It was 4:10 when the house exploded with sound. Ariel

leaped from the bed, disoriented, stumbling over Snookie, who was circling the room in a frenzy. A continuous, high-pitched wail bounced off the wall in double time to a shrieking whistle that seemed to be coming from all the doors and windows. She knew instinctively it was the alarm system even though she'd never tested it out. With trembling fingers she punched in the code that should have turned the room silent in the space of two seconds. The wailing and shrieking continued.

"I can't turn it off," Dolly screamed from the hallway. "It won't take the code. Do something, Ariel, or we'll both be deaf. Get Snookie out of here—this is going to hurt her ears." She obeyed her own instruction and opened the French doors. Both women stared at the dog as she literally sailed through the open doors. She hit the top of the steps when both feet touched the ground for the second time. Then she was in mid-air, landing gracefully a split second later. She was a streak of black silver beneath the glow of the floodlights, heading into the darkest reaches of the garden.

"Do something, Ariel."

Ariel punched in every combination she could think of, but the alarm continued. "Why isn't the alarm company calling? They're supposed to call within three minutes." She was shouting to be heard over the deafening din.

"The phone's dead," Dolly screamed.

"It's not *dead* dead. The alarm company freezes it or something for those three minutes. Just wait, the dial tone will come on." Lord, how desperate her voice sounded.

"It's been more than three minutes and the line is still dead." Dolly was bellowing now. "Oh, God, look!"

Ariel ran to the kitchen door. A parade of red, blue and white flashing lights was racing up her driveway. In the lead was a clanging fire engine. She echoed Dolly's words. The alarm continued to sound. Both women ran out to the driveway where Ariel pressed the buzzer to open her gates. She threw her hands in the air as she tried to shout above the din, to try and explain she didn't know what happened to set off the alarm.

And then there was silence. Ariel sighed with relief, as did Dolly.

Ariel tried to explain again in a normal voice that was coming out as a hoarse scream, that they were both asleep when the alarm went off. "Maybe there's a loose connection or something," she said lamely.

"Ma'am, you own Able Body Trucking, don't you?" a young officer said. Ariel nodded, puzzled. Then she recognized him as the officer who had filed the report of her run-in with Chet Andrews.

"Do you think there's a connection between that to-do and my alarm going off?"

"Anything's possible. Call your alarm company in the morning and have them come out and check the system. A squirrel could have chewed the wires or they could have gotten wet. It's as easy to believe that as it is to believe someone tampered with it. You're sure you paid the bill?"

"Of course I'm sure I paid the bill. I always pay my bills. Squirrels stay in the trees because of the dog. It hasn't rained in two weeks. My phone is still dead so perhaps you'll do me a favor and call the alarm company for me. And I'd appreciate it if you'd call the telephone company, too. Dolly will get you the numbers."

"Phone's back on," Dolly said. She held out the receiver so Ariel could hear the dial tone.

"I guess I can make the calls myself, officer. I'm sorry all you men had to come out here. Can we get you anything to eat or some coffee?"

"No, thanks, Ma'am. We'd rather it be a false alarm than a tragedy."

The women waited until the last cruiser backed through the gates. Snookie stood sentinel, her ears alert, the hair on her back at attention. The moment the gates clicked shut, the dog turned and walked sedately ahead to the house. She waited patiently for Ariel to open the door, then stepped aside and did a brief circle of the terrace before she walked into the house. Satisfied that things were under control, she sprawled out in front of the door. When her huge head dropped to her paws, Ariel relaxed.

Neither woman said a word as Dolly measured coffee into the wire basket of the percolator. Ariel slid thick slices of bread into the toaster. "All we do is eat," she grumbled. "I just had a fried egg sandwich a few hours ago. I'm going to have to run ten miles on the treadmill today to work this off." This last was said as she melted butter to spreadable softness in the microwave and scooped wild strawberry jam into a small bowl.

Dolly bit down into the golden toast. "Ariel, did we make a mistake coming here?"

"I don't know, Dolly. I hope not. You're referring to the problems at the trucking company, I assume."

"Everything in general. You don't look happy. If you aren't happy, I'm not happy. Snookie is the only positive thing that's happened since we moved here. I guess what I'm trying to say is if you want to go back to L.A., it's okay with me."

"I can't quit now. That wouldn't say much for me. Let's see it through to the end, then make a decision. Besides, who would buy a trucking company with someone like Chet in the background?"

"You did."

"I didn't know about him. It was Mr. Able's place to tell me. Since he chose not to mention it, I have to believe he didn't think the man would be a problem for me. Of course, I could be wrong. I can even understand him being afraid and not saying anything. Older people deal with fear differently than younger ones. They feel more vulnerable. This just makes me mad."

"Time to get ready for the day, Ariel. It's 5:30. Spruce up—Lex Sanders will be at the office. It won't hurt to put a little of that sinful perfume behind your ears, and I'd wear those drop earrings with the little clusters of pearls. Maybe you should get dressed up today—you know, a tailored suit or maybe that frilly brown and white polka dot dress with the wide leather belt. Not for Lex Sanders, for the feds. They might be more respectful if you appear businesslike. The pink Donna Karan suit. Easy on the makeup."

"Do you want to pick out my underwear, too?" Ariel snapped.

"Only if you want me to."

"Well, I don't."

"Do you want me to call you after the alarm people leave or should I just head for the office?"

"Come to the office. We're so far behind in our billing it's going to take us weeks to catch up. The Witherspoons from Georgia are due in this afternoon. They want 25 of our rigs, which will bring us a pretty penny. We need to get our bills out so some revenue comes in. Okay, you take care of things here and I'll do what I have to do. Sometimes, Dolly, I don't tell you how much I appreciate you. I do, you know. I can't imagine what my life would be without you. We're going to work this out, and things will get back to normal. See you in a bit." She tapped her leg, a signal that Snookie was to follow her.

Forty minutes later, Dolly said, "You look like a movie star, Ariel Hart. You really look good, my friend. You're going to have those feds and Lex Sanders eating out of your hand. You eat like a truck driver and as far as I can see, you haven't put on a pound. That suit looks the same on you as it did back in Hollywood."

"And on that thought, I'll leave you. Do I really look good, Dolly?"

"He's going to eat his heart out. Keep watching his eyes. Eyes are the mirror of one's soul. I believe that."

"I'm outta here." Ariel grinned.

She laughed aloud when she climbed from the Range Rover and heard wolf whistles as the skirt hiked well up her thigh. She gave a thumbs-up salute as she crossed the lot to the office. Seated on the front step was Lex Sanders. She pulled up short, sucking in her breath.

"Breakfast. Doughnuts. Delectable jelly and thumb-licking cream. I had the girl throw in two bagels with cream cheese. Hot coffee, real cream. And napkins. You aren't going to turn me down, are you? I don't think there's anything more . . . appealing than a girl with sugar on her lips."

Ariel stared at the man on the step dangling the doughnut bag. She wanted to tell him to take a hike, to get off her property for letting a whole month go by without a single phone call. Then she'd deliver some blistering dialogue about holding her personally responsible for his loss. She was going to tell him so, too, to his face. Coldly, of course. Obviously he was going to ignore what she'd said earlier on the phone. Mr. Lex Sanders needed to be put in his place, and she was just the person to do it. She did her best to marshal her thoughts so that when she did start to talk she wouldn't get flustered. Then he winked at her, the doughnut bag his peace offering.

Ariel laughed, and then giggled and couldn't stop. Between giggles, she tried to explain her late-night or early-morning breakfasts and the alarm system going out as she fished inside the bag for one of the jelly doughnuts. She really didn't want the doughnut or the coffee, but she knew she was going to eat and drink because she didn't want Lex Sanders to walk out of her life. So much for telling him off.

"Winsomeness does not become you. I've already had two breakfasts. Those things will kill you," she said, pointing to the doughnut bag.

"I like that suit. I like your hair like that, too, and you smell sweeter than a summer peach." He dangled the bag again as he followed her into the office.

"If this is your version of an apology you don't want to hear what I think of it, now do you?"

"Actually, I do. I was out of line, and I apologize. You're making me crazy, Ariel Hart. My life was on a steady course until you arrived and turned it upside down. Nobody in this world who knows me would ever say I'm good with women. I probably shouldn't admit that because it will give you an edge. Neither party should have an edge. It should be what it is—two people being honest with each other. I have some personal baggage I have to deal with. I imagine you do, too. I'm trying to clear mine away in my own way. What exactly am I guilty of, Ariel? Tell me so I don't do or say it again."

"You . . . what you did was . . . you led me to . . . it wasn't nice what you did. We're adults and should act like adults, not adolescents. I actually thought about going to bed with you, and what do you do? You know what you did and don't think doughnuts and flattery are going to change a thing. How many jelly doughnuts did you bring?" Sugary lips. God.

"Four. Did you really think about going to bed with me? It's only 6:15—how could you have had two breakfasts already? I came down early so I could try and explain to you about the jukebox and Coke and bubble gum machines. I wanted to tell you myself why those things mean so much to me. Again, I'm sorry about the things I said. I don't do things like that. It's part of . . . you turning my life upside down."

"I'm not easy—you need to know that." God, did she just say that?

"I never thought you were. I'm not, either," Lex said huffily. "I didn't *ask* you to go to bed, so why were you thinking about it?"

His voice sounds crafty, Ariel thought. "Maybe you didn't ask me, but you were thinking about it. That's what men do. Women think about it and then make the decision either to do it or not. It all depends on the moment. Anything else is kind of calculated and then all the spontaneity flies out the window."

"Spontaneity, huh? Like if I locked the door and suggested we go for it right here on this gorgeous desk? Is that the moment?" He leered at her and couldn't believe his own words.

"It's something to think about, but not today. I like to take my time when I make love."

"I do, too. Imagine that!" He sounded, he realized, like he'd just found the Holy Grail.

Ariel laughed again. She leaned across the corner of her desk until their eyes were level. "Just how much sugar do I have on my lips?"

"Not nearly enough. It'll do for starters, though. How much do I have on mine?"

"Just enough."

He kissed her. Ariel strained into him, her lips meeting his. Time stood still for the first time in her life. She wanted more when his lips promised the best was yet to come. Later, she swore kissing Lex Sanders was like drowning in a pool of sweet nectar. She was the first to pull away. She cleared her throat. "I liked that."

"I can do better under different circumstances. How about dinner this evening at the ranch? Or dinner here in town? I can buy a toothbrush and one of those disposable razors."

"Dinner here in town. No toothbrush and razor, though. Now, tell me about those machines that were hijacked."

He told her.

"Okay, I'm sorry. I understand better now. The feds will get them back."

"This wasn't a hijacking for money, Ariel. It was done to me personally. Those machines are going to be destroyed. If it was Chet and his cronies, it's my personal opinion that he's going to take an ax to them. He might try to sell the tractors or hide them until things calm down. I'll never get my machines. That's a given."

"Can they be replaced? Aren't there other dealers who specialize in memorabilia like that?"

"All kinds. All over the country. The problem is the owners don't want to part with them. It's not a question of money. A collector doesn't think in terms of money. It's a part of life, the past, memories. Part of my goddamn life I never got to experience. But, to answer your question, maybe in another thirty years. I'll be eighty and won't give a damn then. I don't like what happened at your house. Coming on the heels of the hijacking, I think it's a warning. I'm willing to bet you five dollars that the alarm company tells you the system was tampered with."

"That's a sucker bet. I already figured that out myself," Ariel said as she fed Snookie pieces of the jelly doughnut. "I also know you can't accuse someone without proof, and neither one of us has any. Maybe we can hire a private detective to keep Chet under surveillance, and maybe they can track his whereabouts last night and during the time of the hijacking. I'd be willing to split the cost if you think it's a good idea. I even know a private detective who might be interested."

"I think it's a good idea. I'll be more than happy to split the cost."

"I'll call today. I have some work I have to do, Lex. Perhaps you might want to visit with Stan. Sometimes those guys know more than they let on. He might open up to you. By the way, I spoke to Mr. Able last night. Don't be surprised if he shows up at your door."

Lex laughed. "He's coming in tomorrow around noon our time. I didn't have the heart to tell him not to come. He wants to help. This is just my personal opinion, but I think he's dealing with some guilt where you're concerned. He thinks he should have told you about Andrews and his cronies."

"Even if he had, I'm not sure it would have made a difference to Ken Lamantia. He went by the bottom line. He's a law abiding citizen like I am. We expect, because we respect the law, that things will be taken care of by the authorities. I still believe that because I need to believe it. A John Deere tractor isn't something you put in a paper bag and sell on a street corner. I'm sure the authorities will get a lead when who ever did the hijacking tries to peddle those tractors. The odds of ten people remaining silent, I would think, would be just about nil. I could be wrong, of course, and then there's always the possibility that one or more of Andrews' cronies will get mad over the money split or just plain fed up. Even I know that once the feds get into it, the jig's up. All you have to do is sit back and wait for them to get caught."

"Until that time, a pack of jackals like Chet and his buddies can do an awful lot of damage. I'll be back when the feds arrive. Don't eat any more of those doughnuts unless you call me."

"Oh, do you want to take them home with you?" Ariel asked innocently.

"I love your sense of humor," Lex said cheerily as he left the office.

The minute the door closed behind him, Ariel had the phone in her hand and was punching in her home number. "Wait till I tell you who was here with a bag of doughnuts when I arrived. Did you ever have someone kiss the sugar off your lips? Let me tell you, it's an experience every woman should have." She listened to Dolly's voice on the other end of the line. "*Of course* it was Lex Sanders doing the kissing. We're having dinner this evening, so don't make anything for me. Did I tell him off? I suppose you could say that. Nicely, of course. I got my point across. Oh, by the way, he said he liked my suit, and he said I smelled better than a summer peach. I was impressed. Yes, he is a good kisser. A real good kisser. God, I can't believe I'm telling you all this. I feel like some giddy teenager. I'll tell you the story behind the memorabilia this evening. Did the alarm company call? Oh, they're there now. Call me back."

Ariel walked into the private powder room in the back of her office. She stared at her reflection. She didn't know if it was her imagination, but she thought her lips looked different, more sensual, kind of pouty, like she'd just been kissed. "What a brilliant deduction, Ariel Hart." Her heart started to flutter. She hadn't felt like this since she was a kid. It was true, what writers said in all those midlife articles she'd read: it doesn't matter how old you are, emotion is the one thing that remains a constant. One article had gone on to say that once you got past the age number, the midriff bulge, the thinning hair, the wrinkles, the jowls, all you had to do was sit back and let your emotions take over. The article didn't say anything about facial deformities, though. She sighed mightily as she wondered what God had in store for her next.

The office staff arrived at eight o'clock, pouncing on the bag of doughnuts and the fresh coffee Ariel had just made. It was an ordinary day with old and new business to be taken care of. Ariel settled in behind her desk and worked steadily until ten-thirty, when she was summoned to the outer office.

Two rumpled, tired-looking men introduced themselves as federal agents. Ariel told them what she knew and offered to take them out to the truck apron where they could meet Stan, the drivers, and Lex. She felt pleased and flattered when one of the men said he'd seen her last movie and liked it. "A bit farfetched, but then most things in life are farfetched, like this hijacking." It was a compliment of sorts so she just smiled.

Ariel was about to open the door when Bernice answered the phone and said Dolly wanted to speak to her. She held up her hand for the others to wait. "This might have something to do with our hijacking. Just give me a minute."

The phone pressed tightly to her ear, Ariel listened intently to Dolly. "It's not a problem. I'd rather you stayed there until it's fixed. Call me when the men leave."

The agents looked at Ariel, their expressions expectant. She explained the alarm incident in detail. The agent who said he'd seen her last movie conferred with his partner, then asked for directions to her house. Ariel's eyes narrowed. Obviously he was of the same opinion as Lex and herself. She felt better immediately when she saw him climb behind the wheel of a nondescript black sedan.

From that point on, the day moved like lightning—meetings with the truckers, interviews she sat in on between individual truckers and Agent Navaro, calls to antiques shops, making flyers that would be posted throughout the township, posting rewards, short dialogues with the drivers from other companies over the CB, conducted by Agent Navaro. And all of it was bringing her hours and minutes closer to the time when she could head home to get ready for her date with Lex Sanders.

What to wear? How to do her hair? Which perfume to use? More important, which underwear? Just in case . . .

Agent Navaro intruded in her thoughts when he said, "I guess this wraps it up. We'll take it from here. Be careful, Miss Hart. Are you okay? Your face is red." Ariel looked at him helplessly. Perhaps the agent thought she was going through menopause. Should she tell him she was thinking about her evening with Lex Sanders? Vanity won out. "Actually, Agent Navaro, I was planning my evening. You know, wondering what to wear and what comes after a nice dinner and a little dancing." She winked and smiled. Flustered, the agent apologized. The part that bothered her was the look he gave her, which clearly said he didn't believe a word she said. She decided right then and there that she didn't like the man or his speculating gaze. It was almost like he was saying, *You gotta be at least fifty years old and you're planning a heavy date? Who are you trying to kid?* Aside from that, there was something else about his eyes that bothered her. Later, when she didn't have so much on her mind, she'd think more about it.

She didn't mean to say the words, but they tumbled out of her mouth anyway. "Actually, it's a misconception that a woman's life is over once she turns fifty. What really happens," she said, trying not to smile at the agent's acute discomfort, "is that women shed their inhibitions, throw caution to the winds, in a manner of speaking, and then go for whatever it is they want. Fifty is a number just like thirty-five is a number. Or sixty-five. You would be surprised, Agent Navaro, how many sixty-year-old women in Hollywood can have any man they want. Let me give you a case in point. I'm sure you know Angel Davies. Every single movie she's ever made has been a hit. She's been retired for some time now. Her personal calendar is booked a full year in advance with men who want to have breakfast, lunch, and dinner with her. Do you know why? She's interesting! She has a brain, she's a fine actress, she's warm and compassionate. Angel wrote a book not too long ago and shared some of her intimate secrets. She said, to a man, most of her dates tell her they don't want to do the bar scene, don't want to dance the night away when they have an early call, don't want to have their masculinity tested on a daily basis by long-legged, breast implanted, peroxide blondes. They told her they look for a sense of humor and comfortable, pleasurable hours spent in the company of a woman they respect and like. If sex happens, it happens. If it doesn't, that's okay, too. Women, as they age, are not dead. I'm not dead, and I'll be damned if I know why I'm even talking to you like this. I guess it was the look on your face when I said I had a date. So what! So what, Agent Navaro?"

"Listen, I didn't mean . . . I'm sorry . . . I . . ."

He wasn't sorry. *Sorry* was just a word. She didn't know how she knew, but she knew the agent's speculating gaze had nothing to do with women, menopause, or anything having to do with sex. He was just saying words. I do not like this man, she thought. "Apology accepted," she said curtly.

Her heart took on an extra beat when she thought about her date with Lex Sanders. Fifty is just a number. Numbers don't mean anything. Emotions are what count, and she was counting.

Agent Navaro offered his hand. "No offense meant, Miss Hart. We'll be in touch."

Ariel nodded. "Mr. Sanders, our biggest client, wants to talk with you. I believe he's in the dispatcher's office. The cargo belonged to him. He's pretty upset, as we all are." She wondered if it was a trick of light or if she actually saw the agent's shoulders stiffen at the mention of Lex Sanders's name.

"Understandable." He was almost out the door when his cell phone rang. He excused himself to take the call. Ariel tried to make herself busy, picking up order forms from one of the girls' desks, placing it on another. Anything to get a clue to the phone call. She wasn't sure why, but she thought it pertained to her.

"That was my partner. The lead wire from the pole to your security system was cut. My man is reporting it to the police as we speak. It will become part of this ongoing investigation. You need to know that the FBI takes precedence over local law enforcement. Have a nice day, Miss Hart."

Inside her office, with the door closed, Ariel gave in to her shaking nerves. She gulped at the coffee Lex had brought. The caffeine would add to her already twitchy nerves, but she didn't care. Somebody had deliberately cut her security alarm. Somebody was on her property. An intruder had invaded her privacy and threatened her safety. She reached down to stroke Snookie's sleek head. How much protection could this dog be? What if someone took it into their heads to harm her dog? She shuddered. She loved the animal sleeping at her feet. Only an insidious person would harm an animal. Was she going to have to hire security guards? "Oh, God," she mumbled.

The phone rang. Ariel pressed the button on the speaker phone. "Ariel Hart. Oh, Dolly, I'm glad you called. Agent Navaro just told me the wire was cut. I can't believe this is happening to us. It's part of the ongoing FBI investigation They're reporting it to the police. I guess it's procedure. Because of the hijacking the feds take precedence. I've been thinking—maybe I should hire some security guards. I think whoever did this wants us to take it as a warning. If it *is* Chet Andrews and his cronies, what good does it do? The whole thing doesn't compute. A hijacking is a federal offense. There's nothing I can or cannot do about that. The damage is done. I fired him, and he knows I'm not going to rehire him. Can a person be stupid enough to do things like this for spite? What else can it be? The FBI has a very high success rate. You don't mess with the IRS and you don't take on the FBI. Whoever it is, is trying to scare us. Get in the car, Dolly, and come down to the office. I don't want you there alone even if they did fix the alarm."

The moment Ariel cut the switch on the speaker phone, she had the yellow pages in her hand. She flipped to the S's and looked up security guards. She called three agencies, got their prices, then called three more to verify that the rates were pretty much standard. She deliberately avoided the large ads and chose one in a little box that simply said, YOUR SAFETY IS OUR BUSINESS. In a matter of minutes she'd hired four men for twelve-hour shifts at the house as well as at Able Body Trucking. The guards, the owner said, had highly trained canines that were part of the deal. She didn't know if she felt better or not, but at least she'd done something.

Ariel did her best to concentrate on the work in front of her, but her thoughts kept drifting to other things—to her safety as well as Dolly's, to Lex Sanders, to what kind of an evening it was going to be. She flushed a bright pink just as Lex Sanders rapped softly, opening the door to her office at the same time.

"I'm heading home. I'll pick you up around seven or is that too early? Why's your face so pink?"

"Seven's fine. My face is pink because I was just thinking about something I said to Agent Navaro. I was trying to defend fifty-year-old women. He made me mad. Why is it that men are considered distinguished as they age and women just get older?"

"Who said that?" There was such amazement on Lex's features that Ariel burst into laughter. "I happen to like maturity in women as well as men. Jesus, I don't think I could handle a twenty-three-year-old. Nor would I want to," he was quick to add. "What's your opinion on that?" Lex asked craftily.

"Pretty much the same as yours." She smiled as she realized she meant what she'd just said. "Youth has its place as does maturity. We had our go-round. You can't go back. All you get is heartache. I've seen it so many times I could write a book about it."

"Dedicate it to me. I'm outta here. See you sevenish." He blew her a kiss.

The moment the door closed, her fist shot in the air. "I think he's mine, Snookie. And that's just fine with me. Forget all that bad stuff I said about him." The shepherd wiggled out from under the desk and did her best to get on Ariel's lap. Laughing, Ariel slipped down off the chair and tussled with the ninety-pound dog. Her hair came undone, cascading down around her face like a waterfall, and her narrow skirt hiked way above mid-thigh as she rolled over and over on the newly carpeted floor. Snookie had her pinned to the floor when the door opened and Lex stuck his head in, then came all the way into the room. He cleared his throat. Ariel burst into uncontrollable laughter as she struggled with the huge dog. Breathless with her own laughter and silliness, she gasped, "Get him, Snookie, but remember, he's a good guy."

Lex was on the floor before he knew what was happening to him. He tussled, but he was no match for the dog growling in his ear as she pinned him to the floor simply by sitting on his chest. Ariel laughed until the tears rolled down her cheeks. Lex was still struggling with the shepherd, who seemed rooted to his chest. "Bring him here, Snookie."

The dog inched off Lex's chest, her two front paws secure on each side of his neck. With her long snout, she pushed and shoved, none too gently, until Lex was face-to-face with Ariel, who was still laughing. She sobered immediately when Lex was a hairbreadth away from her face.

It was a kiss unlike anything she'd ever experienced. It spoke of a thousand tomorrows and more beyond that. She felt warm and safe, secure and desired. She was the first to break away, but only that same hairbreadth. She stared into his gray eyes. "What would you say if I said let's go for it right here?" she asked boldly.

"Ask me."

"The door isn't locked."

"That dog is about the best deterrent I know of. Well?"

Ariel was saved from making a decision when the door opened and Dolly yelled, "We've been hijacked again. You have a run in your panty hose, Ariel. I also have a date tonight with that fed. I gave him a piece of my peanut butter pie and he was hooked. Did you hear what I just said? We were hijacked twenty minutes ago. Am I interrupting something?"

"Not so you could tell," Ariel snapped as she struggled to her feet and smoothed down her skirt.

"Tell me it wasn't my new horse trailers," Lex said.

"I wish I could tell you that, but I can't. It *was* your load. They got it right outside of Ocala, Florida. I'll make some coffee."

"Son of a bitch!" Lex seethed. "It's me those bastards are after." Ariel and Dolly watched him as he slammed his way through the open doorway. He stiff-armed the front door on a dead run. Both women ran to the window to watch him race to the dispatcher's office.

"What about our truck?" Ariel demanded.

"They took the whole thing. I heard them talking when I parked my car. I didn't get all the details. I'd comb my hair before I went out there if I were you. You look . . . like you just . . . well, what you look like is . . . a Cheshire cat. I'm all for mixing pleasure and business. That guy is real nice. I'm babbling, Ariel. The insurance company will start to think about canceling our policy. No one will want to go out without insurance. Whoever is doing this could put you out of business. The criminal justice system works very slowly. Harry told me that. That's his name, Ariel."

"How in hell do you steal an eighteen-wheeler in broad daylight on the road? Where's our driver? Is he okay?"

"I don't know. I told you everything I know."

Her hair in wild disarray, Ariel stomped her way through the office, to the staff's amusement, and out the door and across the truck lot to the dispatcher's office.

"Your man is okay. According to the troopers, the hijackers set up four roadblocks, a mile apart on each side of the road. The only traffic they let through was your man and then they yanked him out, got in, and drove away. They had traffic backed up for miles. They unloaded the horse trailers, and I assume they put them in another rig. Your truck is totaled. They set it on fire," Lex said.

"Totaled!" Ariel gasped. "They'll cancel my insurance."

"Don't report it to the insurance company. Not yet. Let's wait and see what the feds come up with. I think you're going to have to think about hiring some extra help to ride shotgun, Ariel."

"What if my drivers walk out?"

"Then you have a problem. Maybe it's a good idea that Asa is coming here. He might have some idea of how to handle this. I don't know what else to say. My own insurance company is probably going to cancel me. I'm not blaming you, Ariel; let's get that straight. Like you, these guys can put me out of business because I depend on Able Body. Even if I took my business somewhere else, they'd come gunning for my loads. This is a goddamn vendetta. I don't mind telling you I'm pissed."

"You have every right to be angry. The FBI will, I'm sure, be on top of this. Once the hijackers know they've been called in, they'll back off."

"They knew that going in. Hijackers are a breed all their own. They don't think beyond the moment they're pulling their jobs. That type of person never believes he'll get caught. I read a profile on hijackers once, written by a behavioral criminologist. Chet Andrews fits the profile perfectly. I've got to get back to the ranch. See you later."

"Okay, Lex. I'm truly sorry this is happening to us. I wish I had never fired him. If I'd waited, used him a little on short runs, this might not have happened."

"Ariel, this is not your fault. I don't want you blaming yourself. If it is Andrews, he would never be satisfied with short runs. There's very little money in short hauls. He's been planning this for some time. I repeat, Ariel, this is not your fault. The authorities will take care of this. See you later."

Ariel waved listlessly. She turned to Dolly. "You know, if we were back in Hollywood and this was a script, all I'd have to do is turn the page to find out the solution. I need to ask you something, Dolly. When we were back there, did I ever . . . seem to you like . . . you know . . . like I was living in a fantasy world? Did you ever think I couldn't distinguish between make-believe and reality? My lifestyle was . . . so very boring. Is that why it was boring, why I couldn't sustain a relationship? Even now, I find myself thinking in terms of scripts. I weigh it both ways, and I believe I have a handle on things, but do I really? I insulated myself, made friends who lived in the same make-believe world, carried on conversations with people who believed they were characters in whatever movie they were working in. Did that make sense? God, I just don't believe this is happening to us."

Dolly put her arms around Ariel's shoulders. "Ariel, you're the most together person I know. Yeah, sometimes you were boring, but so is everybody else in the world. It was your choice not to be involved in the Hollywood scene. You contributed, you did more than your share of good deeds. They knew they could count on you because you always came through. You gave more than you ever got. You were a friend to everyone and you never asked for anything in return. If anything, you cared too much. That doesn't make it wrong. You were so normal it was scary at times. You weren't a phony like some of the people you were forced to associate with. You always said, underneath they weren't phony, they were scared. You're a good person, a good friend, and a wonderful employer. You had everyone's respect and those friends, the real people, the ones who count, lived in the real world like we did. Stop fretting about reality versus make-believe. So, if this was a script, and you turned the page, whodunit?"

"Chet Andrews, and we both know it. I feel as bad for Lex as I do for myself. He looked so miserable when he left here. It wouldn't surprise me if he calls when he gets home and cancels our date tonight. I wonder what he's doing and thinking right now, this very minute."

What Lex Sanders was doing was grinding his pickup to a stop in the parking lot of his lawyer's office. At the door he settled his Padres cap more securely on his head, took a deep breath, and opened the door. He ignored the receptionist and marched down the hall to Colin Carpenter's office. The attorney looked up over his glasses at the unannounced intrusion.

Lex banged his fist on the desk, his face a mask of something the attorney couldn't define. "I want a divorce!"

"Hell, Lex, I didn't even know you were married. Maybe we should talk about this before we go filing papers. When in the damn hell did you get married? I've known you for twenty years and you've been a bachelor all that time. I hate it when my clients withhold information. Tell me about it, Lex. See, I have my pen and my pad, so let's get on with it."

Lex removed his cap. "It's a long story."

Twenty minutes later he said, "I'll drop off the marriage certificate tomorrow. I want this quick. If I have to, I can cross the border and get it in a few days. I just want to make sure things are legal. Well, Colin, say something," Lex snapped.

"I take it there's someone waiting for your hand. She must be pretty special, Lex. Why didn't you ever tell me about the name change?"

"She *is* special, but I can't . . . won't . . . until it's right. Right for me. In here," he said, thumping his chest, "and up here," he said, tapping his forehead. As to the name change, what was the point? It was a new life and Mr. Sanders was so good to my family and to me, I didn't want to . . . hell, I don't know what I wanted. Don't for even one minute think I gave up on my heritage or my roots or whatever the hell they're calling someone's past these days. I would never deny my blood. I take care of my own."

"I know that, Lex. I'll get on this first thing in the morning. One last thing, what are you going to do if this private dick you hired turns up Aggie Bixby?"

"I'm going to tell her I'm divorcing her. Or you can send her a letter. After thirty-four years I don't think she's going to mind too much."

"You did . . . do. What if she's been looking for you the way you've been looking for her? What if she says she doesn't want a divorce? You're a wealthy man. What if . . . You need to think in terms of *what if*. You could always call off the detective if you don't want to know. Your call, Lex."

"Colin, I honest to God don't know what I would do if that happened. This is hard for me because I'm a practicing Catholic. So was Aggie. I finally met someone I think I can love. I'm fifty-three years old and I don't want to get any older without someone at my side. Until I met Ariel I lived in a goddamn vacuum. By my choice, I admit. Now I want out of that vacuum. Do your best. You can call me anytime. And if you ever want to go riding, come out to the ranch."

"You'll be hearing from me, Lex. Stop worrying. I'll handle this myself."

"Just don't drag your feet, Colin. I want it over and done with."

He was a mile from the ranch before it hit him. Jesus. He'd finally gone and done it. He felt a hundred pounds lighter.

Chapter Eight

A t six o'clock, Ariel stepped from the shower, towel-dried herself, splashed on her favorite gardenia scent, added dusting powder, and then spritzed a matching perfume high in the air. She danced beneath the fine mist, savoring the delicious scent.

Wearing nothing more than powder and perfume, she made her way back to her bedroom where she pawed through her lingerie drawer searching for just the right underwear. Bras, panties, and panty hose sailed in every direction, a lacy bra landing on one of Snookie's pointed ears. She shrugged it off and watched her mistress's strange behavior.

Ariel held aloft a bra that was nothing more than intricate lace panels with straps so fragile they looked like cobweb strands. The panties were equally sinful looking. She waved a pair of sheer panty hose under Snookie's nose. "Yes? No?" Snookie growled. "Guess that means no. I'm of the same opinion. On the other hand, no lady is dressed unless she wears stockings. Thigh-highs should do it." She rummaged some more and came up with a pair so sheer it looked like she wasn't wearing any, which she supposed was the object. A silky slip that was so pretty it could have passed for a dress was next. She pranced back to the closet where she wreaked havoc, pulling out first one outfit, then another, tossing the clothing on the bed, on the chairs, on the corners of the bureau. Other ensembles were tossed on the floor. When her ample closet was virtually empty, Ariel picked up mix-and-match outfits from the floor to hold in front of her before the floor-length mirror.

"I think this is it, Snookie," she said. She pulled a vibrant, electric blue A-line dress over her head. Then she added a single strand of pearls and pearl studs to her ears. Elegant, but not overpowering. She chose shoes and matching purse the color of straw. She spent the last twenty minutes working with her hair. She swirled and teased, combing it out again and again. She piled it high on her head, then she pulled it back into a tight chignon. She still wasn't satisfied and tried a French braid that did nothing for her outfit. She was still twirling and brushing when the doorbell rang at seven o'clock. Frantic she would be one of those keep-'em-waitin' females, Ariel pulled her hair back on the sides, stuck in a pair of combs, fluffed her shaggy bangs, and headed for the stairs, Snookie behind her. She was on the third step from the bottom when Dolly opened the door.

My God, he's handsome, Ariel thought. Wrong. He's more than handsome. Hollywood would love this guy. He's got the kind of face that makes love to the camera. "I like a prompt date," she said.

Lex grinned. "I had my fingers crossed that you weren't one of those females who keeps a guy twiddling his thumbs while they decide what to wear or not to wear."

"Not me. I reach in, grab something, and that's it for the day. Or night. I can't stand indecision," she said with a straight face. Behind her back, Dolly rolled her eyes. Neither Lex nor Ariel saw her; they were too busy staring at one another.

"Be home by midnight," Dolly ordered.

"Yes, Mother." Ariel grinned. "And you'd better be home before me. What time is Mr. FBI arriving?"

"Any minute now. We aren't going out, though. We're going to watch some videos and make popcorn. Saturday we're going to go out to dinner. He doesn't have much free time— he works shifts."

"Does he have a name, Dolly?" Ariel teased.

Dolly flushed. "His name is Joseph Harry Minton. He told me to call him Harry. He was widowed five years ago. He has a grown son he sees twice a year. No grandchildren. He works, for now, out of San Diego. He could get transferred, but he has enough time in that he can ask to stay or refuse the transfer. He rattled it off the way you used to do when you memorized a script."

"Guess he did more than check the facts while he was here," Ariel quipped. "I spent only a few minutes with Agent Navaro, and he seems to think women over fifty are foolish even to think about dating. Did Harry ask you a lot of questions, personal questions?"

Dolly nodded, her eyes puzzled by the question. "So, have a nice evening and I'll be quiet when I get in."

Outside in the balmy April evening, Ariel allowed herself to be led to Lex's Mercedes. "Buy American, huh?"

"I swear to God I would have brought my truck, but I knew you were going to be dressed up and there's all kinds of junk in it. I bought this when I thought I needed a status symbol. I was wrong. The only time I drive it is when I wear a suit to go to a funeral or a wedding or maybe a christening. I apologize."

"I accept your apology."

"My God, what was that? What is that? Get down, Ariel! Jesus, I think someone's blowing up your house."

"What?" Ariel screeched. "Snookie! How did you get here?"

"Through the goddamn window, that's how. I heard the glass break, saw this flash of something hurtling through the air, and thought . . . hell, I don't know what I thought. That damn dog went right through your front window. I call that devotion." He threw back his head and roared with laughter when he saw Ariel sitting cross-legged in the middle of the driveway with Snookie in her lap.

"Ariel, Ariel, I couldn't stop her," Dolly yelled. "She backed up to the dining room and ran like a bat out of hell. I knew she was going to do it the minute she started to run. Good thing the drapes were closed. Is she all right? Is she bleeding? She thought you were leaving her. That's what she thought. Dogs are smart. You always take her with you. This is the first time you left her behind. I'll ask Harry if he'll help me board up the window when he gets here."

"I'll help him," Lex volunteered. "Call the trucking company and have someone bring over a piece of plywood. Thank God your alarm system wasn't on. You won't be able to turn it on until the window is fixed. Why don't we forget about dinner and order in some pizza? If Dolly and Harry don't mind, we can all watch the videos and Snookie will be happy. You're sure she's okay, Ariel?"

"She's got a few nicks here and there, a few traces of blood. I think she scared herself. Look how quiet she is. She's shaking, though."

"I never would have believed it if I hadn't seen it with my own eyes. It must have something to do with her early training at the school for the blind. They're taught not to leave their masters." He yanked at his tie, loosened it, and then pulled it over his head. It went in the back seat of the car along with his jacket. The moment he finished rolling up the sleeves of his dress shirt, he reached down and pulled Ariel to her feet.

None the worse for her aerial feat, Snookie trotted between Ariel and Lex, who muttered something about Snookie not liking anyone getting too close to her owner. Ariel grinned in the darkness.

The pepperoni pizza was delicious, all four pies of it; the videos of Steven Seagal trouncing the bad guys were enjoyed by the men, tolerated by the women. Snookie, her belly full of filched pepperoni, slept through the evening once her cuts and scrapes were tended to. Munching on the pizza and swilling cold beer, Harry proved to be more than entertaining, pointing out Seagal's blunders—things he said the FBI would never allow to happen, at which point he went into great detail about some of his toughest cases and how brainpower won over muscle-power ten to one. "Reality is a lot different from fiction. Isn't that right, Miss Hart?"

"Absolutely." Ariel thought about her lacy underwear and the wicked scenario she'd fantasized earlier. She sighed mightily in disappointment. Lex took the sigh as a sign that Ariel was tired. He was on his feet a moment later, his face a mask of disappointment.

"I've got to be going myself," Harry said. "I'll see you Saturday night, Dolly." He shook hands at the door with everyone, including Dolly.

Lex did the same thing. He winked at Ariel and said, sotto voce, "If it's good enough for the FBI, it's good enough for me." The wicked gleam in his eye turned Ariel's stomach to mush.

"I don't believe this!" she hissed when the door closed. In the blink of an eye, she had the zipper down on the back of her dress. She stepped out of it. "I wore this . . . this . . . and I practically drowned myself in that expensive perfume, and the guy shakes my hand. Did you see that look on his face— in his eyes, actually? All right, so I'm horny. I admit it. What's that I see on your face? Don't tell me it's lust, Dolly! And to top it off, my goddamn dog goes through my front window. How am I supposed to go to bed with a man when my dog won't let him get near me? Now I ask you!" she said dramatically from the top of the steps. Then she started to laugh and couldn't stop. She climbed on the bannister, hiked up her slip and slid all the way down to where a giggling Dolly was standing.

"I have to admit, even on my worst date, I never had an evening like this one," Ariel gasped, tears of laughter rolling down her cheeks. I guess I'm not meant to go to bed with Lex Sanders. He has a great sense of humor, don't you think? It was nice of him to pay for all those pizzas—of which *your* friend ate three. Not to mention the six beers he guzzled."

"Harry offered to pay. Lex wouldn't let him. It *was* nice of him. How do you think Harry will be in bed, Ariel? He wears boxer shorts. I hate boxer shorts. I like jockeys. I saw the outline on his leg. It makes a mark, you know," Dolly fretted.

"It's not like you're an expert," Ariel teased. "How long has it been?"

"He said he hasn't seen anyone romantically since his wife died. For some reason, I don't believe him. I don't even think he was ever married. Just things he said. It all sounded . . . rehearsed. Maybe it's my imagination. He said he threw himself into work. That part didn't ring true, either. I like him, but there's something about him that . . . I guess it's law enforcement . . . that kind of thing."

"They all say that, especially after a divorce. You'll be what they call the transitional woman. If you want him, you'll have to snare him. I would imagine, to answer your question, that he would be the type to be slow and thorough. He's real good looking. But, now I know this isn't going to make much sense, but he looks to me, as does Agent Navaro, as though . . . someone spruced them up. I said it wouldn't make sense. It's just my opinion. Another thing, do you think agents have a . . . routine? You know, stock phrases, things they say to everyone? I don't like Navaro's eyes. At one point I had the feeling he was undressing me with his eyes. Yep, slow and steady. Not too imaginative. If he was married for a long time he's forgotten what foreplay is, like most men. What do you think about Lex? Let's have another beer if we're going to be talking about such serious things."

"Okay, I'll fetch it. Cigarettes, too, right?"

"Bring more than one beer—this might take a while. Lots of cigarettes," Ariel said, snapping the skinny strap of her bra in disgust.

"Gotcha."

"I think," Dolly said, brandishing her bottle of Corona aloft, "that men are stupid. They don't pick up on signals. Take Harry now . . . those boxer shorts are going to be a problem, I can feel it in my bones. I asked him leading questions and either he's stupid or else I didn't make myself clear. My feeling is, he's not into performing. Men think they have to do that, perform. What's your opinion on that, Ariel? I'm about as drunk as you are. Your eyes are crossed did you know that?"

"Who cares? What was the question? Did you give Snookie some beer? You know the rule, she gets what we get."

"No, I did not," Dolly said, enunciating each word carefully. "Somebody has to be sober. What if what's-his-name comes back and tries to break in?"

"Then Snookie will go after him and hold him at bay. I'll get my gun and shoot him. How does that sound?"

"Real good if you can see straight enough. I like that slip. Bet you could get away with wearing it as a dress."

"That's what I thought. You should see my bra and panties. I had this wonderful fantasy evening planned, and it all fell apart." Ariel looked at her empty bottle and motioned for Dolly to hand her another. "They look like soldiers all lined up like that. That's very original, Dolly."

"Takes practice." She hiccupped as she flipped open Ariel's beer. "Your friend, what's-his-name, sure ordered a lot of beer. I know, he thought he was going to stay all night and then Snookie did her number and it all went down the drain. That's very funny, Ariel."

"So funny we're sitting here in our underwear stinking drunk. That's not funny, Dolly. Actually," she said, swigging from the bottle, "it *is* kind of funny. It used to be man and his dog. Now it's woman and her dog. Shit!"

"Oh, Ariel, I feel so bad for you. Tell me about your fantasy. Can you remember it?" she asked, peering into her beer bottle. "I'm not horny anymore. Are you, Ariel?"

"Nope. What did you ask me again, Dolly?"

"I can't remember. We drank ten bottles of beer. That's a lot," Dolly said stiffly. "Did you hear something?"

"Nope. What was the question?"

"I remember, I asked you about your . . . your . . . think, Ariel. Oooh, look at that lovely smoke ring I just blew."

"It's pretty. We should be smoking a joint. When was the last time we did that?"

"When we were thirty years old, maybe twenty-five. Is it important to know exactly when?" Dolly asked fretfully. "I heard something. You better get your gun, Ariel."

"If you heard something, why isn't Snookie barking?"

"She's drunk like we are, that's why."

"You got my dog drunk, Dolly! You should be ashamed of yourself. Now who's going to protect us?"

"You are, with your gun," Dolly said smartly. "Tell me about your . . . fantasy. That was the question. In detail. Everything."

"Everything?"

"I already told you about Harry's boxer shorts so you have to tell me. You said you would. Is it good, Ariel?"

"Oh, yes," Ariel sighed. "I didn't even wear panty hose because they're a pain to get on and more of a pain to get off."

She giggled when she held out a shapely leg to show Dolly her thigh-highs. I'm wearing this scandalous underwear. Paid a fortune for it and never had the right occasion to wear it. This was the occasion and look what happened. I was going to let him take it off."

"All of it?" Dolly's hand flew to her mouth in pretended shock.

"Yep. Then I was going to take off all his stuff. Myself. Everything, even his shorts."

"What if he wears boxers?" Dolly mumbled. "I'm going to be very disappointed," Ariel sing-songed. "I like tight buns and you can't appreciate tight buns in boxers. Is that how you feel about Harry?"

"Uh-huh. Then what?"

"Then I was going to check out . . . you know . . . see how big . . . or small . . . whatever . . . and get him to the bed. Touchy, feely, that kind of thing. How come I'm telling you my fantasy?"

"Because I asked you," Dolly said. "I hear something again. Snookie, wake up! She won't get up, Ariel."

"Because she's drunk. Do you want me to get my gun?"

"Yes-I-do!"

"Okay. I'm not going outside. Whoever it is has to come in here and then I'll shoot him. Only if he comes in, Dolly. Do we agree?"

"Yes." Dolly opened the last two bottles of Corona. She watched as Ariel trotted over to the mantel for the gun. She blew imaginary dust off it, then stuck it down between her breasts.

"That's not a good idea, Ariel. You're so drunk you might shoot off your nipple and then where will you be?" She doubled over, howling with laughter.

"Nippleless. Without a nipple. Bosom with no nipple. Rosy crests. That's what they call them in romance novels. I'll just put it here on the steps beside us. Since we're probably going to sleep here it's a good place. The living room is lopsided, Dolly. I never noticed that before."

"I don't care. Do you care, Ariel? What else were you going to do to that guy?"

"Lex?"

"That's the one," Dolly giggled.

"I was going to have my way with him. I was going to ravage and savage him. I was going to . . . do all those things those heroines do to the heroes in romance novels. I learned a lot reading those books."

"Be spa-sif-ick," Dolly said.

Outside in the bushes, underneath the boarded-up window, Lex Sanders peeped through the two pieces of plywood he and Harry had nailed to the window frame. He clapped his hand over his mouth so he wouldn't laugh aloud and give himself away. He'd returned because he was worried about the window. His intention was to check on the two women, and then spend the night in the car watching the house. Now, though, he saw that his work was cut out for him. Who was going to put the two of them to bed? If he was any judge, neither one could hold her liquor. He knew both of them would be heading for the bathroom soon. He didn't see the gun, but he did see Snookie sound asleep by the steps. He continued to listen.

"Plunder, too. Ravage, savage, and plunder. Everything, Dolly. All the things I never did . . . all kinds of things. Triple orgasms. That's possible. I read it when I was at the dentist's. In *Cosmo*. He gets one, I get a triple."

"How?"

"How? You work at it. That's how. He works at it. When it happens, I'll tell you and you can have Harry try it. It's an experiment. I don't feel so good. That pepperoni pizza must have been bad. I have to go to the bathroom. Ooohhh, this room is really lopsided," Ariel said, holding on to the banister.

Outside in the bushes, Lex slapped his leg, howling silently. This couldn't be the Ariel Hart he knew and lusted after. But it was. He was shifting his weight from one leg to the other when a neighbor's cat jumped from the bushes, hissing and scratching. He let out a stifled yelp as he moved sideways. A second later something whizzed by his ear and he felt his hair part down the middle. He hit the ground with a thump. He risked a quick glance upward and saw four round holes in the freshly nailed plywood. "Jesus Christ!" he bellowed.

Inside, Ariel looked at Dolly and then at the gun in her hand. "I shot somebody. Somebody is out there. I hit somebody and I couldn't even see what I was shooting at. Dolly, let's go see who we shot."

"What's with that *we* stuff? If you shot him, why do we have to look at him? Let him lie out there till the milkman comes in the morning."

"Okay," Ariel said agreeably. "The doorbell's ringing."

"If you shoot through the door it will probably stop. We won't look at him till morning either."

Ariel brought the gun up to shoulder height, squinted, and jerked backward when she heard her name called from the other side of the door.

"Ariel! It's Lex Sanders. Open this goddamn door!"

The two women looked at each other. They both mouthed the name *Lex* at the same time. "Look at it this way, Ariel. You're getting a second chance to salvage . . . blunder, and what was that other thing you were going to do?"

"Ravage."

Ariel opened the door a crack. "Lex! What are you doing here?"

"I came back to check on you and Dolly. I didn't like leaving you here with that open window. Were you shooting through the plywood? Why, for God's sake?"

"He wants to know why, Dolly," Ariel sing-songed.

"If he wants to know, then you should tell him."

"What should I tell him?"

"The truth," Dolly snapped. "All those three things we said. You shouldn't have had that last beer, Ariel. Oh, I'm going to be sick."

"So am I," Ariel said, bolting for the downstairs lavatory while Dolly headed for her bathroom off the kitchen. Snookie slept on.

Lex leaned against the bathroom door frame, his arms crossed against his chest. When Ariel was finally finished throwing up, Lex squeezed toothpaste onto a toothbrush and offered it to her.

"How could you stand there and watch me go through that?" she asked.

"I have to tell you it wasn't a pretty sight."

"Go home," Ariel said around the foam in her mouth.

"I like your outfit. It's sexy."

"That's what I thought when I put it on. You're too damn late. Go home."

"I heard you, you know."

"You what?"

"I heard you and Dolly talking. Very interesting conversation."

Ariel dropped her head into her hands. "God, I just got the grandmother of all headaches. You shouldn't believe anything you hear standing outside a plywood window. Everyone knows plywood distorts vowels ... words ... sayings. God!"

"I don't think I ever heard that before. Are you sure?" His face was so blank, so innocent looking. Ariel groaned.

"Come on, I'll take you up to bed and get you settled in. I'll sleep downstairs on the sofa. It was my intention to sit outside in my car until morning. I can't leave you here like this with a drunken dog who's sleeping it off."

"I can go to bed by myself, Mr. Sanders."

"I don't doubt that a bit, but the stairs are tricky for someone in your condition. I wouldn't want you to topple backward and fall on that sleeping dog."

"Oh. All right, you can help me up the steps, but at the top you turn around and go back down. Okay?"

"Okay. Hold on to my arm. See, I told you it was tricky," Lex said when both of Ariel's feet came down on his own right foot.

"I'm not embarrassed, you know," Ariel said.

"I'm glad. Just three more steps. Atta girl. You made it."

"Did you think I wouldn't?" she snapped.

"There was a moment there when I wasn't sure."

"Wiseass," Ariel retorted. "This is my room. You got me here safe and sound and you should leave now. Anything else wouldn't . . . look right."

Lex grinned as he poked his head into Ariel's room. "For some reason I thought of you as a tidy person. Tiki would never allow this."

"Like I care. Listen, it takes a lot when a woman has a date. You have to try . . . you can't decide . . . why am I explaining anything to you, anyway? Go home!"

"Why indeed?" Lex chuckled. "I'll see you in the morning. Sleep tight, Ariel." He kissed her lightly on the forehead. "I meant to tell you earlier how good you smelled. Sort of like a warm summer garden on a star-filled night."

"Really? That's one of the nicest things anyone ever said to me."

"If you give me a chance, Ariel, there are all kinds of nice things I can say to you."

"Okay, but say them tomorrow," she said, getting between the covers. A second later she was sound asleep.

"Sleep well, Ariel," Lex said as he turned out the light and closed the door.

Downstairs he checked on Dolly, who was asleep in the bathtub. He scooped her up and carried her in to her bed. Satisfied that Snookie was okay, he settled himself on the sofa, Ariel's gun on the table next to him.

Eventually he slept, his dreams full of a woman named Ariel Hart. The woman of his dreams slept peacefully, her own dreams filled with memories of a dark-eyed young boy who reminded her of the man guarding her house and her person.

Chapter Nine

Ariel awoke shortly before dawn. The late night hours flashed in front of her, a kaleidoscope of memory. She swung her legs over the side of the bed and was sorry she'd moved so quickly. Her head throbbed, her stomach churned, and her mouth tasted like old rubber boots. She brushed her teeth three times, using half a bottle of mouthwash. She grabbed three aspirin, chewing the hateful things and then swallowing water slowly. She brushed her teeth again, all the while swearing that she would never, ever, as long as she lived, get drunk again.

She felt every one of her fifty years as she made her way to a steaming shower that helped ease the tension between her shoulder blades. Dressed in jeans and a T-shirt, Ariel opened the door to the second floor deck to let Snookie out. She stood at the railing to watch the sun struggle to the horizon. A new day. Thank God. This new day, like all her yesterdays, would be whatever she made of it.

Snookie nuzzled her leg. She reached down to stroke the dog's huge head. "I've done some stupid things in my life, Snookie, but last night was the stupidest. I gave you beer when I shouldn't have. I drank too much, and I know better than to do that. But, the worst thing of all is, I shot off my gun with no idea of what I was doing because I was drunk. That's why people shouldn't keep guns. People like me, anyway. I could have killed Lex Sanders. If I hadn't given you that beer you would have barked to let me know he was out there. I don't know what's happening to me. I'm supposed to be a responsible adult and what do I do? I act like some lovesick teenager? C'mon, baby, I'll get you something to eat and make some coffee for myself. By the way, you and I are going to have to have a little talk about that stunt you pulled last night. But, we'll have it later. I love it that you love me, I really do."

Snookie, lady that she was, walked sedately next to her mistress as they made their way downstairs. When they reached the bottom of the steps, the hair on the back of her neck stood on end. She growled deep in her belly, waiting for a command from Ariel.

"It's okay, Snookie, those are Lex's shoes. He must be in the kitchen." She dropped to her knees to cradle the shepherd's face in her hands. "He's a friend. Now, smell these shoes, get his scent, and don't forget it. You take care of him, too. He's part of that little talk we're going to have later. God, you're gorgeous. Bet I could get you in the movies, but then they'd ruin your life and you'd be on a time clock and they wouldn't let you be Snookie anymore. I'd have to go back to Hollywood, and wouldn't that be something? Well, that isn't going to happen. We have a new life now, and it's pretty good, all things taken into consideration."

"You look rested, Ariel," Lex said. "I took the liberty of making coffee." He poured her a cup as he spoke. "I've got to get back to the ranch. Make sure you get the glazier here as soon as possible and don't forget to notify the alarm company. Don't be embarrassed. Each of us is entitled to do something . . . out of the ordinary at least once in our lives.

It's really my fault, anyway. I should have called or knocked on the door and told you I was out there. You reacted."

"I could have killed you. I'm really sorry. Last night was a culmination of a lot of things for me. Things I shouldn't have done, and will, believe me, never do again. I *am* embarrassed. I acted very foolishly. I do apologize. Thanks for staying over and thanks for making the coffee."

"My pleasure. Do we still have a date on Saturday?"

"I'd like that."

Lex winked at her and grinned. "As soon as I find my shoes I'll be out of here."

Snookie raced out of the kitchen and returned with the shoelaces to both shoes clamped between her teeth. She placed them in front of Lex, then backed off to stand next to Ariel.

Lex laughed. "Here's your shoes, what's your hurry? That's some dog, Ariel."

"I know."

"If anything else happens, give me a call. By the way, Dolly fell asleep in the bathtub. I put her in bed. You might want to check on her."

"You seem to have experience handling drunks," Ariel said quietly, her face pink with shame.

"I've had my share. See you Saturday."

"I'll look forward to it." She thought he was going to kiss her, but he just smiled and left. She smiled, too, when she saw Snookie go over to the door and lie down directly in front of it. Her head dropped to her paws, but her eyes were on Ariel as though to say, everything's okay now.

The week rushed to a close, and before Ariel knew it, it was Saturday. Things were under control at Able Body Trucking and she was excited about spending the evening with Lex.

"It's a casual date," Ariel said. "I don't think Lex Sanders is the suit and tie type. I was the one who said we should have Italian or Chinese and perhaps take in a movie. He looked so relieved that I felt relieved, too. So, I'm wearing my rainbow-colored skirt, white tee, and the blue linen jacket. Espadrilles and straw bag. I don't think you can get more casual than that. Comfort seems to be what we both prefer."

"I'm all for that. I haven't heard from Harry so I don't know if we're on or off. Either way is okay. I did enjoy our time the other night, though. If it's meant to be it will be. He makes me . . . not exactly nervous . . . maybe apprehensive, but isn't that the same thing? Forget it."

"Do you notice, Dolly, how we're both mellowing out? We were both so . . . stressed all the time. Even now with everything going on you'd think we'd be out of our minds with anxiety, but we aren't. Maybe it's because we have some money in the bank and we know we have that cushion."

"Imagine this scenario, Ariel. You marry Lex Sanders, I marry Harry, you live at the ranch and I live wherever, and you sell the trucking company back to Mr. Able. He'd buy it in a heartbeat."

"My God, Dolly, you should be writing for the movies. You're moving pretty fast here, aren't you? Did you mean that part about marrying Harry and moving away? We've been together for so long . . . what would I do without you? We're like a pair, a matched set. Snookie loves you. God, Dolly, now I have to worry about Harry popping the question."

"It won't be for a while, if it even happens. Maybe never if I can't put my finger on whatever it is that bothers me about him. I'm probably overreacting, but I think he really likes me. A woman can tell these things. Like the way you know Lex Sanders is wild about you. I forgot how nice it was to be with a guy. It was just a thought, Ariel. Flip that coin over and look at your side. Let's say you did marry Lex Sanders.

What would you do with me? Lex has his own housekeeper who, you said, has been with him for a long time. He's not going to let her go. You know me, I could never work with someone else, doing busy work."

"If that ever happened, we'd work something out. I'd never cut you loose, no matter what the circumstances. We've been through too much. We're a package deal. Is that why you've been so cranky lately?"

"Partly. Listen, Ariel, I think I'm starting to go through my changes. I've been getting hot flashes at night and you're right, I'm cranky and irritable. On top of that, along comes Harry. At this stage. I want it to be something, you know, work out, but there's something . . . I just don't know. I hope it's my hormones or lack of them making me feel this way."

"Why didn't you say something, Dolly? We're going to make an appointment with a gynecologist first thing Monday morning. He can prescribe pills for you and give you some estrogen or whatever it is they give for hot flashes and crankiness. You don't have to tolerate it. For God's sake, Dolly, I thought you would have gone to the doctor at the first sign."

"I didn't want to admit that's what it was. I still don't want to admit it. You're right, though, I should have gone to the doctor months ago. How about you, Ariel?"

"So far, so good. I try not to think about it, but just the other day, I blasted Agent Navaro. He thought it was a hot flash. He said his wife is having them. You know what? I don't think he even has a wife. Don't ask me how I know that or why I even think it. I just damn well do. Maybe I am starting and am too dumb to know it. I blush and flush a lot. Little things are starting to bother me. A hijacking doesn't bother me half as much as running out of half-and-half for my coffee. Let's not talk about this anymore, okay?"

"You know what the worst thing is, Ariel? It's knowing half your life is over and this next half isn't going to be as good because of . . . of . . . all the things you have to go through. You dry up. Your skin flakes. And, of course, children are out of the question. It's all over. You damn well age is what you do. And it shows. We're looking at our mortality. I just started thinking about that lately. What have I done with my life, Ariel. Not much. I didn't make a mark. What am I going to leave behind? Everyone is going to remember Ariel Hart. You did something with your life. I wish I'd listened to you and gone for my degree. What will they put on my tombstone? Nothing but my name."

Ariel's stomach started to churn. Dolly needed her to say just the right thing. But, what was the right thing? Please, God, make this come out right.

"I don't know if my career was preordained or not. What I do know is I would not be where I am if it wasn't for you. You made it all possible. You took care of me in every sense of the word. You were there for me through the good times and the bad. You're a caregiver, a nurturer. I know I could never be what you are. God's hand was on both of us, I guess. It could just as easily have been you who was the actress and me the caregiver, but I know you would have fired me after the first day. You're better than a nurse, you're better than a shrink, you're that very, very, rare person called *friend*. Everyone says they have friends by the bushel, but if push came to shove, most would be reduced to zip or maybe one friend. One solid, good friend in life makes a person rich. You're the one person in this world I would trust with my children, if I had children, and my money. The one person, Dolly. You're my family, the sister I never had, my mother, my grandmother, my aunt. You are that wonderful person. You care, Dolly. Not just about me, but about everything. Do you have any idea how often I wish I was more like you? I do, every time something goes wrong and I can't do it on my own. That's pretty damn often. Now, this is my last word on this subject. If you go before me, I promise your tombstone will say, 'Dolly Delaney' on the first line. Under that, it will say, 'Friend, Sister, Mother, Grandmother, Aunt.' That's in the order of importance. You're on your own if I go first." She tried to laugh for Dolly's benefit. Instead, she burst into tears. The two women clung to one another, their tears mingling. Snookie howled at the strange sounds, trying to wiggle her way between them.

"Now what?" a voice said through the screen door. "What happened? Why didn't you call me? Jesus, what happened? Somebody better tell me something." Lex Sanders roared. Snookie nudged the screen door open, sniffed his shoes, then went back to try and separate the two sobbing women.

"Is this one of those female things men aren't supposed to understand?" Lex demanded as he checked out the new front window and the furnishings to reassure himself things were all right in the Hart household.

Ariel wiped at her eyes, as did Dolly. "We were talking about our mortality."

"Why?"

"Because we passed the half-century mark and things start to happen to a woman. I don't suppose you thought I was that old. I am. I'm going to be fifty-one!" She made it sound like she was going to the moon on the next shuttle.

"I'm going to be fifty-four," Lex said importantly. He felt out of his depth.

"Oh, sure. Fifty-four for a man, especially if he's rich and unattached, is like hanging out a red flag for every twenty-year-old within a hundred-mile radius. You need to know, though, that those twenty-year-olds just want your money and whatever they can get out of you. Think about it—why would a beautiful young girl want a middle-aged or old man? For what they can get, that's what. I'm an authority on the subject so don't even think about arguing."

"I agree. Why else would I still be a bachelor at the age of fifty-four? Why are you getting so upset over something so silly?"

"Because, men grow distinguished and women just get older. Now that you brought up the subject, why haven't you gotten married again? The odds, especially in California, of a man like you not getting married are about one in three million." Her voice was sounding suspicious.

Lex winced visibly and threw his hands in the air. "Is this where I go out and come in again and we start over, and you go to repair your makeup or whatever women do when they cry?"

"No. What you see is what you get. I'm ready if you are." Ariel squared her shoulders as she brushed past him. "As you know, Snookie will be joining us so I hope you picked a place where we can eat outside. Burger King will be fine. Snookie is partial to their french fries."

Hands on hips in the driveway, Ariel stared at Lex's pickup. "I don't mind riding in your truck, but where is Snookie supposed to sit?"

Lex sucked in his breath. "In the back?"

"Snookie is not a job dog. She'd fall out. I keep her in a seat belt. She's a seat belt dog. This is a problem."

"Does this mean we stay home and order pizza again?"

"No, it does not. Why don't we take my Rover? If we don't take my Rover then yes, we stay home."

"I bet you want to drive, too."

"Of course—it's my truck."

"Tell me something, do you lead when you dance?" Lex guffawed as he hopped into the passenger-side of the truck.

"Sometimes. If my partner has two left feet," Ariel snapped. "In the back, Snookie." The shepherd sat back on her haunches, barking loudly. "In the back, Snookie," Ariel said, holding the door open. "She wants to sit in the front."

"Now, why did I know you were going to say that?" Lex said, getting out of the car to allow Snookie to take her place in the passenger seat.

"Because you're intuitive. Listen, I'm not embarrassed over this."

"Hell, that never entered my mind." He was still laughing. "Since we're going in your vehicle, with you driving, and your dog in the front seat, am I to assume you're picking up the check?"

"You expect me to pay, too?" Ariel asked in outrage.

"This is the 90's. Women pay. This is one hell of a date, Ariel Hart."

"Yes, it is. Do you want to eat in the car or sit at one of those tables? It's kind of breezy."

"I like eating in a car with a woman and a dog who knows how to fasten her own seat belt. It's very romantic. Are we going through the drive-in?"

"We are unless you want to get out and go inside, in which case you'll have to pay. It's your call," she said, swerving into the parking lot.

"The drive-in is just fine. I'll have two Whoppers, two large fries, a Coke, and a milkshake. Whatever they have for dessert is okay with me."

Ariel leaned out of the window to place the order. "Six Whoppers, hold the dressing on three of them, five large fries, three milkshakes, one Coke, and three apple tarts." She slipped the Rover into gear and moved up to the take-out window, paid, pocketed her change, and said, "Do you want to eat in that parking space over there or would you like me to drive us somewhere?"

"I like eating in parking lots with a woman and a dog. I never did that before. They say everything in life is an experience," Lex said.

"I've heard that, too," Ariel said through clenched teeth.

"You encouraged me to take this dog, so you need to take half the responsibility for . . . for this date."

"Yes, I did. Did you hear one word of complaint out of my mouth? No, you did not. I even said this was romantic. So there. I do have a question, though. How are we going to do the ketchup thing with our french fries?"

Ariel sniffed. "You need to take some responsibility for this dinner. You figure it out."

"I say we skip the ketchup." Ariel looked in the rearview minor to see him grinning from ear to ear.

"Fine. But I like ketchup. So does Snookie."

"Then I'll open all of the ketchup packets and dump them in the Whopper box. Is that okay with you?"

"Three boxes. I like my own ketchup. I don't like other people sticking their fries in my ketchup. Snookie doesn't, either."

"I hate that dog," Lex said.

"Right now I do, too."

"How are we going to get this relationship off the ground with that dog glued to you? Do you think there's a way to outwit her?"

"No. She seems to know what I'm going to do before I do it. She's very tuned to me. She loves me. I'm hers. It's your fault." She reached for the two bags of food and the tray with the drinks which she handed over the seat to Lex. She drove to a parking spot and turned off the engine. Snookie undid her seat belt, shifted her huge body, and leaned over the seat. Lex parceled out the food. The dog waited patiently for her box of ketchup, turned around, and sat down. "She's a dainty eater," Ariel said.

"I see that," Lex said. Ariel clenched her teeth.

"Is this a fun evening or what?" Lex said as he stuffed a wad of french fries into his mouth.

"Damn right it is," Ariel snapped. "I can't remember when I had such a . . . nice date." She exploded into laughter.

"I'm thinking of this as a test. Of what, I don't know," Lex said.

In the front seat, Snookie stirred and then fastened her seat belt.

"She's ready to go," Ariel said around the food in her mouth. If we don't go now she'll try to start the car and turn the wheel. She's very smart."

"I'm not finished," Lex grumbled.

"Well, guess what? Neither am I?" Ariel said, her burger clutched between her teeth as she backed the Rover out of the parking space. Snookie woofed softly. "She likes to ride. Where to now?"

"You're in charge. Drive me around until you get tired."

"Then what?"

"Then what *what?*" Lex said.

"Then what and where do you want me to go?"

"I have an idea. Let's go back to your place and hash over that conversation you had with Dolly the night you shot at me through your window."

"That was a private conversation."

"Maybe so, but it was about me so I think that gives me the right to hear all the parts I missed. Yes, that's what we should do." He pulled his legs up and stretched them out, leaning back with his arm over the back of the seat.

"Wrong!" Ariel said.

"Then drive me home. You're no fun," he said with pretended petulance.

"To Bonsall? You aren't exactly a barrel of laughs yourself."

"Don't like that, huh? Okay, this is my best offer, my only offer, my final offer. Let's go back to your place, rip off our clothes, and make wild, passionate love."

"You got it!" Ariel said, making a U-turn in the middle of the road. Her ears felt warm and then hot.

In the back seat, Lex's feet hit the floor. His heart started to pound.

In the front seat, Snookie barked, her ears going flat against her head.

"What's that mean when her ears go back like that?" There was worry in Lex's voice.

"That means she's pissed off. I told you she's smart. She knows exactly what we just said, and she also knows it doesn't include her. Start thinking, and remember that she went through the front window. She might kill you. I wouldn't want that on my conscience. Maybe some herbal tea. She likes that—it has a very calming effect. We could give her two cups. She'll chew through the door if we don't let her in the room."

"I wasn't prepared for an audience," Lex said. "Maybe some brandy in the tea?"

"Absolutely not. I learned my lesson. We need a plan."

"A plan is good." Lex grinned.

"We'll go up to my room, turn on the television. We'll all have tea. I'll make a whole pot. We'll have a fire. She likes to lie by the fire. She'll think we're going to settle down. If we don't make a lot of noise, it should be okay."

"I've been known to roar like a lion. A lusty lion."

Ariel swallowed hard. "I've been known to squeal a time or two myself."

"We'll work it out." There was absolutely no confidence in Lex's voice.

"I hope so. I'm in the mood."

"Brazen hussy."

"You better be worth all this trouble."

"Define the word *worth*." There was such worry in Lex's voice, Ariel smiled in the darkness. "You made that up about those triple orgasms, right?"

"Nope."

"I'm fifty-four."

"I know. I'm going to be fifty-one. That means I'm just hitting my stride."

"I never heard anything like that. How do I know it's true?"

"'Cause I read it in *Cosmo*. Helen Gurley Brown is up on all that stuff. If you can't believe *Cosmo* who can you believe?"

"I hardly know you. You can't expect . . . perfection the first time out."

"I am expecting it. Are you trying to say you can't deliver?" Ariel wanted to laugh so hard she had to clench her teeth at the worry she saw on Lex's face in the rearview mirror.

"I'm not saying that at all."

"Good, 'cause we're home."

While Snookie did her last evening visit in the garden, Ariel prepared a pot of herbal tea and poured milk and sugar into separate bowls. "Do you take lemon, Lex?"

"No. I like milk in my tea. I don't think I ever drank herbal tea." He reached for her just as Snookie appeared at the kitchen door. He dropped his arms, picked up the tray, and said, "I'm just here to serve the masses."

Giggling, Ariel led the way up the steps, Snookie in between them. In her room, with the door shut and then locked, she set about lighting the fireplace. Lex put the tea tray down on the hearth. Ariel spread out a champagne-colored satin comforter on the floor along with mounds of pillows. "Take your shoes off," she ordered. "When you take off your shoes, she relaxes. She knows you aren't going anywhere." She kicked her espadrilles into the corner before she settled herself on the floor next to Lex. She poured three cups of tea, setting Snookie's on the side. The shepherd drank daintily and waited for more, her eyes on both of them, watching to see if they were drinking. Three cups later, Ariel leaned her head into Lex's lap. "It takes a while for her to nod off. Talk to me, tell me things about you I don't know. Start with the day you were born," Ariel said lazily.

Lex eyed the shepherd, who appeared as alert as ever. His own eyelids felt heavy as he muttered something about weighing seven pounds.

"That's how much *I* weighed," Ariel said. "My mother said I was a wailer, that I cried all the time because I had gas. I don't think she wanted me. Once I heard her tell her friend I was a mistake. She never hugged me or kissed me, at least not that I can remember." She sighed. "It was all so long ago. Nobody ever really loved me except two people. Dolly and . . . and . . . a friend of mine. Dolly still loves me and now Snookie loves me. I like the feeling."

Lex yawned. It took him a few seconds to realize Ariel was sound asleep in his lap. He risked a glance at Snookie, who was eyeing him warily. He could hardly keep his eyes open. Maybe he should just close them and go to sleep. "I hate your guts. You know that, don't you?" he said to the shepherd. "I don't really. I love dogs, but you're one big, king-size pain in the ass."

Lex stared down at Ariel. She was so pretty in sleep, a golden-haired angel. His hands moved and he found himself tracing the outlines of her chiseled features. He stopped, not because Snookie growled, but because he remembered another time long ago when he'd done exactly the same thing. Again and again he allowed his fingers to trace the outline of her eyes, her chin, her nose, and then the whole of her face. It felt the same, perhaps a little larger, perhaps a little more defined, just the way it should feel because it was older. He wanted to wake her, to ask her if Ariel Hart was a name Hollywood gave her, but he didn't. Snookie wouldn't allow it. He wondered if Ariel had a birthmark above her elbow, a pinkish-brown mark. Holding his breath, he inched up the sleeve of her T-shirt. Maybe it was the wrong arm. His eyes on Snookie, he moved the sleeve on Ariel's left arm. There was no pinkish-brown mark. But there was a faint scar the size of a dime. That in itself meant nothing. Even the contours of her face meant nothing.

He closed his eyes, the nerves in his stomach doing battle. He'd been drawn to this woman the moment he set eyes on her. He'd felt something. He sensed that she had, too. After all this time, was it possible he'd finally found his true love? It was about as likely as San Diego getting twenty-four inches of snow in August.

He slept, his hands cradling Ariel's face.

Snookie waited until she heard his deep breathing before she lowered her head to her paws. Even then, she stared at the sleeping couple a long time before she allowed her own eyes to close.

The moment the lacy shadows of the early dawn started to creep toward the horizon, Snookie moved slowly, stretching her long, sleek, powerful body. Gently she nudged the sleeping man's arm. When he didn't stir, she did it again. She inched closer, her pink tongue swiping at Lex's ear. She wiggled her ears when she heard him say, "Don't stop, that feels so good." The busy pink tongue worked its way down the side of his neck and then back up.

Lex cracked open one eye to stare directly into the shepherd's face. He saw the pink tongue and realized the dog was waiting for him to do something. What, for God's sake? Snookie nudged him again, first with her snout and then with her paw. Finally it dawned on him that she wanted to be let out. He carefully inched himself away from Ariel and got to his feet. Snookie trotted after him, waiting patiently while he unlatched the door. She looked back once. Lex stood rooted to the floor.

"Now what?" Lex whispered.

Snookie came back in and immediately dragged his shoes over to the chair. "Time for me to go, huh?" He watched as the big dog took his place on the satin comforter. "Gotcha. I know, this is a test. If I go, you'll accept me easier next time. I'm outta here. I'll leave it up to you to do the explaining."

Lex tiptoed down the steps and went out through the kitchen. Right now he'd kill for a cup of coffee, but he had the feeling if he made any stops along the way the shepherd would be three steps ahead of him, somehow, someway. He couldn't believe he was kowtowing to a dog. He let himself out the kitchen door then drove to an all-night fast food restaurant and ordered two cups of coffee. He sat in his truck, drinking and thinking.

Was it possible Ariel Hart was Agnes Bixby? *In your dreams, Lex Sanders, in your dreams.* How could he find out without actually asking her point-blank? If he did, and she wasn't Agnes, she might laugh at his devotion to a memory. He didn't think he could bear that. Maybe she didn't want anyone to know her background. So many things fit. She spoke of a friend in her youth, but never named the friend. He remembered how Aggie told him she was a mistake, and that her parents didn't love her. He remembered the feel of her face against his hands. Was it possible? Anything was possible.

Lex finished the coffee and headed for Bonsall. He had to remember he had a ranch to run, business to take care of.

At eight o'clock he was on the road again. His first stop was at his attorney's office, knowing Colin worked a seven-day week. "Colin, scratch the divorce. I changed my mind. Send me a bill."

"Lex . . . damn it, Lex, get back here and tell me . . . goddammit, Lex. Okay, okay. Are you going through some mid-life crisis I should know about?" the attorney bellowed.

"Yeah," Lex bellowed back.

His next stop was the offices of the private detective he'd hired. "Forget what I hired you to do. I want you to do something else. He spelled out in detail what he wanted. "Everything. Every written word. By the middle of next week. I don't care what it costs, but it better be within reason. If you can't do it, tell me now. You can. Good."

Lex was back on the interstate. Now, he could attend to business.

Ariel woke slowly, warm and comfortable. "Oohh, you're so soft and snuggly," she whispered. "Do that again. Hmmnnn, I like that." She opened one sleepy eye and gasped, "Snookie!" She looked around, her eyes wild. "Where's Lex? Like I really expect you to answer me. Oh, God," she muttered, dropping her head into her hands. "What I'd like to know is, did you let him leave or did you chase him out? This man is going to think I'm some kind of a nut case."

Snookie tilted her head to the side and stretched her sleek body lazily. She turned, picked up one of Ariel's shoes, and walked toward the door. Somehow, she woofed, the shoe tight in her teeth, and took a few more steps.

"I get it, he put his shoes on and left. Do you want to go out?" The shepherd sat down on her haunches and then lowered her graceful body to a full-length position on the floor. "Guess he let you out, too."

Ariel sat down on the floor next to Snookie. She stroked her, cuddled her, her thoughts busy. A long time later, she said, "If it's meant to be, it will be. I like his sense of humor, though. There's not another man in the world who would have put up with you last night. He's a good sport. I like him. I think you do, too. Let's go downstairs and get some coffee and breakfast. Sticky buns sound real good. Maybe some scrambled eggs to go with them. Bet Dolly's already up and cooking."

The red brick kitchen was dim and empty. Ariel flicked on the overhead fluorescent light. The white lighting allowed her to see that Dolly's door was open and her room empty. In all the years they'd been together, Dolly's room had never been empty in the morning. She felt an immediate sense of loss and wasn't sure why. To cover her confusion, she measured out coffee, poured water, and gave Snookie her breakfast. Then she poured a glass of orange juice and ate a stale doughnut. No sticky buns and scrambled eggs this morning.

When the dog finished her breakfast she waited for her vitamin and a second pill that guaranteed a glossy coat. "Go ahead, have a run for yourself. Maybe we'll go for a walk later. God, I hate Sundays."

Ariel drank her coffee while Snookie meandered all around the yard. When she finished the pot, she called the dog in and headed upstairs to take her shower. The day loomed ahead of her. She wondered what Lex was doing, what he was thinking. She knew she was falling in love with the rancher. She felt flustered and out of control for the first time in her life.

Back downstairs, dressed in baggy jeans and an equally baggy T-shirt, Ariel made a second pot of coffee. While it perked, she walked out to the gate for the Sunday paper. She was halfway through it when Dolly, Harry, and Agent Navaro appeared at the back door. Ariel peered over the top of her granny reading glasses. "Good morning."

"Miss Hart, we want to talk to you about something. Two of your trucks were hijacked during the night. We just found out an hour ago. One in Oklahoma and one in Arizona. Your truck in Oklahoma was hijacked at 4:10. The Arizona hijacking took place at thirteen minutes past midnight. We're looking at the proverbial brick wall. Andrews is delivering appliances for Sears. We're having him watched. He said he was home watching television. We can't prove that he wasn't."

"He did it," Ariel said, her tone stubborn, her face a mask

of fury. "He might not have driven the truck, but he's behind this one hundred percent. I damn well know it."

"In this country, Miss Hart, a man is innocent until he's proven guilty."

"Keep saying that when they cancel my insurance and I'm forced to file for bankruptcy. What about his cronies?"

"They have alibis, too, but they're weak. We're on top of this. There is something we'd like to discuss with you. But first you should know the workers at the different ranches are being stirred up. We understand there was some kind of meeting last night around ten o'clock. Saturday nights are good for that sort of thing around here. The workers are off, they come into town and spend money. Even Lex Sanders's workers were there. Sanders, from what I've been told, treats his people better than any rancher around these parts. All he asks in return is loyalty. Somebody must be promising something to these people to make them even attend such a meeting. I doubt Sanders even knows about it. We'll be bringing him up to speed today."

"What does all that mean?" Ariel asked. She stared at the federal agent and realized he was just mouthing words, like a brand new actress in front of the camera for the first time.

"I think it means the ranchers aren't going to get their avocados picked if the workers walk out. If you can't get your crop to market, what good is it? Picking is due to start this week. The avocado crops are what keep these ranchers in business all year. Sanders has other interests, but he could take a serious loss if he doesn't get his crops picked."

"I can't believe his people would turn on him like that," Ariel said. "He just put washers and dryers in for them. He bought bicycles and toys for the kids. Maybe they were at the meeting just out of curiosity," she added without conviction.

Agent Navaro's expression was compassionate. "If you promise a hard-working man who works from sunup to sundown a thousand dollars, cash, he's going to listen. These workers have never seen that much money at one time in their life. It's like the pot of gold at the end of the rainbow."

"But then they're out of a job."

"For the moment. Some rancher will hire them. It doesn't have to be Sanders. A rancher is only as good as the people who work for him. The workers know someone will hire them when a crop is ready to be picked. It's not just the avocados, it's the lettuce and all the other produce that's grown around here. That thousand dollars is a veritable fortune."

"But Lex has a school for the little ones and he gives them clean, decent apartments. He cares about his people. I'm sorry, I just can't believe they'd turn on him like that."

"I find it hard to believe myself, but it's going to happen. Probably within the next few days." He sounds like he wants it to happen, Ariel thought. He's just going through motions.

"What will the ranchers do?"

"Get family and friends in to help pick. The fruit rots on the trees. There aren't many options."

"Would it help if . . . God, I can't believe I'm saying this, but would it help if I went to Chet Andrews and hired him back? Lex will never agree to Chet driving for him. Even when Mr. Able owned the company, Lex wouldn't agree to it. Andrews hates both Lex and me. The man is a terrorist, and he's got us all running in fear, but I'll hire him back if it'll stop all this and help the ranchers."

"I think it's gone too far, Miss Hart. The man has no conscience, and he likes the part of the bully. He was born to it. Now, this is what Harry and I were thinking. I understand you have your trucker's license. Your man, Stan Petrie, called early this morning and informed me that Sanders's agent in Nevada has come up with those collectibles he wants. Seems an old retired showman passed away last week and his widow is hard-pressed for cash. She has exactly what Sanders wants.

Petrie is going to arrange for delivery, but I thought what we could do was to pretend you were going to be the one making the run. That way if Andrews hears about it, and I'm sure he already knows, he'll come after you instead of the real shipment. If all goes well, Sanders gets his stuff, we get Andrews, and wrap up the case. We need you to cross the state line. Nevada is just as good as Arizona—it's your decision. In reality, you'll be driving an empty truck with Harry and me in the back. I'm going to give some thought to having other agents follow us in unmarked cars. The reason I want you to drive instead of one of your men is because this is a vendetta on Andrews' part. We suspect it's him, too, so you aren't alone in your opinion. It's dangerous, you need to know that going in."

Ariel's heart raced. She could see a definite gleam in Harry's eyes. "Well . . . I . . . what if something goes wrong? What if they spot you? What if nothing happens? He's not exactly stupid. He might suspect this is a trap and not go for it. Then, what happens to the ranchers and their crops? What if he already knows about Lex's real shipment and outfoxes you? That'll kill Lex. Just how good are you guys, anyway?"

"What you say could well be true. We won't know unless we try. To answer your question about the ranchers, I just don't know. Depends on how much money was promised and how agitated he can get the workers. It's not one of those either-or problems, it's an 'as is', as we say in the business. We do our best. As for Sanders, I hope he gets what he wants. I just don't see any other options. We always get our man, Miss Hart. Does that answer your question?"

"I'll ride with you if you decide to do it, Ariel," Dolly said. "Snookie goes too, right?"

"I guess so. Okay, I'll do it on one condition. I can carry my gun."

"I didn't hear you say that," Agent Navaro said.

"Yes, you did. I want it in writing, too. Otherwise, I won't do it. It's not fair of you to ask, either. I want to help. You forget, Agent Navaro, that I made hundreds of movies and I'm a movie buff and read a lot. You say you'll be there, you promise this, you promise that. But when push comes to shove, I'm on my own. You know as well as I do that a hundred different things could go wrong. That's why they make movies, to show people how it really is. I know you're going to dispute that, but it's a fact. I don't mind being on my own because I can take care of myself as can Dolly. The gun is . . . a safety net, so to speak. I have a permit, and I know how to shoot. The cops say they look the other way, but the way my luck has been running lately, I'll get a trooper who won't." She knew she'd offended him. It was in his eyes, the set of his shoulders, and the tightened lips.

"We have jurisdiction," Agent Navaro said.

"Then you won't mind putting it in writing."

Navaro nodded curtly. "It's going to take a day to set this up. You'll drive up to Nevada—I think that's our best shot— and pick up a rig there. The scheduled driver will suddenly get sick. You'll just happen to be there, gambling, whatever, and offer to bring it back. Once it goes out on the air we'll wait a reasonable length of time, then you pick up the truck and we'll take it from there. Some of those drivers are like gossipy old women when it comes to talking on that CB. They talk in some kind of code, but I got the gist of it. Curled my hair, I can tell you. Sanders collectibles go out at the same time you take to the road."

"Thanks for telling me that. When do you think this is all going to happen?" Ariel asked.

"Sometime tomorrow. If you don't have anything planned for the rest of the day, why don't you head up to Vegas? We'll have someone drive your vehicle back. Check in at the Mirage, have dinner, play the slots or do whatever you like, then call Stan here in dispatch over the CB. Make it sound like it's a two-day getaway. You're the actress. I'm sure I don't have to tell you how to act. We'll be in touch."

"What about Snookie? They aren't going to let her into that big, fancy hotel."

"Trust me, they'll let her in," Navaro said, flashing his badge.

Ariel's expression was dubious. Suddenly she wanted to snatch the agent's badge and mangle it.

"I'll pack," Dolly said.

"When you get there, go up to the desk and tell them your name. Your room will be ready and so will your key. No fuss, no waiting in line, none of that. When you're ready to leave, just put the key on the dresser and walk out. Do me a favor, though—don't let the dog mess on the carpets." When Snookie growled menacingly, Agent Navaro backed up a step.

"Okay."

"We can see ourselves out," the agent said.

"You're crazy, Ariel," Dolly said when the door closed behind the two agents.

"How come you didn't say that when they were standing there proposing this little jaunt?"

"Because I was so flabbergasted, I couldn't think of anything to say. I knew you were going to do it so why should I get all upset? I can read you real clear, Ariel."

"Didn't come home last night, huh? So tell me, how'd it go?"

"We had a nice time of it. I think I expected more. How'd it go with Lex?"

"You don't want to know. Snookie took over the evening. It was a nightmare. I'll tell you about it on the way to Nevada. I think I can do this. Do you think I can do it, Dolly?"

"With your eyes closed. You're talking about driving the rig, right?"

"All of it. This isn't a movie, you know. This is about as real as it gets."

"Harry says he's a good agent, but I think he's sloppy. By *sloppy* I mean he doesn't dot his i's and cross his t's. I thought FBI agents had to be perfect. He said he has dozens of commendations. He has a blurry picture of himself shaking hands with Dan Quayle. I was impressed. Agent Navaro is the senior agent by three months. They work well together, Harry said. They'll take care of us. Are we taking any dress clothes?"

"One dress. Nobody gets dressed up in Vegas. You want to be comfortable when you lose money. I'm going to change into slacks and a T-shirt, and I'm bringing only an overnight bag. Bring Snookie's blanket. I washed it this morning. It's in the dryer. You know we're going to have to eat in our room or at drive-in restaurants."

"You spoiled her, Ariel. She thinks she's a person. Look at her face. She knows we're talking about her. Jeez, my life is changing right in front of my eyes."

She sounds so happy, Ariel thought as she climbed the steps to the second floor. She deserves to be happy, and I want her to be. Tears blurred her vision as she threw cosmetics and underwear into her overnight bag. Snookie paced, uncertain about what was going on. "I think Dolly's in love, Snookie," Ariel whispered tearfully. "I think it's great, but I'm really going to miss her if she leaves. It's going to be me and you, kiddo. We'll manage, I suppose. Boy, am I going to give her a wedding. It'll be the biggest shindig ever. I'll invite every single person I know to make sure she gets lots of presents. So what if it's tacky? You can stand guard with a white carnation in your collar. God, I *am* going to miss her."

Snookie put her paws on Ariel's shoulders and licked at the tears on her cheeks. Ariel cried harder. Snookie then did something that made Ariel forget her misery for the moment. She felt the shepherd's paws circle her neck and back, and then somehow, her paws were patting her back, the way a mother comforts a child. "You *are* something else, do you know that?" The bad moment was over.

As soon as the women were on the interstate, Ariel said, "Now, I want to hear everything. Don't leave anything out. Swear."

"I swear," Dolly giggled. You know that song the Pointer Sisters used to sing, "*I want a man with slow hands . . .*"

Lex Sanders closed the barn door behind him. He was sweating like a Trojan with all the work he'd done these past four hours. The noise coming from the workers' apartments made him turn to stare across the cobblestone courtyard. "What the hell . . ." It wasn't a saint's day, there was no fiesta of any kind, so what was going on? Today was Sunday and his workers, ever respectful of the Sabbath, usually did nothing more than sit on their stoops or under the trees, reading their Mexican papers or playing cards. The women served food in wicker baskets and the children played quietly. They were like a gaggle of geese now. Normally he did not interfere in their private lives, but today it looked like he was going to have to break his own rule because from all appearances, something serious was happening.

The women were arguing, the children were crying, and the men were shouting at their wives, who seemed to be ignoring the loud, blustery voices. He waited a moment to see if he could make sense of it. His heart leaped in his chest when he finally understood: his people were leaving. The men wanted to go, the women and children wanted to stay.

Lex whistled shrilly between his teeth, and was rewarded with instant silence. "What's the problem? Why do you want to leave? We're getting ready to pick in a few days. How can you do this? I want an explanation and I damn well want it NOW!"

"Money, Señor Lex. The Marino ranch is promising every worker a thousand dollars to sign on for the picking season. That plus our hourly wage. We wish to do this, Señor Lex."

Lex's head reeled. A thousand dollar bonus to these people was like a hundred thousand to someone like himself. Where in hell was Marino getting that kind of money? He was a newcomer to the area, buying out several other small ranches and combining them into one. "Where will you live? What about the children's schooling? There are no sanitation accommodations for families. Have you thought about that?" Obviously the women had; they were weeping again. His eyes narrowed. "Who promised you this money? When will you get it?" His voice was so hoarse, he hardly recognized it as his own.

"When the crop is picked and taken to market," one man said. "Señor Marino's foreman is the man who spoke to us."

"Just like that! You've worked for me for fifteen years, some of you as long as twenty-five, and you're going to leave me high and dry right before picking season? I've taken care of you, seen to it that your children are educated, your elderly taken care of. I give you excellent housing, good working conditions, make sure you have medical, dental, and eyeglasses, and you do this to me? Get off my property, and don't think you're coming back when Marino doesn't pay up. You'll be damn lucky if you get your wages, let alone the bonus."

The women then did something he never thought he would see. They verbally attacked their men, their words faster than bullets. They were so angry they were shouting in English— for his benefit he presumed. Why, he didn't know. The bottom line, though, he understood; the women weren't leaving. It wasn't such a serious situation, he would have laughed when the women, as one, said, "If you go, do not come back to our beds. No more papa for the children, no more grand-papa for the children. The dogs stay, too. Stupido! We can stay, Señor Lex? We will pick, even the children."

"Of course you can stay. This is your home." He eyed the men warily, waiting for their response. He didn't believe for one second that they would leave.

But they did. The women wailed. The children shrieked their unhappiness. When the men didn't turn around, the women chased them with brooms and mops. They cursed their men, their anatomy, their brains, and their ancestors. But their shrill cries had no effect at all on the mass exodus.

"Lock the gates, Señor Lex! Lock the gates! No good hombre!"

When the huge iron gates closed behind the men, Lex stared at the circle of women and children. There was no way he was going to get his avocados picked. He knew the women were as good as their word; they'd work a twenty-hour day if they thought it would help him, but it wasn't the kind of work the older women should be doing. He didn't doubt for a minute that they'd come up with a system that involved the children to ease their workload. He shook his head.

Because he didn't know what else to do, Lex picked up the phone and called Ariel. When the answering machine came on, he hung up, something he'd never done before. He headed for the shower. If he didn't hurry he was going to be late picking Asa up at the airport. If he was smart, he'd call Hawaii and find out if the old man really left this time. He'd cancelled out the last three times. But then again, if he was smart he wouldn't be in the position he was in now.

His mind raced as he lathered up. He had to talk to the women. Better to let that go until he returned with Asa. Jesus Christ, where to start? Cross the border? He knew he could bring in illegals if he really wanted to. He knew everyone at the border. If money changed hands he could manage it. He didn't want to do it. That wasn't what he was all about. That would be going backward, stooping to a Chet Andrews level. He prided himself on being an honest, hard-working business-man. Fair and just. He didn't break rules. Until now. Maybe if he viewed it as an option, and only an option, it would sit better on his conscience.

Pulling on clean jeans, he bellowed for Tiki. "Call Asa Able and see if he got on the damn plane this time. I'm not driving all the way to the airport to see thin air get off the plane. If he's still diddling around, tell him he can hitchhike the next time he says he's coming. I have a goddamn crisis on my hands and I don't need this crap!" He was still bellowing. Tiki nodded, her eyes fell as she waddled out the door and made her way back to the kitchen.

"Señor Able left on the plane, Señor Lex," Tiki said, meet-ing her boss at the bottom of the steps. "Do you want some-thing special for supper?"

"Supper!" The word sounded mysterious, alien, coming from his mouth. "Throw something in a pot and let it sit on the stove. I don't have time to eat or think about food. I don't know when I'll be back. Is the guest room clean?"

"Señor Lex! Of course it is clean and it has fresh flowers, too. I am a good housekeeper."

"I know. I'm sorry."

"Señor Lex, I will call on my nephews and their friends. They will help. There are ways for them to come here. Maybe twenty or so. Nieces, too. They are not afraid to work. You tell me okay, I cross the border for you."

Lex hugged the old woman. "I'll let you know, Tiki. This is a hell of a Sunday. It was a hell of a Saturday, too." He pulled on his Padres baseball cap and yelled over his shoul-der. "Tell the women I'll talk to them when I get back. I don't know when that will be, though. Call Frankie, too. Maybe she can talk some sense into those men."

"Bad idea, Señor Lex. Be better for the young educated men to talk to their relatives. Maybe not so good, too. The elders will demand their respect and the young ones will have no patience. You created a monster, Señor Lex, by sending them to college. Maybe it won't work," Tiki said dramatically. She threw her hands in the air as she trundled back to the kitchen.

She was probably right, Lex thought. Education was not one of his workers' priorities. He'd pushed education, but he'd seen the looks on the men's faces when a son or daughter graduated, often with honors, and took their place in the business world. The elders had their niches and were contented. The women always wanted something better for their children. He'd never been able to figure it out and he knew he wasn't going to find an answer now either.

There was one bright spot on his horizon: after picking up Asa, he could stop by Able Body Trucking or Ariel's house. Her house would be better. His shoulders straightened a little at the thought.

Chapter Ten

It was seven o'clock when Ariel turned the Range Rover over to the parking attendant who was eyeing Snookie warily. The shepherd walked gracefully next to Ariel on her Gucci lead. People turned to look and point at the huge dog. One capricious female, who Dolly said later looked like a lady of the evening, came a little too close, her hand extended to pat Snookie's head. The shepherd stopped in midstride, her ears flattening against her head, and growled ominously. The woman backed off, her voice shrill and angry. "I'm not staying here if they allow vicious animals like that. What kind of place is this?"

"Her garter belt's too tight," Dolly said. Ariel giggled as she reached for the key the desk clerk was holding.

"We're in room 711. We need to remember that. It could be lucky."

"Why? We aren't going to be able to leave this room. What good is a lucky combination?"

"I didn't hear anyone say we couldn't leave the room with Snookie. The only thing Navaro said was not to allow Snookie to mess the carpets. I'm willing to chance going into the casino with Snookie. The feds are in control. We'll just say that Agent Navaro said it was all right. Providing we want to gamble. I'm for anything that doesn't allow me to sit and think about the next forty-eight hours. Let's shower, change, and test our luck. You take the bathroom first. I want to call Lex. He's liable to call tonight and . . . I'd just like to let him know where we are."

Dolly winked, her grin stretching from ear to ear. "I do believe the lady's in love," she sing-songed on her way to the bathroom.

Snookie leaped onto the bed, gave a mighty yawn, stretched out full length, sighed, and closed her eyes.

Ariel read the instructions on the telephone, pressed the right numbers, and placed her call. "It's Ariel Hart, Tiki. Is Lex there?" She listened, her eyes widening at Tiki's babbling. "They all walked out on him? My God, what's he going to do? If he calls home, will you give him a message? He has a phone in the truck? Do you know the number? No. Okay, tell him to call Agent Navaro and he'll explain things.

"Dolly!"

"What's wrong?" Dolly yelped as she ran from the bathroom, her hair and body full of soapy bubbles. Snookie opened one eye, looked around, and went back to sleep. Ariel repeated her conversation with Tiki.

"What does that mean to us, Ariel. Us personally? Is it all connected? Should we be doing something? What? All the ranchers?" Her voice was so disbelieving, Ariel shuddered.

"What can we do here in Las Vegas? I don't know anything about ranching. To answer your question, I guess it is all connected if Chet Andrews is working for the man who bought Tillison's ranch. He's some kind of Wall Street wizard. I have a good mind to call Ken Lamantia and Gary Kaplan and ask them if they know Drew Marino. What good the information will be is beyond me, but I'm going to do it anyway. Go wash off those bubbles before your skin shrivels up."

Ten minutes later she shouted, "He's a legitimate Ivan what's-his-name, the one indicted for insider trading, the one who went to that white collar prison. Money out the kazoo. According to Ken he's one of those people who lives on the edge. He made his money, tons of it, probably billions. Now he wants to be a gentleman rancher. Ken said the writeup was on the front page of the *Wall Street Journal*. He says within two years he'll be the biggest rancher in the state of California. He's prepared to buy out the other ranches if they go under. Nobody has any ethics anymore. Can you imagine doing that to people whose ranches have been in the family for generations?"

"Where have you been, Ariel. It's been like that since the beginning of time. You stayed in Hollywood too long. This is reality, this is the way it works on the outside. We lived in a fantasy world."

"I don't like it one damn bit," Ariel snapped. "People like Drew Marino shouldn't be allowed to get away with things like this."

"Everybody says that but nobody does anything. That's why the Drew Marinos and the Chet Andrews of this world get away with the things they do. Your turn, my dear," Dolly said with a low, sweeping bow.

"Dolly!" The call came from behind the bathroom door.

"Now what?" Dolly shouted back.

"I have an idea. Today is Sunday," Ariel said behind the shower curtain. "Call everyone we know in Hollywood. Tell them I'm having a country-western party on Thursday night. Call the airlines, charter planes, hire some buses, do whatever you have to do. Call everybody and have them call everyone they know. Everyone in the universe knows Hollywood has the biggest heart in the world. Actors helpings ranchers. They'll go for it, I know they will. They'll end up making a movie about this, wait and see. We need a prize and some newspaper coverage. Call downstairs and ask how we can get another phone up here. Order room service, too. Get Snookie a T-bone steak with mushrooms and gravy. Rice and carrots, too. Get a couple of root beers. She loves root beer. Did I forget anything?"

"Who's going to play our parts in the movie?" Dolly asked. Ariel gurgled with laughter.

At one o'clock in the morning, Ariel unplugged the phone. "My faith in human nature has definitely been restored. It's true what they say, Dolly. Hollywood takes care of its own. If everyone who committed to this shows up, we can get all the ranchers' avocados picked. Next thing we have to do is provide food. You know, that hoedown stuff. I said it was going to be a party and it's going to be a party. The women at Lex's ranch will do the cooking. I'll call Tiki now and ask her. If she says no, we switch to Plan B and have it catered."

"We're saving the day," Dolly said as she finished her last call. "Now, who takes the avocados to market? It's not enough to pick them. We have to pack and load them."

"Hey, I own a trucking company, remember? Worst possible scenario is all the women who took the driving course, take to the road. The other ranchers have their own truckers. Our men will drive, too, if the other companies don't want to get involved, and they probably won't because that tycoon will promise them the moon to drive for him. Mr. Wall Street just took on Hollywood. I wonder how long it will be before he realizes he's met his match. I can't wait to see who plays *his* part."

"In your wildest dreams, Ariel, did you ever think something like this would happen?"

"Nope. I say we take Snookie for her walk, stop for a nightcap, throw a few bucks in the slots, and call it a night.

We did real good, Dolly. I feel like . . . I never felt like this before. Everyone was willing to help. No one asked for money. God, the word never came up. When I called Zeke Neuimer, head of the stuntmen, he said he'd transport his people himself. I didn't think he'd even remember me. Hollywood is literally going to shut down while this is going on. I'll take a full-page ad in *Variety* and list the name of every person who shows up. And pay for it myself.

"C'mon, Snookie, let's hit the great outdoors and find a patch of grass for you."

It was like daylight outside with more people walking around than during the day. They watched, mesmerized, when Steve Wynn's volcano erupted. "Hollywood couldn't have done it any better," Ariel sighed.

"I wonder how much money changes hands daily in Vegas," Dolly said.

"We can't count that high. It's so gaudy you have to love it. Do you know, Dolly, they have drive-through wedding chapels? I swear to God. No waiting. They have all these package deals. They have one for $500, one for $389, and a real cheapo for about $150. Some of the places give you a bottle of champagne and a real orchid. That's class. If either one of us gets married in the near future, I say let's come here and go to the drive-through. That would be a memory we'd never forget, and it would make a perfect ending for the movie. What do you say?"

"I say we go for it. Okay, Snookie's ready to go in. I have five bucks for the slots—how much do you have?"

"Seven."

Thirty minutes later, Ariel was up by twenty-five dollars and Dolly had lost her seven. "That means you buy the drinks. I'll have a piña colada. It's three o'clock in the morning. We have to be up at seven, don't we?"

"I don't plan to leave a wakeup call, if that's what you

mean. We sleep until Navaro calls us. Or Snookie wakes us. I'll have a piña colada, too." She handed Dolly ten silver dollars.

"Don't you think it's funny that not one single person in this casino has said a word about Snookie? This is a gambling town. What are the odds of that happening?"

"I guess you don't mess with the feds. I don't think the odds have anything to do with it. Okay, let's head upstairs and go to sleep. It's been a hell of a day."

"You feel better about Hollywood now, don't you?"

"They didn't let me down. I'm very grateful. Not for myself, though. I'm grateful that it'll help the ranchers. Their life is hard enough without some scumbag making it worse. You're right, though. I feel damn good."

"I hope both of us still feel good and confident when we take to the road tomorrow."

"You had to bring that up, didn't you?"

"It's a fact, Ariel."

It was ten o'clock in the morning when the call came from Agent Navaro. Ariel copied down the address of the trucking company, called the front desk to order a cab, and then called her dispatcher back in Chula Vista. She trilled the message she'd memorized, and Stan did his part.

"We'll roll at exactly twelve o'clock. When we pick up the truck, Navaro and Harry will already be in the back. Everything's set. Funny, I don't feel jittery at all. Personally, I don't think Andrews is going to fall for this. It's just a gut feeling I have. I think he's got himself entrenched with that financial wizard and from what Navaro says, it's a pretty cushy job. He won't risk blowing it. Even a terrorist knows when to strike and when to lie low. You going to spend that $380 you won last night on sexy underwear?"

"Jeez, Ariel, what's my underwear got to do with anything? I can only concentrate on one thing at a time." The sound of the zipper closing on her overnight bag was so loud in the quiet room, Ariel jumped.

"Just making conversation. I'm ready. Where's the key?"

Dolly tossed it on the dresser as per Navaro's instructions.

An hour later Ariel was checking out the rig she was to drive. She settled herself behind the wheel and took a moment to feel the power of her position before she flicked the switch of the CB. Her announcement was loud and clear. She signed off, jammed the Glock under her belt in the back, and then pulled her sweatshirt down around her hips. She looked at Dolly's pale face and at Snookie, who seemed to be grinning. "Okay, we just wait for the dispatcher's signal and we're outta here."

"Aren't you supposed to say something flippant like, 'let's rock and roll'?" Dolly said through clenched teeth.

"Only in the movies. You keep reminding me this is real life. Would it make you feel better if I said that?"

"Maybe. I don't know."

"Okay, baby, time to rock and roll." Ariel grinned as she shoved her foot down on the clutch, her eyes on the dispatcher. "If those guys in the back aren't holding on tightly, they're going to be slipping and sliding all over the place. We've got some wide turns coming up. Six, seven hours at the most and we're home. Let's talk about the party."

"Party, my butt. Let's talk about all the hard work involved. We'll all be too tired to party when we're done."

"It doesn't matter. It's the mingling, the talk about a job well done. So what if no one swims or dances. A party's a party. We'll get thousands of balloons."

"No one will have the strength to blow them up," Dolly said.

"They come blown up. You pay extra. Let's talk about love, sex, and good-looking men. It'll make the time go faster."

She wanted to talk about Lex. Wanted to hear Dolly tell her again that the man loved her even though she was beginning to suspect Lex's true feelings.

"What kind of wife do you think I'd make, Dolly? I botched up my first two attempts."

"You weren't in love then. This is your time in the sun. You'll be in a position to give back for all the good life has given you. Together. That's the best part. But to answer your question, you'll be a good wife because you're a good person. All your fans would give a collective gasp if they knew how insecure you are. You have to think positive from now on."

"Yes, Mother," Ariel said.

"Turn on the CB and let's listen to these gossipy men. I get a kick out of them. It'll make the time go faster."

"Yeah, I'd like to find out the exact location of that place that gives a two-hour massage with Cool Whip and strawberry syrup."

The sun was past the horizon when Lex Sanders rolled into the Able Body's truck lot. Asa hopped out of the passenger side, spry as a frisky pup. "Jesus, Lex, this place is a sight for sore eyes and my eyes have been mighty sore these past months. Stan, it's good to see you. How's Miss Hart treating you and the others?"

Lex watched the grizzled old man clap his dispatcher on the back. He handed over a putrid-smelling cigar and then fired up one of his own with a lighter like a blow torch. He wasn't a tall man, but what he lacked in height he made up in girth. Hawaiian food must agree with him. Or else, he was doing a lot of sitting. Lex would bet his last dollar he was up on every single episode of the daytime soaps. And the game shows, and the cop shows. The guy probably never slept. His blue eyes, the color of faded denim, were full of dismay as Stan told him how well the new owner was treating him and the others. He finger-combed his spiky gray hair that stood out on the sides in little tufts. His wrinkly skin wasn't just tanned, it was leathery and weathered-looking.

He was dressed the way he'd been dressed for the twenty-five years Lex had known him—baggy blue jeans, plaid cotton shirt, heavy work boots, a four-pack of the evil-looking cigars in his breast pocket.

"You need to be looking at the renovations, Mr. Able. Miss Hart spent a lot of time and money decorating the old place. Spiffy now. Flowers and all. Pink bathroom with artificial flowers, colored soap, pitchers on the wall . . . fluffy carpet on the floor. Lots of changes."

Asa growled something indistinguishable that Lex couldn't hear. He grinned.

"Door's open. I saw Bernice's car in the lot so she must have come in early. What time do you expect Miss Hart, Stan?"

"Sometime late tonight. She's in Las Vegas. Drove up there yesterday. Thought you heered all that from them FBI fellers. She's driving a rig back. It's a trap." he said importantly.

"What?" Lex bellowed.

"Shhhh. Don't you be giving away FBI secrets. I told you in confidence. That agent, he didn't tell me I wasn't supposed to tell you. Seein' as how you're sweet on Miss Hart and all, thought you should know. Them people who got your juke-box, they come up with another set of stuff for you. We're bringing it back on another load. Miss Hart is playing a decoy so's your stuff gits here the way it's supposed to. Bet that makes you real happy, huh?"

"Yeah, yeah. Jesus, what's she hauling?"

"Them two FBI agents in the back. Told you it was a trap." Stan slapped his leg as he cackled in glee.

Lex's voice was full of outrage. "They're using a woman as bait! I goddamn well don't believe this."

"Two women and the dog." Stan cackled some more.

"Everything's pink and green! Seashells! My spittoon is gone! So's Teddy!" Asa sputtered.

"Get in the truck, Asa! We're going to Las Vegas! Give me the route, Stan, and don't even think about telling me you don't have it," Lex said. He shoved the slip of paper Stan handed him into Asa's gnarled hand.

"Vegas! Hot damn!" Asa said as he settled himself into the truck and buckled up. "Burn rubber, boy. I have money to spend, and these old eyes want to look at some purty girls. 'Course, I'll tell my wife all about it when I get home."

"She won't care, Asa."

"Now, ain't that the truth! Why are we going to Vegas?"

Lex told him.

Asa rubbed at the stubble on his chin. "I'd never have allowed that if I still owned this company. Women are not supposed to be used as bait to trap a crook." His voice was so virtuous, Lex almost choked.

"I'm going to ask her to marry me. Soon. One of these days. Maybe over the weekend. Maybe later on, when all this business with the workers is settled. Maybe I won't. I might not have anything left to offer her. How could they do that, Asa? How is it that she agreed? She doesn't look stupid. They probably gave her some of that patriotic crap they dish out. Hung a guilt trip on her."

"Maybe she did it for you. Women do all kinds of silly things when they love a man. Men do silly things, too, like right now. You could get us killed if you try and stop that truck, and don't tell me that isn't your plan. You're gonna pull that truck over and then me and you are gonna get in it and them women and dog are going to get in this here truck."

"Zip it up, Asa. That isn't my plan at all."

"Then what is your plan?"

"Goddamn it, I don't have a plan. Well, maybe I do. We'll follow behind her. You got a better idea?" Lex growled. "Why didn't she call and tell me what she was doing?"

"Them FBI fellows swear everyone to secrecy. Seen that in a movie. Miss Hart made lots of movies. She knows the drill. Stan, now, he never could keep anything to himself. She's doing it for you, son, and we both know that."

"I don't want her doing stuff like that for me. I want her home safe and sound."

"This is the 90's, son. Women don't want to stay home safe and sound. My wife is making seashell jewelry and she peddles it on the sidewalk. Now, don't that beat all hell? She's making money, too. We have one whole room full of nothing but flowered clothes."

In spite of himself, Lex burst out laughing. "What would be even funnier would be you telling me you help her make the jewelry."

"Just once in awhile. Got four cabinets full of pineapple. I hate it. I hate Hawaii. I hate all that sun, all them mirrors. Everything is yellow and green. The furniture, I mean. Do you think Miss Hart will sell me back the business?"

"After this is all over and if she agrees to marry me, your chances are looking pretty good. What about your wife?"

"I'll visit," Asa guffawed. "Relax, son. There's not much you can do right now. If she's taking off at noon, we'll be about two hours from Vegas. I say we sit and wait for her to come rolling by. I don't have a bad feeling about this, Lex. I think the feds made a mistake on this one. A trap only works if you have someone ready to step into it. Chet is not going to bite. Trust me and my years of knowing that scum. He's frying other fish right now."

They drove in silence. Occasionally, Lex turned the radio on, listened for a while, and then turned it off. In between he smoked and coughed as Asa enjoyed his obnoxious cigars. He heaved a sigh of relief when the older man dozed off. He drove steadily, his eye going occasionally to the speedometer, careful to stay at sixty-five. The radar detector was a single eye, glaring at him like a Cyclops.

Lex did everything he could think of so he wouldn't think about what was happening back at his ranch. He ate peanuts, chewed gum, chainsmoked, hummed under his breath, and stuck his head out the window to draw in deep breaths. But it wasn't until he was into his third hour on the road that he settled down.

Forty minutes into the fourth hour, two things happened: Asa woke, and he blew two back tires simultaneously. "And what the hell are the odds of that happening?" He snorted his disgust because he knew he only had one spare in the back of the truck.

"Things seem to be going from bad to worse, son. You got any kind of patch kit in the back? Best get on the horn and call Triple A, but first you gotta get off at the next exit. This shoulder is too narrow."

Lex did as instructed—and missed Ariel by fifteen minutes. He spent the thirty minutes he waited for Triple A kicking the back tires, cursing in two languages, kicking the front tires, smoking, and banging the hood of the truck. Seventy minutes later he was southbound, knowing full well Ariel had passed him.

"This is a goddamn exercise in futility," Lex muttered. "Asa, call Stan and see if there's a way to get in touch with the agents or Ariel. Stan can get on the CB and report back to us. At least we can get a location, and then I can speed up or slow down if it turns out they're behind us. They've got to be ahead of us. I'd bet the ranch on it. Jesus, Asa, if Ariel weighs 110 pounds it's a lot. I still can't believe she can drive that eighteen-wheeler."

"And I can't believe she decorated my offices in pink and green and has seashells all over the damn place. I left Hawaii to get away from seashells and those damn sunset colors. It's not . . . manly."

"That's because Ariel is not a man. When you buy it back you can hang zebra wallpaper. Call Stan!"

"He's gonna call us back. He hasn't heard a thing. All he knows is Ariel took to the road at noon. You're probably right that she passed us when we were having our repairs done. Patience, son. If anything went wrong, Stan would have heard."

"She's got four hours to go. A lot can happen in four hours. Hang on, Asa. I'm going to floor this baby. I'll decorate my Christmas tree this year with the tickets I get."

The truck phone buzzed. Asa growled a greeting, listened, nodded, and replaced the phone. "So far so good. Stan told her Big Daddy, that's me, and Junior, that's you, were having car trouble and would meet her for supper. He was afraid to say too much. If she's as smart as you say she is, she'll figure it out. She's an hour ahead of us. You're going eighty, son. I wonder what it's like to go a hundred miles an hour or as fast as the speed of light, or is that sound? You got twelve cylinders, son, let's go for it!" Asa cackled gleefully.

"Jesus, Asa, when did you get so daring?"

"When I started making seashell necklaces."

Twenty minutes later, the radar detector squealed at the same moment a state trooper's siren went off. "Shit!" Lex said succinctly. He slowed down and pulled over to the narrow shoulder. "Pretend you're sick, Asa. You look kind of green. Guess high speeds aren't what you thought they were. Stringing seashells might be your forte after all."

Lex stared at the trooper's spit and polish uniform, his black, mirrored sunglasses, and his chiseled features as he handed over his license, registration, and insurance card.

"It's not his fault, officer. I'm having a gallbladder attack and my boy here was just trying to get me home because I ain't goin' to no hospital to die. Want to die in my own bed. Give us our ticket so I can get home to my missus and my bed. Ohhh, sweet Jesus, this hurts." He threw his head back against the headrest and clutched his gut, having no idea where his gall bladder was.

"Okay. These are your options—I can escort you to the hospital or you can drive at a safe speed. I clocked you at 97 miles an hour. I'm not giving you a ticket this time because my own father is just as ornery as yours is, and I understand. I'm going to radio ahead so take it easy. Don't suppose you take your medicine, either."

"Makes me sicker," Asa growled.

"That's what my father says. Ask the doctor to change it."

"We'll do that, won't we . . . Dad?"

"Darn tootin'," Asa growled again. "Want my own bed. That's all I want."

Lex slipped the truck into gear. "Thanks, officer." He offered up a roguish wink, but couldn't see if the officer returned it with the sun glaring off his sunglasses.

"Should have been an actor. Maybe Miss Hart can get me a part in a movie."

"I thought you wanted to buy back the company," Lex said, his eyes going to the rearview mirror.

"That, too."

Lex drove at sixty-five, his eyes constantly checking his side mirror and the rearview mirror for signs of trooper patrols. Ninety minutes later he was satisfied there were no police, so he pressed down hard on the accelerator. Asa's head snapped backward. "A warning would have been nice," he bellowed.

Thirty miles down the road, Lex slowed. "I think that's her up ahead. Call Stan and see if I'm right. Describe the car behind her. I think it's a white Ford Mustang, New Jersey license plate AWA-397. On her left, slightly ahead, is a Chevy Blazer, Arizona plate, but I can't make it out. I'd say the Blazer is riding shotgun and the Mustang is backup. I can't see what's directly in front of the truck. What they usually do in the movies is switch up. Probably another car or truck up ahead and one behind us. Then, when the time is right, they all converge. Lots of manpower and lots of bucks involved. We're gonna coast now."

"We're coming up to the Pine Valley exit. If anything is going to happen, it'll be soon." Ariel swiped at the perspiration beading on her forehead. "Snookie is calm—I don't see anything strange. I think this was a bum idea, if you want my opinion. And I wouldn't bet the rent on it, but I think that's Lex Sanders about three vehicles back. If something happens, his presence won't help matters. Everyone around here knows Lex and his truck. Asa probably sticks out like pink skin on an elephant. This is a bust, I can feel it."

"Thank God," Dolly said. She fed Snookie a dog bone, but not before she took a bite of it. "These things are awful."

"Dolly, I have this . . . this bad feeling suddenly. You aren't going to like or believe what I'm thinking. I could be wrong, but somehow, I don't think so. It all hit me when I got up this morning. I started to equate this whole thing to a movie script. Dolly, if this was a script, do you know what the kicker would be?"

"I don't have the foggiest, Ariel."

"Well, I do. Scripts, like stories, have a beginning, a middle, and an end. There's a bad guy and a good guy. Usually you know what the klinker is by the middle. We thought it was Chet Andrews. Actually, it is Chet Andrews. But there's another one. I don't think those men in the back of the truck are FBI agents at all. I think they're men in the employ of Drew Marino. I think Marino is out to destroy Lex Sanders as well as the other ranchers so he can become the big gentleman rancher the way he was that famous Wall Street tycoon. Those guys, there was something about them from the beginning. They were slick, but they weren't polished. They knew a little bit, but not enough. I never personally looked at their badges up close. I didn't like Navaro's eyes from the gitgo.

You said there was something about Harry that made you uneasy. They asked a lot of questions that had nothing to do with business. There were twenty different ways they didn't compute. I don't think I'm wrong, Dolly."

"What's it mean, Ariel?"

"God, I wish I knew. I would imagine Lex's second set of collectibles is being hijacked as we speak. And we unknowingly helped it to happen. I don't know what to do. When we get back, they'll climb out, apologize, say something to appease us, and go their merry way. Our insurance will be cancelled for sure, as will Lex's. Those collectibles are things, and Lex can get by without them. We're down to basics now—his livelihood. The avocados. If this was a script, and I turned the page, I'd see a fire in progress. Now, they don't know Hollywood is coming to the rescue. Then again, maybe they do. If they had someone listening to our phone calls last night, they know. What that means is, between now and Thursday, they burn him out or drop poison from planes over his trees . . . something to destroy his crops. The other ranchers, too. The next page in the script is blank. What's the answer, Dolly?"

"Oh, Ariel, I don't know. I can't comprehend people being so vicious. We have to call the real FBI. Alert all the fire departments. What can we do about planes with poison?"

"We can't do anything, but the real FBI can alert all the airfields, even the small, private ones. There has to be a way to put an end to this. Am I crazy, Dolly?"

"No. It all makes sense. We fell for it, too. They must be snickering up their sleeves as we speak. I hate that."

"They think they have us fooled. I say we let them keep right on thinking that. We call the FBI from a pay phone. Arrange a meeting. They'll take it from there.

"Do you want to know something else? This all would have gone off without a flaw except for one thing. Asa Able sold out to me and didn't tell anyone, not even Lex, until it

was a done deed. The hijackings were just a . . . just a way
for Andrews to get back at Lex. That was personal. The big-
gie was . . . is Marino. He wants the whole thing and if I hadn't
come along, he would have gotten it and there would be no
trail leading back to him. He would be just another business-
man taking advantage of someone else's misfortune. He'd
have his fifteen minutes of fame and then he'd be plain old
Drew Marino, wealthy rancher. It's making more and more
sense. I'm taking the back road and heading back to the lot.
We need to come up with a story for those jerks in the truck.
Let's say you had an ulcer attack and I had to get you back to
your doctor. Practice looking sick."

"I don't have to practice—I *am* sick. They snookered us,
Ariel. How'd that happen?"

"I can't tell you exactly, but I imagine it was when Dave
Dolan said he was calling the FBI. Somebody must have in-
tercepted or made the call. Offered to make it, I should say.
Then these two guys show up, flash their badges, and that
was it. I should have checked it out. It's my fault. I can't believe I was so stupid."

"It wasn't just you, Ariel. No one else picked up on it. Lex
talked to those guys for a while. Stan talked to them, and so
did Bucky, the dispatcher. Hey, I went to bed with Harry!
That should show you how smart I am. Don't blame yourself, Ariel."

"Easy to say, Dolly. Let's get our stories straight. We'll be
back home in about twenty minutes. So, this is what I think
we should say . . ."

"*Now* what the hell are they doing?" Lex demanded.

"This is just a guess on my part, Lex, but I'd say they're
heading back to the lot. I think something's wrong. I don't
mean something physically wrong. I think their plan, whatever it is, has gone awry or else Miss Hart has had enough of

this game playing—and that's what it is, Lex, game playing," Asa said.

"It's funny that you should use that term, Asa. For the past hour I've been thinking the same exact thing. It's all a game, the whole thing. The hijackings, the workers walking off, this stupid run, us chasing them. Think for a minute. Who comes out on top when this comes to an end? Not me, that's for sure. Not the other ranchers. Not only will I be ruined, but so will Able Body. Ariel can't operate without insurance. I can't, either, but then I won't have to worry about that because I won't have anything to insure. The only person who wins is that guy who bought up Tillison's ranch. This might be a bit farfetched, but I'd wager he'll try to buy Ariel out when she starts to go under. Then he has a lock on the whole thing. Andrews will probably run the trucking company. Five bucks says that's his payoff for all the dirty things he's been doing. Does it make sense, Asa?"

"Christ Almighty, it does, son."

"Well, it ain't over till it's over, Asa. I'm not giving up. There has to be a way to outwit those bastards."

"You only have a couple of days till picking starts. If you can get the fruit picked are you willing to send it out in Miss Hart's trucks with no insurance? Only a fool would do that. You ain't no fool, son."

"I can cross the border, Asa."

"And open another can of beans? The border patrols will be down on you in the time it takes your heart to beat."

"There are ways."

"Not legal, there aren't. Don't you go doing something stupid, now. It's damn unfair is what it is. Somehow we'll work this out. I have a hunch Miss Hart is on to something. She didn't follow instructions and she's heading back to the terminal. That has to mean she's taking the reins. I say we take her out to supper."

Lex told him about Snookie.

"So, I'll pretend I can't see good. I can't, you know. Got a cataract on my left eye. Can't take it off till it gets ripe. Did you ever hear of such a thing?"

"Yeah, yeah, I did. I'm sorry about that, Asa."

"It makes no never-mind, Lex. Got one good eye. My hearing's good and so is my sense of smell. When you're my age that counts. Another mile to go."

Ten minutes later, Lex swerved into the terminal lot. The first thing he saw was Ariel's Range Rover parked in her usual space. So, someone had driven it back. He'd wondered about that. The second thing he saw was Ariel climbing down from the cab, Snookie behind her. She walked to the rear of the truck where Dolly met her. She opened the trailer. The two agents emerged, rumpled and disgruntled. The third thing he saw was Snookie heading straight for him at a dead run. He planted his feet firmly on the ground, grabbed Asa's arm for added support, and waited for the big dog to pounce on him. It occurred to him to wonder why Ariel wasn't calling her back. Then he saw the note in the dog's collar. He palmed it as he stroked her sleek head. "Good girl," he whispered. Snookie took a second to sniff his shoes and then raced back to Ariel.

With his back to the two agents, Lex read the note. *Meet me where you first saw Dolly and me. Bring Mr. Able. Leave now.* He stuck the note into his breast pocket before he motioned for Asa to climb back into the truck. With the engine running, he leaned out to shout to Ariel, "How about lunch tomorrow at the ranch?"

"Sure thing," she called in return, waving airily.

"Well, this was certainly an exercise in futility," Ariel said. "Tell me something, did either one of you or your superior, whoever that might be, think this through?"

"Of course we thought it through. We also told you it might come to nothing. My question to you is, why didn't you follow orders and head for the Sanders ranch?"

"Because it was a stupid order and I'm not a stupid person. Even I knew nothing was going to happen on that stretch of road, and I was right. Now, if you'll excuse me, I want to find out if Mr. Sanders' load is safe. Until now I thought the FBI was a top-of-the-line government agency. At this point in time I wouldn't give you five cents for the whole outfit. Maybe what I'll do is call the FBI personally and complain. They need feedback from ordinary people like me. Yes, that's exactly what I'll do. I'll be sure to say flattering things about you so nothing derogatory goes into your file. I played a female FBI agent once, so I know the drill."

Navaro's face took on an intense look. Harry looked green in the dim twilight. The sound of cars and trucks rumbling in the background seemed to add to both men's discomfort. The sensor lights outside the offices sprang to life, lighting up the entire parking lot.

"That probably isn't a very good idea. My people take a dim view of calls like that. You're wrong—it will go on our records. It won't look good for either of us. I need to remind you again that we said it was a long shot. Everything's in place—you just need to be patient. Why don't Harry and I buy you ladies dinner and discuss this whole matter and see if we can't come up with something we can sink our teeth into. We do need to rest up a little, though, and I need to check in with the office. The biggest steak in San Diego—how does that sound? With the government picking up the check." Navaro chuckled to show how amused he was.

"Not tonight. We'll take a raincheck, won't we, Dolly? I'll decide tomorrow whether I'll call and complain. I want to present my side. Why don't we schedule a meeting here, let's say, tenish? Is that okay with the two of you?"

"Well, sure. Ten it is."

The women watched the men walk over to a dark green sedan, climb in, and drive off. "What do you think the odds are they'll show up tomorrow at ten? Did you see that look on Navaro's face? He's pissed off, big time. Another thing—when we get into the Rover, don't say anything. Just follow my lead. If this was the same script we were playing with on the ride down here, someone would have planted a bug in the truck. I want to check with Stan to see if there's any news on Lex's jukebox. Oh, and when I stop the truck at the restaurant, I'll just say, we're here, or something like that. If there is a bug whoever is listening will think we're home."

"What if they follow us? Don't they have to follow you within a mile or something so they can listen? They might be brazen enough to show up. This is getting scary, Ariel."

"Tell me about it. Things like this only happen in the movies, Dolly. I don't know how it works in real life. I guess we'll find out soon enough. My big worry right now is how I'm going to get Snookie into the restaurant. A hundred dollar bill and the promise that she'll sit under the table might do it. If that same waitress is working, maybe Lex can charm her."

Ariel motioned for Stan Petrie to join her. "Have we heard anything from the driver with Lex's load?"

Stan massaged his whiskered chin. "Not for the past two hours. Can't reach him on the CB. I called the ranch and he hasn't arrived. Didn't think he would, but sometimes those fellows can burn up the highway. Tim Ryan is a hell of a driver and he knows the score. He did say something funny, though. Guess he thought I'd catch on. I don't know what it means. He said R. R. Hood was heading east with all her goodies. Do you know what that means, Miss Hart?"

"Who's R. R. Hood?" Dolly asked.

Ariel laughed. "Dolly, shame on you. Don't you remember when I played that FBI agent, my code name was Red Riding

Hood or R. R. Hood? The goodies are Lex's collectibles. East probably means Ryan is taking a different route, but east could just as easily mean north, south, or west. My guess would be he'll come in from the back and drive that rig through the fields. Something like that. I'm not saying . . . listen, if you can come up with something better, let's have it. It's a damn possibility. We'll spring it on Lex and see what he thinks. This is where we'll be for the next hour or so, Stan. Get the number from information. If you hear anything, have us paged."

"Sure thing, Miss Hart."

"See you tomorrow, Stan. In the truck, Snookie."

Cold, frosty Corona beers sat on the table waiting for the women the moment they sat down. Snookie settled down under the table and went to sleep.

"Thanks for taking care of Snookie's arrangements. How much did it cost you?"

"A hundred bucks."

"She's worth every penny. I'll pay you back."

"If you don't, I won't be able to sleep tonight." Lex did a Groucho Marx thing with his eyebrows. Ariel smiled.

"Listen up," Ariel said as she motioned the others to lean in toward the center of the table. "This is what I think. Just hear me out." She spoke quickly, ending with, "I'm sure there's a bug in the car. What I think you need to do, Lex, and this is just my opinion, but I do think it will work. When we leave here, you and Mr. Able head out to all the other ranches and tell them Hollywood is coming on Thursday. Actually, they'll probably start arriving tomorrow. There have to be accommodations. We're going to get your avocados picked and we'll get them to market, too. Trust me."

"Jesus. How'd you do that, Ariel?"

"I asked. That's all it took. I think I have it all covered, but there are bound to be some screwups. Food, sanitation, sleeping arrangements are up to your ranchers. Tents are coming tomorrow. You'll need Tiki and the other cooks to keep the flow going. I'd go real easy on the beer until we're done, then you can have it flow like a river. Did I forget anything?"

"This is amazing, isn't it, Asa?" Lex said in awe.

"Yep. All of Hollywood? Who's going to make pictures while all of this is going on? Will they really shut down?"

"You bet. Hollywood loves a cause."

"You must be somebody real important for them to do this," Asa said.

"No. I'm just somebody who sold them short. I'm sorry about that. Maybe it's because I never asked for anything for myself. Maybe they feel they owe me, but I don't think so. They're doing this to help, pure and simple. They're good people. You'll see."

"Here's our food. I took the liberty of ordering filet mignon for Snookie. I figured you could cut it up and she wouldn't mess the carpet with the bone. Her french fries and ketchup are on a second plate."

"Thanks." Ariel cut the meat in small pieces, then squeezed the ketchup on to the plate and slid it under the table. "Boy, is this good. I'll have another beer, if you don't mind. I want Sinful Chocolate Thunder for dessert. With vanilla ice cream and soft marshmallow drizzled all over it."

"You got it!" Lex chortled.

"When are you calling the FBI?" Asa asked.

"When we're ready to leave. There's a pay phone by the front door."

"I don't think you should go back to the house tonight, Ariel. Go to a hotel. I'll call a friend of mine who's a cop and have him watch over you guys. Asa and I will head out to the ranches. It's going to be a long night and I don't want to have to worry about you."

"That's sweet," Ariel said as she scraped the last of the potato out of the skin.

"That's because I'm a sweet guy." Lex grinned from ear to ear. "If this was a movie, what would come next?"

A devil perched itself on Ariel's shoulder. For a moment she looked thoughtful. "Well, the script writer would probably clear out this place for starters. He'd make sure there was a very, as in very nice, lounge area inside the ladies' bathroom. He'd have me say I was going in to powder my nose. Then he'd want me to look over my shoulder, enticing you with my bedroom eyes. You'd get up and trip over Snookie who'd be trying to chew off your leg. You'd give her the rest of your steak. You'd race to the lounge. We'd both lock the door. Because this is the 90's, I'd take off your clothes. Little by little. All the while I'd be nibbling your ear and whispering sweet nothings."

"Yeah, yeah, then what?" Lex was breathing so hard, Ariel laughed.

"Then the director yells CUT! and says, that's it for today."

Asa's fist crashed down on the table. "I liked that!"

"So did I. When do we get to rehearse?" Lex demanded.

"The minute we get those damn avocados to market," Ariel said sweetly.

"Put it in writing."

Ariel scribbled on a napkin. "You better not lose this. You have to present it at the time rehearsal starts."

Lex folded the napkin and stuck it in his breast pocket, buttoning the flap securely. "Guess we have to get to work. Let me use the phone first to call my friend on the police force. I'll have him make the hotel arrangements for you. All you have to do is show up. I'll call you from the different ranches."

"Be careful, Lex."

"You too, Ariel."

She wanted to kiss him. It looked like he wanted to kiss her, too. She felt her legs go rubbery at the thought of melting into his arms. Instead, he picked up the phone, his left hand covering his breast pocket. He winked at her. She felt dizzy as she puckered up to blow him a kiss. It pleased her to see his hand start to tremble.

"You shameless hussy," Dolly hissed.

"Dontcha love it?" Ariel hissed back.

"I do!" Asa cackled.

Chapter Eleven

They came in private planes, stretch limos, Ferraris, Mercedes-Benz, trailers, pickups, motorcycles, roller blades, and one young starlet, along with her companion, raced up on a skateboard. Television crews jockeyed for position, satellite dishes sprouted like young seedlings, and as far as the eye could see, actors, actresses, camera crews, techni-cians, directors and producers worked side by side.

The newspapers described the day as glorious. The news anchors had a field day as Hollywood turned out to help one of their own. Ariel tried to set them straight and insisted it was simply goodhearted people helping other people in need, but the media ran with their lead: Hollywood helping their own. Eventually she gave up and pitched in. What did it matter as long as the job got done?

By mid-afternoon there was a routine that was, as one actor put it, "as slick as a greased pig." Ariel looked around in awe. How was it possible to just pitch in and do what had to be done with no squabbling about top billing, better accommodations, makeup and costume faults? She swigged from a can of cold Pepsi, saw an actor she'd worked with many times, and handed it over. He finished it at a gulp. "Thanks,

Ariel, that was real good. Miss you, sweetie." Then he was gone. She laughed out loud.

"My God, was that Tom Hanks? Ariel, was it?" Dolly demanded.

"That was a very nice man who said he missed me. I think he meant it. Do names really matter, Dolly?"

"Jack Palance helped me drag my basket over to the truck. At least I think it was him. It sounded like him, but with that hat and his sunglasses, it was hard to tell and I got tongue-tied. Somebody said Heather Locklear is over there and she's got on the cutest bib overalls I've ever seen. She broke all her fingernails and didn't even get mad. That says a lot, Ariel."

"Yes, it does. Time to get back to work. I'm relieving Charlie Sheen. That guy needs to take a break. He's been going non-stop. I promised to bring him a soda. His dad is working like a Trojan. It's great, isn't it, Dolly?"

"Did anyone tell you Dolly Parton and Reba what's-her-name are going to sing tonight if they don't fall asleep?"

"Nope, I didn't hear that. Who rigged up the lighting?"

"Those guys from Universal. There's this grizzly old guy who's the boss. He said he loves a skinny woman with long hair. I offered myself right then and there. He said he'll see me at supper. Like we're really going to have supper. Food wagons are going all day and into the night. No such thing as supper. Maybe I'll take him a plate. Ariel, I picked 84 bushels of fruit. How many did you pick?"

"I lost count. My back says it's a lot. My arms are numb. See you later. Hey, have you seen Lex?"

"A long time ago, maybe around noon. He was talking to the feds. The real ones. Then I saw him go off in his truck. I think he's the one who organized the workers for the other ranches. It's working, Ariel. It's absolutely amazing how everyone just fell to and started to work The best part is no one is giving interviews to the press. This whole thing renews my faith in mankind."

"Yep—me, too."

It was one in the morning when Ariel, a hot dog in one hand, a soft drink in the other, gingerly lowered herself to the ground. "I don't know if I have the strength to lift my arms to eat this," she muttered to no one in particular.

"Someone over by the cook wagon has a whole case of liniment. Got a tube in my pocket if you want some," a voice drawled.

"Clint! Gee, it's nice to see you. You came all the way from Carmel?"

"It's not that far, Ariel. We miss you. You happy here?"

"Yeah. Yeah, I am. I fought it at first, but yeah, I'm happy. I appreciate you coming, Clint. Hope I can return the favor someday."

"No need. You made my day." He dropped a tube of ointment in her lap before he walked away.

"This seat taken?"

"Nope." She was still holding the hot dog and soda can in the same upright position, unwilling to feel the pain she knew would follow if she tried to lower her arms.

"How's it going, Ariel?"

"The truth?"

"Of course. You gonna eat that dog or just hold it like that?"

"I can't move my arms. I'm starving. I've never been this tired in my life, Sly."

A huge hand guided the hot dog toward her mouth. "Eat it and then I'll rub your arms. You should work out more."

"I should do a lot of things. It was wonderful of you to come. All the ranchers appreciate it. They would have been wiped out without all of you. God, this is good. Want a bite?"

"All those nitrates?" He took a huge bite and munched contentedly.

"Do you think, Sly, if we had sixteen Rambos shooting the avocados off the trees, it would go faster?" Ariel asked wearily. "By the way, you're lookin' great."

"Same goes for you, kiddo. I heard about your operation. You should have given us a chance, Ariel, before you cut and ran. You of all people should know we take care of our own. We deserved a chance."

His voice sounds so sad, she thought. Her own sounded just as sad when she said, "My face was my life. I didn't want pity. And I needed to lay some old demons to rest. I'm okay with it. I really am. I can truthfully say, this is the second most wonderful thing that's ever happened to me."

"Atta girl, Ariel. If you ever need me, you know where to find me. This is a good thing you're doing. None of us will ever forget it. Can I have the rest of that hot dog?" Ariel shoved it in his mouth. Then she held out the ointment.

Fifteen minutes later she was back at work.

By noon of the following day, the "Hollywood Warriors," as the media referred to them, took a collective break for a hot meal. They were exhausted, weary to the bone, as they wolfed down the barbecued spareribs, T-bone steaks, and pan-fried potatoes. Iced tea and soda pop flowed like waterfalls.

Ariel found herself leaning up against one of the trailers with a can of soda and a cigarette. She wondered how she was going to continue for another two days. She listened as one of the media announced their progress over a loud-speaker.

"Ariel, are you okay?" Lex Sanders asked.

"Tired, but okay. How about you?" He was dirty and un-shaven, but the light in his eyes was for her and she knew it. She thought she'd never seen a more endearing face. She smiled. "I just heard that guy say the first five trucks are loaded and ready to go. How's it going at the other ranches?"

"Real good. There are some people here I'd like you to meet." He motioned with his hand and six men, all as dirty and unshaven as Lex, advanced with their hands outstretched. "These are the ranchers I told you about. They want to thank you personally for getting all these people here to help us. The lot of us would have gone under without your help."

One by one the men introduced themselves and shook hands. Ariel looked at her own hands with dismay. They were dirty, with blisters and broken nails. She gamely held out her hand and did her best not to wince as they shook it.

"Any news on Mr. Marino and the workers he pirated away? Are the feds here?" Ariel asked.

"They were. Actually they were helping pick a short while ago. They have this van with a Fax and all kinds of fancy equipment. One man is inside taking care of business. Don't know what happened to Navaro and Harry. I gave them a pretty accurate description and they were running a check. They're long gone, Ariel."

"I feel so stupid. How could I have fallen for their story?"

"The same way the rest of us did. We all thought we were dealing with a Chet Andrews mentality while in reality Marino was the guy pulling all the strings. So far, though, they can't tie him to the hijackings."

"Did your collectibles get here, Lex?"

"Yep. They're inside the house. Tim transferred them to a pickup and threw a tarp over it. His brother drove it in sometime last night. He left your rig parked on the side of the road ten miles away. Stan sent someone to fetch it. Smart man, deserves a bonus."

"Oh, Lex, I'm so glad you got them. I was so worried."

She threw her arms around him and hugged him. "You smell," she said, wrinkling her nose.

"You don't exactly smell like a wildflower yourself. When this is all over, let's hit the hot tub together. Hell, I'll even invite Snookie in."

"Really, Lex. That's the nicest thing anyone's said to me in days."

"If you give me half a chance, I can say nice things to you till the end of time. Hey, isn't that Charles Bronson over there?" His voice was full of awe.

"Sure looks like him. He moves pretty good for a senior, doesn't he? Bet this takes him back to the time he made that picture with all the watermelons."

"I saw that! Good movie. Time to get back to work, Ariel."

"Do I really smell, Lex?" she asked fretfully.

"Uh-huh."

The hours crawled by. It was way past sundown when Ariel, Snookie at her side, reached for a glass of iced tea. She carried it over to the side of one of Able Body's rigs and gingerly lowered herself to the ground. It was an effort to sip the iced tea, but her throat was so parched, she forced her aching arms to lift the drink to her lips. She set the glass down and motioned for Snookie to come closer. "I need to sleep for just a few minutes," she whispered to the dog. "I know you can't tell time, but do your best to wake me in thirty minutes." She was asleep the moment the words were out of her mouth. Snookie circled the sleeping figure once, twice, and then a third time before she lowered her huge body to stand guard. Her ears stood at attention when three men stopped a foot away. She listened to the voices, her ears picking up the different tones. Reassured, her head dropped to her paws. Her eyes were bright and alert.

"That's Ariel Hart. I used to see her on the lot from time to time. They say she's one nice lady. She always smiled at me or waved. I wouldn't have missed this for anything, even if I have to work with you, Van Damme."

"I think we should think about making a movie together, Seagal."

"Count me in, gentlemen. How about I write the script? We'll call it Rambo something or other, but Seagal, that pony-tail has to go."

"No way! Call my agent."

"Mine, too," Van Damme said.

"Who gets top billing?"

"We'll do it in alphabetical order."

"Sounds good."

The three superstars offered a jaunty salute in Ariel's direction. Snookie woofed softly.

They moved off, three of Hollywood's top box office draws, to do what they came to do—to help one of their own.

When Ariel woke, the moon was high in the sky. She looked at her watch. Damn, she'd slept for five hours. So much for a thirty-minute catnap. The moment she stretched to wakefulness, Snookie was on all fours. "So, you aren't perfect after all. I'll have to see if I can teach you how to tell time. When this is all over. My toenails hurt, my earlobes hurt. I damn well hurt. Time to get to work. I don't think I ever went to work at three-thirty in the morning." She dropped her head as far as she could before she did a slow rotation to relax her neck muscles.

On her way to the section of the grove where she was working, she met Lex, the back of his pickup full of crates of avocados. She waved. "Where have you been?" he yelled.

"Getting a manicure!" Ariel yelled back, never breaking her stride.

"Don't forget we have a date with my hot tub."

She spun on her heels and headed back to the pickup. Lex stretched his head out the window. "Kiss me." He did. "I liked that. Do it again." He did. "How'd you like that?"

"I can truthfully say I've never been kissed like that."

"Hrumph. You ain't seen nothing, Lex Sanders. Wait till I'm cooking on all cylinders. I hope you're up to it! Do I still smell?"

"Uh-huh. Listen, I normally operate on all twelve cylinders. What nobody knows but me, and now you, is I have a reserve. You, lady, are the one who ain't seen nothing yet!"

Ariel laughed all the way back to the avocado grove. "You know, Snookie, I hope the anticipation doesn't prove to be better than the actual event. I'm tingling. I don't think I ever tingled before. Maybe I'm numb from all this work." Snookie barked loudly, her tail swishing back and forth. "And then there's you. I really gotta figure out what to do with you. How can I go to bed with a man when you won't let him get near me?"

"I say you blindfold the damn dog," a delightful voice purred.

"Raquel! Is that the best advice you can come up with?"

"Short of hanging her on a hook, it is. She looks like one of those dogs who wouldn't think twice about going through fire or a plate glass window. I don't have that problem," she went on. "This is a good thing you're doing, Ariel. I'm glad to be a part of it. Hey, there was some guy looking for you a couple of hours ago. He looked a little scummier than the rest of us—pot belly, needed a shave real bad. And, he smelled. See you—gotta get this basket over to the truck. When this is all behind us let's do lunch."

"I'd like that."

Chet Andrews. Would he dare set foot on Lex's property? Yes, she answered herself. He definitely would dare. What did it mean? She took a minute to look around. How could she ever find him in this crowd? For all she knew he might have her in his sights this very minute. She shivered.

Ariel worked for another two hours before she paused for a coffee break. She watched the sun come up as she made small talk with two cameramen she'd worked with for years. She knew them well enough to ask after their families. "This is so wonderful, the way you all came out to help. I wish there was something I could do to show everyone how grateful I am."

"Since when does Hollywood need a thank you?" one of the men said.

"They deserve some kind of recognition for what they've been doing. The word *wonderful* doesn't quite cover it. You guys been taking pictures?"

"We got some real good shots. We'll make you up a video and send it on. Unless, of course, you're planning on coming back, in which case we'll show it to you on the big screen. It'll go in some basement. You gotta record everything in this business. You never know when you'll need it."

"Gee, suddenly it's quiet. Where is everyone?" Ariel asked.

"Getting ready to head out to the last grove. Most everyone is over by the cook tent getting fortified for the last fourteen hours. That's how long Mr. Sanders said it would take to finish up. Somebody said there's over 700 people here. That doesn't count the media, who, by the way, have been working just as hard as the rest of us. We gotta get going. See you around, Ariel. Give me a couple of weeks to get the video ready."

"She ain't got a couple of weeks," a surly voice said. "She ain't hardly got any time at all. Now ain't that true, Miss Ugly Movie Star?" a voice hissed from the semi-darkness, a voice only Ariel heard.

She didn't think it was possible to have her blood run cold, but it did. "Mr. Andrews. No, that isn't true at all. What are you doing here? What do you want?" She risked a glance to her left. The two cameramen were almost out of sight. There was no one around but her and Snookie. She licked at her dry lips.

"This is all your fault, you bitch. Everything was going just fine till you showed up. I was set for life until you fucked things up. You ain't gonna get away with it. My men have you and that dog in their sights. We'll plug him in a heartbeat."

"Easy, Snookie. Stay," Ariel said in what she hoped was a calming voice. "There are hundreds of people here. It's over. The real FBI is here. They know all about Drew Marino. Whatever you're planning now will only make it worse."

"It can't get any worse, bitch! You and that Mex, you did this. It don't matter no more. You're gonna get yours, right now, right here. And then that Mex gets his."

Keep him talking. Think, Ariel. This isn't a movie. He wants to kill you and Lex. He *will* kill you. She looked around to see if he was telling the truth about his backup. In the early morning light she thought she saw shadowy figures everywhere. Her hand went to Snookie's collar. Did she dare risk the dog's life? She moved to stand in front of the panting shepherd. Under her breath she whispered, "Find Lex and Dolly."

In the blink of an eye, Snookie was through the shrubbery, an elusive streak of speed that confused the man in front of her. Her shoulders slumped. Where would he shoot her? In the chest, in the head, in the gut?

"I'm just gonna pound you to a fucking pulp. I'm gonna smash up that movie star face of yours till there's nothing left. I'm not gonna kill you—you're gonna die on your own."

"Murder's murder. It doesn't matter how I die. They'll lock you away for the rest of your life, maybe send you to the gas chamber." For the life of her she couldn't remember if the state of California had the death penalty.

Andrews scoffed at her words.

Ariel did her best to focus inwardly as she sought to bring Master Mitsu's teachings to the forefront of her mind. Defense against multiple assailants. Pretend this is a movie, Ariel. You just stepped onto the set. Picture the page of the script, remember the lines you learned last night. Relax. Focus. Turn inward. Take the unorthodox "southpaw" stance. Depend on your right foot and hand. Remember, you have to be able to use both your left and right proficiently. Be cognizant of all your assailants' positions. Focus. Shit!

You can take this guy, Ariel. You're in shape. He's a tub of lard. Yeah, two hundred and fifty pounds of lard. I'm tired. My arms ache. My back hurts. He's going to try and bearhug you. You counter with a left front kick to his groin, step back, grab his arm, and flip him to the ground with a twist of his body. Finish him off with a straight punch to the face. If he gets up, go for the groin and throat-chop him with your left and punch with your right. If he's still moving, give him a side kick to his chest. Fini. Yeah, yeah, on the mats that's the way it goes, not here.

Ariel's breathing was ragged. She needed to be calm, focused. From somewhere, the outer perimeters, she sensed movement. Andrews' men? Lex? Her friends? She saw stiff arms and huge hands, big as ham hocks. He was wiggling them, trying to terrorize her. She dropped down to a semi-crouch, her own arms loose, her stance secure. Focus, Ariel. Don't take your eyes off him for a second. Snookie's bark almost made her lose her stance. Focus, Snookie is okay. She's bringing help.

Suddenly, she didn't want help. Her adrenaline kicked in. She turned her hands palm side up. She wiggled them backward. "Come and get me, Mr. Truck Driver." The air around her stirred. Fast movement. Not her friends. His people. They were leaving. It was just her and Andrews.

Focus. He's scared. More scared than you. He's pure fat. On your worst day you could take this guy. Master Mitsu said you could. Believe.

"Bitch!" Andrews roared.

"Bastard!" Ariel roared back as her right foot shot out, delivering a side kick to the side of Andrews' forward knee, causing him to drop. She moved like lightning, trying to drag him aside so she could stomp his face, the exact thing he promised to do to her. He wiggled free, was on his feet, his hamhock hands slashing the air between them. He landed a stiff blow to the side of her cheek and neck. She felt warmth on her cheek and knew the skin was split. She shook her head to clear it as she sidestepped and did a pirouette any ballerina would have been proud of, her forward foot jamming into his groin. From somewhere she heard applause. God, she had an audience. Don't think about that. Focus.

"Somebody do something!" It was Lex's voice. Again, she sensed movement. She knew instinctively that someone was holding him back. Focus.

"No!" It was her voice. She was going to finish this herself. She had to finish this. She moved. Andrews, for all his poundage, lunged, jabbing her in the chest. She reeled backward, stunned.

She heard Dolly's voice saying, ever so shakily, "She can do it. Leave her alone." And then even more quietly, "She *needs* to do this. I don't know why, but she does."

It was true.

"Ugly, fucking bitch! Your tinseltown didn't want any part of your ugly face. I'm gonna make it even more ugly."

She saw the pipe then. Maybe it was a stick. She wasn't sure. "You and what army? Who do you think you are? You hijack my trucks, steal my loads, and terrorize my workers. I played by the rules all my life and I'm not going to let some scumbag like you ruin these people who worked all their lives to make a living. Do you hear me, you piece of shit?" She heard the roar of applause. Andrews heard it, too. For just one brief second, he lost his focus.

Ariel took advantage of the brief second to spin away from him, her right foot swinging high and wide. She caught him on the side of the neck. She spun around again. This time her foot knocked the thick stick out of his hands.

She lost her focus then, doing everything she'd been taught not to do. "You son of a bitch! Terrorize my family and friends, will you? Never again. You steal a man's life and destroy it! I'll show you what the word *destroy* means. Family means nothing to you—you don't even take care of your own children. Mr. Able did it for you. No more!" Her breathing out of control, Ariel was in the air, on the ground, her legs and arms attacking like a swat team. She pummeled and battered, her mouth spewing words she didn't know she knew. When he was down, when she was sure he wouldn't land a blow in her direction, she called for Snookie. "Sit on him!" The shepherd growled, the skin peeling back from her canines.

"CUT!"

"What?" Ariel gasped as she staggered over to Dolly, who was running to meet her. "What's he talking about?"

"You know these Hollywood types," Dolly whispered. "Are you okay, Ariel? He got you good a couple of times. Your cheek is bleeding. You did good, real good. I think Lex needs to hear you say you're okay."

"I'm okay," she said wearily as she leaned into Lex's arms. "I bet I smell worse now, huh?"

"Who cares? There's a couple of people over there who want to shake your hand. I heard them say they couldn't have done it any better. Don't know if they'll own up to that or not."

"It doesn't matter."

"For a woman that wasn't bad at all."

"Thanks, Steven."

"I can give you a few pointers, but I don't think you need them."

"Thank you, Jean."

"We're making a film together. I'm going to write in a part for you. Picture this: you take on these two guys in a black lace leotard and spike-heeled shoes. Top billing. You up for it?"

"Not in this lifetime, Sly, but thanks for the offer."

"I have to sit down, Lex," Ariel said, slumping against him.

He was crooning soft words to her, words Dolly used from time to time when she was hurting emotionally. Words her mother never said. Suddenly she wanted to cry. Her shoulders started to shake.

"Let it go, Ariel. There's no shame in tears." She blubbered, because he said she could. He wiped her grimy cheeks with his dirty shirt sleeve. She cried harder. For the would-haves, the could-haves, the should-haves. Then she cried for sheer happiness.

"I'm okay now. Let's finish up this job and get all these wonderful people out of here. I need some peace and quiet."

"That won't be for a while, Ariel. Don't forget the party tomorrow," Lex reminded her.

"Oh, God, I forgot about that."

"I didn't. Tiki and the other women have it under control. Dolly is supervising the whole thing. These friends of yours deserve the best we have to offer. There's going to be all kinds of music. So, now what?"

"Back to work," she said. "I'll see you later."

"We still on for that hot tub assignation?"

"You bet!" She whistled for Snookie, who came on the run.

* * *

It was a party to end all parties. Truckloads of food from the finest caterers in Los Angeles seemed to disappear within seconds, only to be instantly replaced. Champagne fountains gurgled continuously. Everywhere, as far as the eye could see, people danced and laughed. It was like a thousand Christmases all rolled into one.

"Party's over," Lex said jovially. "You need to say goodbye to your friends."

"Yes, I need to do that. *Thank you* seems so inadequate."

"I don't think they even expect that, Ariel."

"I know that, too. Isn't it wonderful?"

Ariel stood next to Lex and the other ranchers, shaking each hand, saying all the grateful words she could think of. The responses warmed her soul. Words like 'anytime baby, just call, my pleasure, I'd do it all over again, glad to help, just call.' They were words of genuine sincerity. Tears dripped down her cheeks.

The last three guests to leave pulled up short. "So, how about an electric blue leotard with silver spangles and bright red spike-heeled shoes?"

"I told you, not in this lifetime. Thanks for coming."

Three sets of dark eyes stared at her. As one, they said, "Thanks for inviting us. You take care now."

When the huge gates were closed and locked, Lex drew her close. "We have a date."

"Yes, we do. What's all that noise?"

"The women beating up on their men. They came back last night."

"And of course you took them back."

"Of course."

"Okay, I'm going to get out of these clothes. I'll meet you at the hot tub." Her heart started to beat furiously. This was it. Finally. The moment she'd been thinking about for days, weeks, months.

Inside Lex's house, in the wide center hall, Ariel picked up her overnight bag she'd placed behind a giant cactus in a red clay pot. Toothbrush and makeup, plus underwear, clean jeans, and T-shirt for tomorrow. Her wish list and the little box she'd kept in her night table drawer for years and years. She picked up the bright red canvas bag and headed for the stairs.

Ariel tossed the overnight bag onto the bed in the room Tiki had assigned to her. She kicked off her shoes and struggled to peel off her panty hose. She couldn't help but notice how badly her hands were shaking. Her stomach rumbled alarmingly. Oh, God. She bolted for the bathroom, certain everything she'd eaten, which wasn't much, was going to come back up. Her eyes started to water, her shoulders shook. She was afraid. Pure and simple.

This was the end of the road in many ways. All those years, all those dreams, all those sheets of paper on her wish list. All geared to this point in time.

As she stared at her reflection, she talked to herself, the way she'd always done when she was preparing to do a scene. The end, always think about the end. Happy ever after. You and Lex will live happily ever after. What if . . . what if . . . How do I tell him? What will he think? Will he believe me? When you show him the braided ring, he'll believe you. Maybe he already knows. Maybe you should call him Felix. Maybe it will be better if you don't tell him. Maybe . . . maybe . . . maybe.

Get on with it, Ariel. He's waiting for you. Maybe he's going through the same emotional turmoil. Maybe . . . maybe . . . maybe.

The silvery sequined dress slithered to the floor. The flesh-colored body suit seemed to float in the air with static electricity before it landed on top of the dress. The heavy, spangled earrings thumped down on the vanity along with her bracelets.

The folded towel was buttercup yellow, so thick, so big, so luxurious, it felt better than a mink coat when she wrapped it around herself. She padded out to the bedroom where she fished for her thong sandals.

She was ready.

For her destiny.

Lex Sanders, aka Felix Sanchez, was her destiny. She'd known that from the day she walked up the mountain in her white dress.

She was almost to the door when she remembered the ring. Her heart skipped a beat when she slipped it on her finger.

Now she was ready.

Snookie was on her feet, her eyes following Ariel with adoration. She nuzzled her leg as they walked down the hall to the stairway. At the bottom of the steps, Ariel took a moment to crouch down and talk to the dog. "I want you to be good, Snookie. I want . . . I want you to go to sleep. There are times, like now, when you can relax and let Lex take over. He can take care of both of us. Trust me on this. I've waited all my life for this, Snookie, so help me out here." She hugged the dog, her arms circling the shepherd's neck. "I love you, too. I don't think I could have made it this far without you." Snookie licked at her cheeks. She tilted her head to the side and made a strange noise in her throat. She was on her feet then, nudging Ariel along the hallway that led to the outside patio and hot tub.

The cover was off the hot tub, spirals of steam wafting upward. The water bubbled and churned. Lex was nowhere to be seen. Next to the wrought iron table was Snookie's bed that Ariel had brought along with her. The shepherd looked around before she settled herself, her head in her paws, her eyes bright and alert.

Ariel let the fluffy yellow towel drop to the chair. A moment later she was in the water. She let out a whoop when she felt herself being pulled under. When she surfaced she was grinning from ear to ear. "Now, that's what I call romantic!" she gurgled. "How long have you been here?"

"That was my fourth underwater dip. I don't think I could have done it again. Look at my hands, they're all puckered up."

"As long as it's just your hands."

"Uh-huh," Lex drawled. "You could, of course, check it out."

"Uh-huh," Ariel drawled in return. "It's kind of hard to tell under the water."

"You could be right. Maybe after, when we get out, when we're listening to records on my jukebox, sipping our Cokes, and chewing our bubble gum."

"Now, why didn't I think of that?"

"Because . . . because . . . I'm smarter and I . . . Ariel, I have to ask you something. I think I'm right. I'm almost one hundred percent sure I'm right, but . . . it sort of crept up on me in degrees—one minute I was sure, the next minute I wasn't. It was all these little things . . . things I remembered, things I never forgot. Things I wouldn't allow myself to forget. See that folder over there on the table? There are things in it I want you to see."

"I don't need to see them, Lex. She held up her left hand, wiggling her fingers so he could see the braided ring. He brought his own left hand up from the depths of the water to show her his ring. Ariel smiled.

"How long have you known?" Lex asked hoarsely.

"For certain? Not that long. From day one, you reminded me of someone. When you laughed, the sound touched my soul. I wanted it to be you. I even hired a private detective to try and find you. The report was so devastating, I wanted to cry. When . . . when I had to make a decision about where to go and what do, after my surgery, this was the only place I could think of. I had been happy here. Because of you. I tried to locate you. You must believe that. But, when that lawyer I hired told me there was no record of our marriage, I fell apart. Then Hollywood beckoned. Oh, Lex, all those years. Wasted. I want to cry now, just thinking about that."

"Shhhh. It's okay. We found each other. Maybe you were meant to find me and me you. Think about all the good you've done since you've been here. We would have gone under without you and your friends."

"But the trouble *happened* because of me."

"No. You have to stop believing that. If it wasn't you, it would have been someone else. Only the names would have changed. You can't blame yourself for any of this. Listen, I have to ask you something. I heard about all those offers that were coming your way. They want you back. It's okay with me. I know this is the 90's and women want careers. I know I can be an understanding husband."

"I don't want to go back. I don't want to be Aggie Bixby, either. We aren't Aggie and Felix anymore. We're Ariel and Lex, and that's the way it should be. If Asa still wants to buy back the company, I'm willing to sell out. I'd love living here with you. I want to catch up, make up, for all those missing years."

"Do you mean it?"

"Damn right I mean it. Lex, at some point during the party, I heard that Marino split. Just up and left the ranch. Is it true?"

"As far as I know. He was a bloodsucker, but other than pirating away our workers and hiring Chet, he really didn't do anything wrong. He had nothing to do with the hijackings. He's probably back in New York bilking someone out of their mutual funds. He's one of those people who's always one step from the edge. Andrews is out of your hair. Life looks pretty rosy from where I'm sitting."

"What about Dolly and Tiki?"

"Tiki is ready to go home. I've given her a little house in the hills. She has lots and lots of grandchildren. The decision was hers. She's been talking about it for over a year. You need to know something else. My people are going to be damn disappointed if we don't get married here. They've got it all planned. The weddings last three days, sometimes four."

"Four days! What do you do for four days?"

"Eat. Sing. Dance. You get lots of presents you stick in a closet and give out at Christmastime to other people. It's fun. I'm up for it if you are. They aren't going to like that ring, though."

"Tough. I don't want another one. This will go with me to my grave. I mean that, Lex."

"I know you do, and I feel the same way. I don't know if you want to hear this or not, but I gotta tell you anyway. I'm puckering up. All over."

"Oh, God, let's get out then."

They did.

Dripping wet, they pressed their naked bodies, slick with water, together. Somehow, Ariel managed to reach behind her for the thirsty yellow towel that was half on the chair and half on the ground.

"Do you really think we can make it into the house, down the hall, up the stairs, down another hall to my room, wrapped in one skimpy towel?" Lex drawled.

"I was wondering about that. How about, I keep the towel and you run ahead?"

"How about I keep the towel and you go first? Look, I can solve this in a heartbeat." The towel was gone suddenly, sailing backward, landing in the hot tub. "We walk naked into your new home. Or, I can carry you over the threshhold. Your call, Mrs. Sanders."

"Carry me. All the way."

"My bed's turned down. Clean sheets. I even bought a bottle of gardenia perfume and spritzed the pillows. Hell, I spritzed the whole room. It's ready. I'm ready! Oh, Jesus," he bellowed suddenly, going down on one knee.

"What's wrong?"

"I think I threw my back out."

"What? I don't want to hear that! Do you hear me, Lex Sanders?"

"It's not any worse than your dog screwing up our evening. By the way, where is that dog of yours?"

"Sleeping. As in sound asleep. For the night. Down by the hot tub. Till morning. That's like six hours away. Six hours! Do you have any idea what we could do in six hours?"

"Tell me!"

Ariel squatted down next to him. She told him in great detail. He was on his feet in a flash, towering over her, his eyes dancing with merriment. "I just wanted to give you a taste of your own medicine."

They were in the bed then, thrashing and laughing, tickling, kissing, romping, having the time of their lives. "I've been known to scream," Ariel said and laughed.

"Can't be worse than my bellowing. House is empty. We can do whatever we want."

"We can't wake Snookie up."

"God, no!"

"Can you make love to me the way you did the first time? Do you remember all the things we did and said? I remember everything."

"So do I. We aren't those same people anymore, Ariel. Wait a minute," Lex said, swinging his legs over the side of the bed. "I had a plan. Get up. Put some clothes on. We're going to do this right."

"Now?"

He was already pulling on his jeans and shirt. Her eyes wide, Ariel pranced down the hall to the room she'd been in earlier. She didn't bother with underwear. She pulled on her jeans and shirt and met Lex in the hall at the top of the steps.

"C'mon," he said, taking her by the hand.

In his office the Wurlitzer stood out like a machine from outer space. She smiled. The dream. Now, she understood. "Want a Coke? Some bubble gum?"

"Yeah. Three red bubble gums."

"No, you need at least six in your mouth. You need to work up a good spit. Then you drink the Coke. We can blow bubbles. You any good at that?"

Ariel thought about her pricey porcelain and how gum stuck to her caps. "I can try."

"Can I buy you a Coke?"

"Absolutely."

"Wanna dance?"

"With the Coke and gum or without?"

"I don't know. I never did this before. What do you think?"

Ariel set her soda down and stuck the gumballs in her pocket. "I would very much like to dance with you, with your arms around me. Then, when we're finished dancing, I think you should light that fireplace and buy me a Coke and some gum. How does that sound?"

"Is that how they did it back then?"

She wanted to tell him she was as green about teenage protocol as he was, but instead she said, "If memory serves me right, it is. I was never allowed to hang out the way the other kids did. Does it really make a difference?"

"Yeah, it does. I've waited for this moment all my life. I want it to be right."

Ariel sat down, cross legged, on the floor. "Let's talk about it. We've both seen movies on how it's done. We should do whatever feels right to you . . . to us."

"Do you think I'm crazy, Ariel?"

"Oh, no, Lex. Not at all. This is your dream. I want it to be right for you. We can't move on until you're happy with your memory. It's too important. To both of us. I'm just so delighted to be a part of it. I want to be a part of everything in your life from now on. So, are you going to ask me to dance?"

"I'm not a very good dancer. And, I'm in my bare feet. Pick a song, Ariel. I would have let you pick the tune if this happened thirty years ago."

"Really?"

"Of course. I was always a gentleman."

"You were, Lex. That was one of the things I loved about you. You were always so gallant. Of course, at the time, I really didn't know what *gallant* meant. The money, please." Lex handed her a dime. She dropped it into the slot and pressed a button. She turned to step into Lex's arms as Hank Williams's golden voice gave life to "Your Cheating Heart."

At first they were all over each other's feet as they circled the room. Then they both relaxed at the same moment, their bodies glued to one another. "You fit just right in my arms," Lex said.

"I was just going to say the same thing. Boy, this dancing is making me thirsty. How about buying me a Coke? I'd like some bubble gum, too, if you have enough money," Ariel said shyly.

Lex threw his head back and laughed. "My pleasure." He dropped money into the slot and waited for the Coke to settle into the opening. He plucked it free, uncapped it, and handed it over with a flourish. Then he bought himself one.

"We should make a toast," he said. "Think, Ariel, what should we drink to?"

"Let's drink to Hollywood. If it wasn't for Hollywood, we wouldn't have found each other. Then we can make a second toast to long life and happiness."

"I like that," Lex said. They clinked bottles before they each took a healthy swig. "Jeez, two gulps and it's gone. Guess when we were kids we didn't think about that, huh?"

"I wasn't allowed too many sweets. My mother said they'd rot my teeth. I can't wait for those bubble gums you promised. I want all red ones."

When they sat down by the fire again, Lex had two Cokes under his arm and a fist of the colorful little gumballs. "Let's see how many we can chew at one time."

Later, relaxing against a pile of pillows, the juke box playing softly in the background, Ariel said, "That was fun. Was it all you expected it to be?"

"And more. Because of you. Without you, I probably would have played the juke once, drank one Coke, and chewed a few gumballs. Then I probably wouldn't have done it again. This was perfect. We have a lot of catching up to do."

"What I want to know is when are we going to bed?" Ariel said, blowing a bubble the size of a grapefruit in his face.

Lex, in turn, blew a bubble almost the same size. He moved slightly so that the two bubbles were actually touching. Their eyes locked just as the bubbles burst. Sticky, pink gum plastered both their faces. Ariel burst out laughing as she tried to peel it off. "I think you should lick it off, chew it off, something. You said this was going to be fun. Is this?"

"I'm having a hell of a time." Suddenly his breathing was ragged and husky. He fell back against the pillows, taking her with him. He found her eager mouth, returning her kisses with a bittersweet ardor. Hers were the softest lips he'd ever kissed. His kisses wandered over the planes of her face, to the dimple in her chin, in the waterfall of silvery hair.

His hands caressed her body, finding it as beautiful as he remembered. He drew in his breath, sighing in contentment as womanly curves fit snugly against manly muscle.

Ariel exerted pressure against him, forcing him to his back where she followed, her knees tightly clamped to his sides. She looked down into the face that was as dear to her as it had been once, so long ago. Love swelled deep inside her. Her hair created a curtain as she bent to kiss him . . . long, loving kisses meant to touch the soul and stir the senses.

Lex smiled up at her when he felt himself being taken within her. This was Aggie, the Aggie he loved . . . his equal, sharing the best of herself, giving, always giving.

Their joining was loving, tender, and filled with joy. It had been too long since they had been together this way, equally hungry for what each could bring to the other.

"Ahhh," Lex said.

"Oh my," Ariel said as she snuggled into the nest he made of his arms.

The only sound in the private room Lex had never shared before was the rustling of their bodies against the pillows and the soft sound of their murmurings. Ariel nestled against him, burrowing her head into the hollow of his neck, the silky strands of her hair falling over his shoulder. She breathed the scent of him, mingled with the fragrance of her own perfume. Her fingers teased the light furring of his chest hairs; her leg, thrown intimately over his, felt the lean, sinewy muscle of his thigh.

They were like light and shadow, she silvered, the color of moonlight, and he dark, like the night. He held her, gentle hands soothing her, bringing her back down from erotic heights.

It was the best of all times, these moments after making love, when all the barriers were down and satiny skin melted into masculine hardness. This closeness was the true communion of lovers who had brought peace and satisfaction to one another.

Ariel burrowed deeper into Lex's arms. He drew her close, his arms tight and protective. He loved this woman. He nuzzled the softness of her neck.

She sensed the immediate change in him and allowed herself to be carried with it. One moment his arms cradled her, soothing her, the next they became her prison, hard, strong, inescapable.

His hands were in her hair, on her breasts, on the soft flesh of her inner thighs. He stirred her, demanded of her, rewarded her with the adoring attention of his lips to those territories his hands had already claimed. And when he possessed her it was with a joyful abandon that evoked a like response in her—hard, fast, then slower and sweeter.

She murmured her pleasure and gave him the caresses he loved. Release was there, within their grasp, but like two moths romancing a flame, they played in the heat and postponed the exquisite instant when they would plunge into the inferno.

"Ahhh," Lex said.

"Oh my," Ariel said.

"Woof," Snookie barked softly.

"Ahhh," Lex said.

"Love me, love my dog," Ariel said.

"Forever and ever," Lex said.

"And then some. C'mere, Snookie."

The shepherd trotted over to the pile of cushions. She lowered her massive head and licked Lex's face. Then she walked around to Ariel's side and licked her face. She woofed once, then twice. They watched as she trotted toward the door. She inched it closer to the jamb, allowing just enough room to get out into the hallway.

"Ahhh," Lex said.

"Guess that makes us official," Ariel said.

"Guess so," he said as he smothered her face with kisses.

"It's wonderful. We get to love again, and again, and again," Ariel said.

Chapter Twelve

"It's sad when you pack up belongings," Ariel said. "At least this time, I know it's for good. Why do I feel like we just did this? I wish somebody would tell me where this stuff comes from."

"You're a pack rat. You have your first pair of knee socks. Ariel, I need to talk to you. Serious stuff. Don't turn away from me. We can't . . . avoid this . . . Both of us know it isn't working. I don't like Bonsall. You and Lex don't need me, you have each other. That's okay, it's the way it's supposed to be. I'm selfish, I want things to be the way they've been for the past thirty-five years. It can't be, and I'm realist enough to know it. You know it, too, you just don't want to look it in the eye and deal with it."

"Dolly, what will you do? What's wrong with Bonsall? Mr. Able said you could stay on here and work that goldarn computer and he's willing to pay you handsomely. You could drive down every day. I wouldn't make demands on you, Dolly. Please . . . don't go."

"Shhh," Dolly said, taking Ariel in her arms. "You know better than anyone that nothing in this life is forever. This is your time, Ariel, to be the wife you always wanted to be with the man you love. He needs you. You'll have each other. We'll always be friends, that will never change. I'll be a phone call away. We'll visit. I'll be back for your wedding and yes, I'm going to be your matron of honor. I think it's wonderful that you two are getting married all over again."

"Please, Dolly, don't go. I'll try and spend more time with you. Lex will understand." Ariel hated herself for begging, for showing her raw emotions.

"Don't you see . . . did you hear what you just said? You said you would try. Lex is your top priority now, not me. Of course he'd understand because he is a good, kind, caring man. But, it will get old real quick. There are no choices here, Ariel, no options. It's what it is." Dolly continued to cradle her best friend in the whole world, crooning softly.

"Dolly . . ."

"Don't even think about it, Ariel. You cannot choose between Lex and me. I'm okay with this."

"You still haven't told me where you're going. God, Dolly, this is worse than . . . than having someone die. You aren't getting any younger. You're almost . . ."

"Sixty! Go ahead, Ariel, say it. It's a damn number, and let me tell you something else. One of the stunt coordinators who came to help pick the avocados has been calling me. Actually, I kind of like him. He's my age and he has a little house up in the hills. Okay, it's a big house up in the hills. The property has a cottage on it and he's promised me he'll rent it to Carla, who, by the way, just snagged herself a real good role on one of those nighttime soaps. I'm going to be taking care of both of them. You know, cooking, cleaning . . . whatever. I have enough money put by so I'll be comfortable. I know how to be frugal, and in a few years I can draw on my social security."

Ariel flopped down on the side of the bed. Dolly was right, nothing was forever. How stupid she was to think things would remain the same. Selfish, too. She stared at her dearest friend and wondered if she had to make a choice, who she would choose, Dolly or Lex. She shook her head to clear her thoughts. "So you're going to take care of Carla and what's-his-name. Is it really what you want, Dolly? If it is, then I can accept it. I don't want you to settle for something as a way out. We can talk this to death and come up with something. I want you to be happy. If you aren't happy, I can't be happy. That's the bottom line."

"It sounds, Ariel, like you don't believe what I'm telling you," Dolly said with an edge to her voice.

"Of course I believe you. In all our years together, I never once questioned anything you said, and you damn well know it. If you're having second thoughts, now is the time to voice them so we can work it out. *We,* Dolly. You and me. There wasn't anything we couldn't settle or solve when we both worked at it."

"I like Max. He likes me. Who knows, maybe it will lead to something. I think I'd like it if it did go somewhere. You should see his house, Ariel, it's gorgeous. He has a big garden, grows his own vegetables, and he has all kinds of berry bushes and he loves blackberry pie. We have a lot in common. We both know the movie business. He doesn't cat around. You have to be careful today."

"If he's so damn wonderful, why do you have to clean up after him? Why can't you get an apartment and date him? Just how old *is* this guy? Another thing, Dolly, old men are usually looking for someone to take care of them in their twilight years. They're looking for nurses! I read that in . . . in something."

"So what!! He's agreed to pay me $750 a week. He says he'll contribute to my IRA's. He'll be paying for my social security and health care and boy, are they good benefits. He has his own little business he hires his stuntmen and provides all kinds of good stuff for them. I'll be on the payroll. What more could I ask for? Plus, I get to do all the cooking and baking I want to do. You know how I love to watch men eat."

"What's this paragon of virtue's name?" Ariel asked sourly.

"Max Petrie."

"What about Carla?"

"She's doing all right. She told me to tell you she asked for a sizable advance so she can pay you back some of the money she owes you. She held out for some big bucks and she got it. She said it was the only way she could ever get enough money together to repay you. I'm real proud of her. Are you proud of her, Ariel?"

Ariel burst into tears. "Of course," she whispered. "I told her more than once she didn't have to pay me back. I helped her because I wanted to and because she needed help and no one else cared. I never expected to be paid back. She's my friend, for God's sake. I don't want her money—tell her to bank it. She has no nest egg at all."

"You have to take it, Ariel. It's important to Carla to repay you. You're just upset that she doesn't need you anymore. You should be happy for her, and for me. Look at us—you, me, Carla—we're all coming out on top. My big question is, what are you going to do all day up in Bonsall? You know, after Lex goes off to work. How are you going to fill your hours? Did you get that far in your thinking, Ariel?"

Ariel listened to the edge creeping back into Dolly's voice. "No, I haven't given it a whole lot of thought. You rammed me between the eyes with your decision. I'm trying to sell this business back to Mr. Able, trying to get this house ready to be put back on the market, and then there's my wedding. It's turning into some kind of national event. If you want something off the top of my head, I've thought, a little, about opening a small acting studio in town. I also thought, a little, about maybe opening a children's theatre. They're just thoughts at this time, but they do keep coming back so I know I'll pursue something. I'm not going to stagnate on the ranch. It won't be an all-day thing-weekends, four or five hours a day. Lex offered to help. It's something we can do together if we decide to go ahead with it."

Dolly stared at her for a long time. When she was satisfied that Ariel was telling the truth, she grinned from ear to ear. "That makes me feel a little better about leaving. I'd hate to think of you turning into some dumb, fat, happy housewife eating bonbons and watching your old movies all day long."

"Not likely. I wish you were staying long enough to give me some cooking lessons. That pile of cookbooks on the counter scares the hell out of me."

"Doesn't Lex like egg and ketchup sandwiches?" Dolly teased.

"If you put refried beans on the top, he does. Actually, he'll eat anything. He's not a bit fussy."

"That's good, Ariel, because you can't cook worth a damn even using a cookbook. You could hire someone."

"I thought about that. Tiki promised to come out and help. There's always Lean Cuisine. God, Dolly, I'm going to miss you. You aren't even gone and I feel so . . . so . . . alone. So many years, Dolly. I wish . . . I wish I knew what the future holds for both of us. Scratch that, I don't want to know. Besides, I'm tired of wishing my life away."

"Now, that's the Ariel I know and love. C'mon, let's get cracking here. If we put some gusto into it, we can get this done in another hour and haul it all up to Bonsall."

"What am I going to do with all this stuff, Dolly? Lex's house is furnished. His stuff is all so . . . manly. There isn't a doodad in the whole place. I need a few ruffles and frills. He said I could redecorate, but I think he was . . . he likes things the way they are."

"Then why don't you keep this house instead of selling it?

You could come down here whenever ranch life . . . you know, gets to be too much. You spent a fortune decorating this place. It's not like you need the money. This is the 90's, you know. Women do things like this all the time. They don't want to give up what they worked for all their lives, not to mention their identities."

"I have thought about it. However, while Lex didn't come right out and say so, I know he would see it as temporary on my part. Don't ask me how I know this, I just do. Both his feet are firmly planted in another decade and I don't even know which decade it is. Part of me wants to keep things the way they are, the other part—the part that loves Lex heart and soul—wants me to give it all up so I can snuggle in with him. God, did you hear what I just said? I'm not making a decision today. Like Scarlett, I'll worry about that tomorrow."

"Tomorrow is going to come sooner than you think, Ariel."

"I love you, Dolly, I really do."

"And I love you, Ariel Hart Sanders."

Ariel smiled through her tears, knowing Dolly's eyes were as wet as her own.

"This is . . . ah . . . really . . . tasty," Lex said.

"You're lying, Lex. It's awful. I never said I could cook. In fact, I made a point of telling you I couldn't and you said, and this is a direct quote, we'll live on love. It's meatloaf. That was your next question, wasn't it?"

"I'm not complaining. This is my second slice. What's this green stuff?"

"Brussels sprouts. Dolly said I should cut up onion and celery, but we didn't have any, so I substituted. She said that's what makes a good cook. I don't like to cook, so that means I'll never be a good cook. I know the rice is sticky. Dolly said I was to put my finger in the water up to my knuckle. She didn't say which knuckle. I guess it was the first one." She was so agitated she started to cry when Snookie wouldn't touch the meatloaf on her plate.

"Ariel, honey, it doesn't matter. We can eat frozen food. It isn't important to me. We can hire a cook. Now," he said, moving his chair closer to hers. "Now, tell me what's really wrong. It's Dolly, isn't it? Call her, Ariel."

"I already called her seven times today. I can't call her again. Am I so insecure I can't get by without my friend? I want to be happy for her. Look at Snookie! She won't eat, she doesn't want to play. She misses Dolly, too."

"Let's face facts here, Ariel. Snookie isn't eating because she doesn't like your cooking. That will change someday. They have gourmet dog food. I'm sure she misses Dolly. And the reason she isn't playing is because . . . she's . . . I wasn't going to tell you this until Frankie confirmed it, but your dog is in the family way."

"No! How'd that happen?" Ariel gasped.

"In the usual way," Lex drawled.

"Oh, my God, I have to call Dolly."

"There you go! Now you have a reason to call her. Go for it, Ariel."

She was off the chair like a shot, punching out Dolly's number, a smile on her face from ear to ear.

Lex leaned back in his chair, his eyes misty with pain as he watched his animated lover talk to Dolly. He winced when he heard her say, "Of course you can be the godmother and yes, you get the pick of the litter. When can you come down? That's wonderful. Bring some food. The meatloaf was awful, but Lex ate two slices. I'll be here, Dolly.

"She's coming down tomorrow. It's a whole month since I've seen her. She said she'd stay overnight and then she'll be back in time for our June wedding. Ohhhh, life is good, isn't it, Lex?"

"The best," he said quietly. "Let's go for a walk. Snookie can use the exercise."

Twenty minutes into the walk, Lex said, "Are you happy, Ariel?"

"Of course I'm happy. But I do miss Dolly. I don't expect you to understand, but try. Please. It's important to me."

"If you had to make a choice, Ariel, could you do it?"

"Dolly asked me the same thing. I didn't have an answer for her, either. If you absolutely must have an answer, the best I can come up with is, I'd walk away from both of you. You both mean so much to me, each in a different way. I just wish she was a little closer. You know, a neighbor. I never knew my neighbors. I guess it's my fault—I never had the time to explore friendships. I have this feeling, Lex, that Dolly isn't happy. She'll never admit it. She liked Bonsall, she told me so, then she changed her mind. In the beginning, I had no time for her, and I think she took it as rejection. I know her so well. This was a way for all of us to save face, whatever the hell that means."

"Let's put our heads together and see if there isn't a way to get her back here."

"Really, Lex, do you think . . . is it possible?"

"Asa's younger brother, recently widowed these past ten years—at least that's the way Asa puts it—is coming to San Diego to help Asa out at the trucking company. Maggie doesn't want any part of it so Pete said he'd pitch in. Asa says he's a cranky curmudgeon, just what Dolly needs. Maybe we could sort of . . . you know . . . make her forget Max. How do you know she's not happy?"

"I can hear it in her voice. She's putting up a real good front. Don't forget, I know Dolly better than anyone in the world. Besides, Carla called and said Dolly was miserable and she made me promise not to tell she called."

"It has to look like it's Dolly's idea to come back," Lex said.

"Lex, look at me. Do you . . . what I'm trying to say is . . . are you . . . were you . . . ?"

"Jealous? Hell, no. I love Dolly. I accepted from the gitgo that you were the banana and she was the peel. I never wanted to change that. Even if I could, I wouldn't. I know how important friends are. I just want you to be happy, Ariel. If you're happy, I'm happy. Let's go back and make a plan." He kept smacking his hands together dramatically.

"I love you, Lex. I really do," Ariel said, snuggling against him, Snookie at her side.

"I love you more.

"That's the right answer."

"How many puppies do you think Snookie will have?"

"Probably around six."

"Can I keep them all except for the one Dolly wants?"

"Absolutely. What's five more dogs?"

"See, that's why I love you," Ariel beamed.

"Is that the only reason?"

"You're good in bed," she giggled.

"How good?"

She was still giggling. "Real good."

"Let's make love on the front porch. Like now."

"On the swing?"

"Those who know me call me a swinging fool." He had her in his arms a second later.

"Ooohhh, I like this, buck naked on a slatted swing," Ariel laughed.

"You ain't seen nothin' yet, lady."

"Show me."

He did.

* * *

On the day of Ariel and Lex's wedding, Dolly arrived, bag and baggage. "Can I come back, Ariel? Is there still a place here for me? Will Lex let me stay? Will he care?"

"Lex!" Ariel shouted.

"My God, what's wrong?" Lex roared as he literally tumbled down the steps, his hair on end.

"Dolly's back. She wants to know if she can stay. She also wants to know if you mind."

"Are you here for good?" Lex asked sternly.

"Forever and ever." Dolly said.

A second later Lex was swinging her around the kitchen, whooping about eating like a normal person, having clothes that matched, and towels that didn't slide off his body. "Name your price. Who cares? Whatever you want, it's yours. When can you start?"

"Now! How about some blueberry pancakes, sausage, scrambled eggs, Kona coffee with real cream, and melon."

"Thank you, God," Lex said, raising his eyes upward. "Quick, Ariel, let's take a shower before she changes her mind."

"Dolly, did something happen?" Ariel called over her shoulder.

"Damn right something happened. Carla snatched Max right from under my nose. I didn't really like him all that much—it was the way she did it. The principle of the whole thing. I made thirty gallons of spaghetti and left it on top of the stove. It was my going away present. All he eats is spaghetti and melon with salt on it. There was no challenge! None at all! Can you believe that Carla?" She banged the frying pan on top of the stove to make her point.

"Why are you laughing, Lex?" Ariel said as she stepped into the shower with him. "We're getting married today—you aren't supposed to see me. Now there aren't going to be any surprises. Why are you looking at me like that?"

"I'm trying to decide if I want to make love or eat Dolly's breakfast."

"No contest. Hurry up, wash my back and I'll wash yours. Breakfast beckons. Tell the truth, why were you laughing? You had something to do with that, didn't you? I get it—that's where you went last week. You arranged all of this. What'd you do, Lex?"

"I offered Carla ten grand to steal Max away from Dolly. In the end I had to pay her fifteen because she said he was an old coot and couldn't get it up. Plus, she said she hates spaghetti. She told me Dolly was sorry the day she moved in and was so miserable all she did was cry and wait for your phone calls."

"Oh, Lex, how wonderful of you to do that for me and Dolly."

"I know. Now, don't give it away."

"Never in a million years."

"Real, honest-to-God food. Hurry up, Ariel."

"I can't wait, either. The hell with the shoes," she grumbled as she raced after Lex. They pulled up short when they saw guests in their kitchen.

"Asa, you're early."

"Yep. Came up early to help pitch the tents. This is my brother, Pete. Dolly invited us for breakfast. I hope that's okay."

"Of course," Ariel and Lex chorused.

The three of them watched as the grizzled Pete proceeded to tell Dolly how to improve her pancakes. "Homely as a mud fence," Asa stage whispered. Lex nodded. Ariel just stared at her friend, who was fawning over the bearded Pete. Nobody ever told Dolly how to cook, but not only was she listening, she was following Pete's instructions.

"I think you just created a damn monster," Ariel whispered. "Where does he live?" she demanded of Asa.

"For now, with me. Who knows where he'll light later on. Maybe hereabouts."

"It better be hereabouts or I'm calling off our deal," Ariel hissed.

"Yeah. We're not giving her up, even to your brother, Asa," Lex said, stuffing his mouth with pancakes. "God, these are good. You outdid yourself, Dolly. These are better than the ones you usually make."

"Do you think so?" Dolly asked sweetly.

Pete cackled. "Told you so, Miss Dolly."

Lex and Ariel both mouthed the words *Miss Dolly* to Asa, who merely shrugged.

"We have so much work to do. The wedding's at four," Ariel said.

"It looked like things were under control when I drove up," Dolly said, her eyes on Pete as she handed him a plate piled high with sausage and bacon.

"He likes to eat," Asa said. "He's real good at cleaning up, too."

"Is he housebroken?" Ariel demanded.

"That, too," Asa drawled. "My Maggie said he knows how to treat a lady."

"Speaking of Maggie, where is she?" Lex asked.

"Sorry to say, she won't be here. She got a rush order for her jewelry and she had to go back to Hawaii yesterday. Sends her best. Present is on the dining room table."

Lex rolled his eyes, as did Asa.

"Now what?" Ariel asked.

"Now we sit and watch as all those people out there get our wedding ready. The band will be here soon. The food is under control, thanks to Tiki and her relatives. I saw the flowers arriving as we were coming down the stairs. The padre will show up about three o'clock. The liquor arrived last night. The only thing left to do is set the tents up. As I said, it's under control."

"Then I'm going upstairs. When you see me next I'll be in my wedding gear."

"I can't wait," Lex said, leering at her. "Listen, I have something I have to do. I'll be back in a little while, okay?"

"Sure." Ariel stood on tiptoe and kissed him soundly. "I'm really going to like being Mrs. Sanders. The official version. Lex, thanks for . . . you know . . . getting Dolly back and all. What you did just makes me love you all the more."

"Ariel, I'd do anything for you. Please believe that."

"I do. God, we're so lucky, so blessed. Go on, but make sure you get back on time."

"Ah . . . excuse me. Dolly, I'm going upstairs. When you have time, no rush at all, come up and . . . help me."

"Sure thing, Ariel. Just let me clean up here. Pete has been telling me that he used to be a rodeo rider, among other things. He's going to teach me how to lasso. Maybe Snookie will let me practice on her. You go ahead, Ariel. I'll fetch us some coffee when I get through here. I'm dying to see that wedding dress. All the way from Belgium. Lordy, Lordy, Ariel, when you do things you do them up right. Does it really have two thousand seed pearls?"

"They said it does. Maybe we can count them . . . together. I think I hear Asa calling you, Pete."

"I think I hear him, too. Just hate to leave this little lady's company is all. You call me for lunch, you hear?"

"We're having lunch?" Ariel asked in surprise. "It's eleven o'clock."

"Pete has to eat lots of little meals, he has a . . . condition."

"Oh," Ariel heard herself saying.

An hour later Ariel held out her arms to Dolly. "We're

both so foolish. I was so miserable, Dolly. I'm sorry things didn't work out for you, but I'm happy you're back. I think you saw Lex's reaction. Things happen for a reason. You always told me that, Dolly, so I believe it. You're here, you met Pete, and if I'm any judge, he looks like he might be interested in you. Oh, Dolly, things are working out, for all of us."

"Ariel, I don't want your feelings toward Carla to change. Like you said, things happen for a reason. She needs someone. I brought her present. She really wanted to come, but the whole cast went to Vermont on location. I imagine she'll call you sometime today."

"No regrets about what's-his-name."

"Are you kidding? That man had two faces. I wanted somebody, Ariel. Do you understand that?"

"Of course. You can't make it happen, though, Dolly. Take today as a perfect example. You met Pete. Who's to say if he's for you? Time will tell, and you'll be the first to know. All I want is for you to be happy. Listen, if you promise not to let Lex know, I'll show you something. Dolly, this man is so wonderful. I cannot tell you how good and kind he is. C'mon, we can sneak out the side door. We have plenty of time. I found it by accident. Actually, Snookie found it. By the way, where is she?"

"Under your bed. Too many people, too much noise. What are you going to show me?"

"You'll see. I wasn't supposed to see it. Lex wanted it to be a surprise. I couldn't figure it out at first. You're gonna love it."

They ran around the side of the house, down and around the stable and garage to a newly landscaped area. "It's behind those trees and bushes."

"What is it? Oh, my gosh, it looks like a Hansel and Gretel cottage. Is it a guest house? It's gorgeous. Look at all those flowers. And it has a front porch with two rocking chairs. Did Lex build this?"

"Every stick, every stone. He did it for me . . . for you, Dolly. It was his way of saying he understood our friendship. He didn't build it so you wouldn't live in our house. He heard you say one of the things you always regretted was that you never had a little house of your own. You should see the inside. He built a little potting shed in the back for all your gardening stuff. You even have your own wheelbarrow. It's purple. And pink and yellow gardening tools and a pair of those high green leather boots. He thought of everything. Your kitchen is a dream. It's got everything. Those super-duper pots and pans that cost a fortune. Two wall ovens, two stove tops, an oversize fridge. You have your own washer, dryer, and dishwasher. It's as state-of-the-art as you can get. Get this—there's a Jacuzzi and a sitdown shower. And a bidet! It washes your tush with warm water. You ready to see it?"

"God, yes. Are you sure it's for me? I don't believe this."

"The deed is on the kitchen counter. You know I can't keep a secret from you. Don't tell Lex, okay?"

"I promise."

"Oh, Dolly, I can just see you here with one of Snookie's pups. Maybe even Pete. It's big enough for a couple. Lex said he was going to put up a white picket fence, but he thought that might be stretching things. He said he'd put it up if you want it. Do you really like it, Dolly?"

"Ariel, I don't know what to say," Dolly gasped as she walked around her new house. "A coatrack. An umbrella stand. Would you look at that fireplace. Lordy, Lordy, I could crawl in there. A circular oak staircase! Lex did all this?" she asked in awe.

"He likes to work with his hands. It's magnificent, isn't it?"

"Oh, yes. Starched organdy curtains in the kitchen. I always wanted them. Pinch me, Ariel. Not so hard! How am I going to pretend I didn't see this when Lex gets around to telling me about it?"

"Something will come to you. Are we lucky or what, Dolly?"

"Yes, we are. *Thank you* doesn't quite cover this."

"It'll do, Dolly. Come on, we better get back. Did you see your name on the doorbell?"

"I sure did. Was he building this when I left?"

"Yeah. He said he started it the day he met us. He admitted he wasn't sure why he was doing it. He was devastated when you left, but he always finishes what he starts. That man just never gives up. I think he knew you'd come back. I even think he missed you as much as I did. We talked about you all the time."

Dolly wrapped her arms around Ariel. "Thank you for being my friend. C'mon, I want to see what two thousand seed pearls look like. Will you be able to walk? Won't it be heavy?"

"Not really. At first I was just going to wear a white summer suit, but Lex wanted the whole nine yards. I did, too, but I was afraid I might look . . . you know, silly and foolish, at my age."

"Who cares?"

"Yeah, who cares?" Ariel said as she linked arms with Dolly.

"It's breathtaking," Dolly said as she fingered the material of Ariel's wedding gown. "It's time for you to start thinking about getting ready. What kind of bubble bath do you want?"

"Gardenia."

"I'll get you a cup of black rum tea to drink while you're soaking. Are you going to be able to manage your hair?"

"I'm piling it on top of my head. I got a manicure and pedicure yesterday. My garter is on the dresser, my shoes

are in the closet. Yep, I'm ready to become Mrs. Lex Sanders for the second time. You know what I mean. You like
that Pete guy?"

"I might."

"That's good enough for me, Dolly. It's what it is, okay?"

"Okay. Two cups of black rum tea coming up."

"You look like a movie star. It's so perfect, Ariel. It was a
wise choice. The gardenia bouquet will finish it off to perfection. I can't say I'm real crazy about your headpiece,
though."

"Me, either. I was looking for something . . . you know,
kind of special, and this is the best I could come up with. It's
too . . . too poufy. What's that noise?"

"What noise?" Dolly asked.

"It sounds like someone's crying." Both women stopped,
their eyes going to the bottom of the bed ruffle. Dolly dropped
to her knees. "It's Snookie, I think she's ready to have her
pups or something else is wrong. I don't know much about
dogs having puppies."

"I don't, either," Ariel wailed. "Quick, see if Frankie is
here. What time is it?"

"Five minutes of four," Dolly called over her shoulder.

"Stall. If you see Lex, send him here, please."

"Ariel, it's bad luck for the groom to see the bride before
the wedding. Okay, okay, I'm going."

"I took a shower with the groom this morning. Go! Go!"

On her knees, Ariel tried to cradle the shepherd's head. She
crooned softly to the dog, stroking her heaving stomach. "It's
going to be okay, girl. Easy, easy. Soon you're going to be a
mother and you'll forget the pain. That's what they tell mothers about to give birth. I'm just repeating what I heard. I was
never a mother, Snookie, so I don't know if it's true or not.
Everything is going to be all right. I promise. Everything *has*

to be all right. We're getting you . . . fixed when this is over. Shhh, maybe some music. Music lulls the soul." Ariel scrambled on her hands and knees over to the stereo unit and flicked the switch. She pushed another button and Frank Sinatra's mellow voice filled the room. "Frank's good," Ariel muttered as she scrambled back to the panting dog. She watched as hundreds of little pearls scattered across the floor. She then noticed the rip in the hem of the gown where her heel caught in it. A tear down the side made her wince. She caught sight of her reflection in the floor-length mirror. Her headpiece was askew, one shoulder of the gown halfway down her arm. "So who cares?" she muttered.

Frankie burst into the room, her medical bag in hand. She was dressed in an electric blue, ankle-length dress. Lex, directly behind her in a dove gray tuxedo, rushed to Ariel. "What happened?"

"I don't know. Things always happen in threes, you know that. First Dolly came back, that was good, then Pete showed up and we think they like each other. That's good, too. And now Snookie, just as we're about to get married. Is she okay, Frankie? Is something wrong? Her nose is warm and she's breathing so hard. Why's her nose warm?"

"Your nose would be warm, too, if you were getting ready to give birth. Get me some clean towels. And some warm water."

"I'll get it," Ariel said as she got to her feet. A loud, wrenching tear sounded in the room. "Oh, shit!" She yanked at the headpiece and threw it on the bed. "There's nothing in the bathroom to hold water. Lex, will you go downstairs and get a bowl?"

"Ariel, take it easy. Frankie's here. Listen, I hate to mention this, but the padre has three more weddings today. He's got ten minutes and then he has to leave. What do you want me to do?"

"Tell him to come up here and marry us. I'm not leaving Snookie."

"A girl after my own heart. I'll be right back."

"What's the hot water for?"

"Nothing. I just wanted you out of the way. Okay, here comes the first one. We had a little trouble with this guy, he wanted to come paws first. We got that all straightened out. Here comes number two."

"Oh, my God, they're so little, so beautiful, so gorgeous. I feel like a mother."

"You ready, Ariel? The padre is here."

Ariel looked up from her position on the floor. She motioned for Lex to stoop down. "Go ahead, Father," she said.

Puppy number seven made his entrance when the padre said, "I now pronounce you man and wife." Lex whistled, Ariel and Dolly clapped their hands.

Puppy number eight arrived as the groom kissed the bride.

Snookie barked ten minutes later when number nine made his entrance.

"She's telling us that's it. Mother of nine!" Frankie grinned. "Now, we need a bed for mother and children. Something warm and, Ariel, turn down the air conditioning. It's too cold in here for the pups."

"Oh, Lex, look how she's cleaning them. She loves them. Isn't it wonderful?"

Thirty minutes later, Snookie was settled with her offspring. When Ariel was satisfied that the shepherd was indeed asleep, she turned to Lex. "I'm sorry. I wanted today to be so special."

"You don't think this was special? Hell, this is something we'll never forget. Hey, I brought you something." Shuffling his feet, his hands shaking, he handed over a circlet of flowers. "They were for your head, but when the pups started to come, I forgot. You got married without it. It's like the one I made for you a long time ago."

She was crying openly as she hugged this wonderful man she'd had the good sense to marry a second time.

"Okay, everybody out!" Frankie ordered. "I'm in the mood for some dancing."

Her gown tattered and torn, the wreath of flowers on her head, Ariel took her husband's arm and descended the stairs, every inch a woman in love.

"Ooohh, look at Dolly. She looks great and I think Pete thinks she looks great, too. I showed her the house, Lex. Don't be mad."

"I know you showed her, and no, I'm not mad. It's going to work out for all of us. I love you, Mrs. Sanders."

"And I love you, Mr. Sanders."

"When do I get to take off your garter?"

"Anytime you're ready, Mr. Sanders."

"I'm ready, Mrs. Sanders."

Read on for an excerpt from Fern Michael's newest novel,
THE WILD SIDE, coming soon!

THE WILD SIDE

#1 *New York Times* Bestselling Author

Fern Michaels

**In an action-packed and thrilling new standalone novel from
the beloved, #1 *New York Times* bestselling author, a former
government agent is drawn back into the world of covert ops
for a very unconventional mission. . . .**

For Melanie Drake, school guidance counselor in a small Vir-
ginia town, the day's challenges typically involve a play-
ground scuffle or a student skipping school. It's worlds away
from her previous career as a vital part of the Office of Special Investigations. There, she devoted herself heart and soul
to covert operations, the riskier the better.

Since leaving, Melanie has cherished her peaceful, calm exis-
tence, with her two beloved retired service dogs for company.
Then a call comes from her former supervisor, Rich Patter-
son. He needs her back for a highly specialized assignment.
An international group of billionaires is known to meet regu-
larly for decadent dinners, and they always hire high-class es-
corts for the occasion. Only the most elegant, well-educated,
and sophisticated women will do. Infiltrating those meetings
could yield information vital to national security.

Melanie's loyalty is indisputable. She's willing to pose as an
escort and glean every scrap of intel that she can. But these
men aren't just wealthy and powerful, they're also exception-
ally ruthless. One slip, and they won't hesitate to eliminate
Melanie, by any means necessary. . . .

Prologue

Melanie Drake was absentmindedly tapping the pen she was holding on top of the yellow pad that sat beside her daily planner. Not quite forty and living in the midst of technology, she was still hooked on pen, pencil, and paper. She was convinced the act of writing something down made a stronger connection to one's memory. It was also a popular means of communication among criminals. No electronic footprint. But more on that later.

Yes, she had a cellphone. Yes, she kept things in her phone calendar, but for Melanie that was backup. As soon as she returned to her office, she would jot down whatever new appointment had been made. Then she would scribble it on the wall calendar that was hanging in her linen closet. If it was in front of her face, there was an excellent chance she would remember.

She glanced at her schedule for the day: routine grammar school guidance counselor agenda. She checked the clock above her door. The yelling, shrieking, laughing voices were about to descend on Jesse Moorer Elementary. Her first task of the day was to maintain order in the hallway.

Miss Drake stood outside her office door and greeted the children as they attempted to stampede their way to their classrooms. "Good morning, everyone. Slow down, please. Mind your manners. Be polite." She must have repeated those words at least a dozen times before the early morning bell rang. Every. Single. Day. And always with a genuine smile on her face.

After years of investigating criminals who clearly didn't follow the rules, she believed bad behavior should be nipped in the bud, meaning at a very young age. She loved being on hand to help shape a new generation of respect and integrity. If she could save one child from a life of felonious activity, then she'd done something good for the world. And that was why Melanie "MelDrake" Drake ultimately became a guidance counselor.

This was the first year of Melanie's second career. Admittedly, it was a bit unusual for someone to start working in the educational system just as they were about to turn forty. Normally it went the other way around. Teachers and counselors entered the field right after college and graduate work; and after twenty years, they retired or entered a different field or started a small cottage business. But Melanie's prior career had taken its toll on her: physically, emotionally, romantically, and spiritually. Yep. It damaged pretty much everything, but it was a means to an end. Luckily it didn't end *her*.